THE MAN IN THE MOUNTAIN

BOOK 1: AWAKENING

BIKRAM DHILLON

CALUMET
EDITIONS
Minneapolis

**CALUMET
EDITIONS**
Minneapolis

SECOND EDITION June 2016
The Man In the Mountain: Book 1: Awakening
Copyright © 2016 by Bikram Dhillon.

Printed in the United States of America.
10 9 8 7 6 5 4 3 2

ISBN: 9781-939548-51-1

Book and cover design by Gary Lindberg

To our many teachers of the past,
remembered and forgotten;
and to you, our teachers of today.

THE MAN IN THE MOUNTAIN

BOOK 1: AWAKENING

BIKRAM DHILLON

MY STORY

I never thought a person could live so many lives in one lifetime, but here I am.

In a way, I guess I'd never thought I would have much to tell. I mean, I'm not really that much different from anyone else. Sure, I've had my ups and downs. Maybe they're a little more up and more down than most, but not by much.

I suppose I wouldn't even be writing this if my life had just kept going along like I thought it would. Well, actually, it probably wouldn't have gone on much longer if it had continued like I thought it would, but I'm getting ahead of myself.

I should go back to the beginning. That was about three years ago. I was a different person then. Three years might not seem like much to you, but my experience that first year changed my life. It was a journey I never expected to take. I want to share that with you now, while I'm still the person I am, because I may not be this person tomorrow.

That may sound confusing, but explaining it is what my story is about. I think you'll understand after I share it with you.

I'm sure I sound hopeful right now, but I can tell you that my story didn't start out that way. In fact, I remember it beginning during a pretty dark time in my life. Before I get to that, though, I should probably tell you a little about myself.

My name is Yosh, which rhymes with Josh. I'm twenty-three years old and I live on my own. In a way, I've always lived on my own. I don't mean I was raised by wolves or anything. What I mean is that after my grandfather, Abe, died when I was nine, I moved around from foster home to foster home. I wasn't a very easy foster kid to take in—or maybe I was just unlucky—and I was bounced around a lot. Anyway, it wasn't what you'd call a stable childhood. I always felt like I had to look out for myself because no one else was going to do it.

Don't get me wrong. There were some fantastic people who took me in. Without them, I probably wouldn't be here. A new home usually started out cool, but just when I'd start to feel at home, my new foster parents would split up, or my foster dad would lose his job, or they'd have to move. The only time I felt like I really had a home was before all that, when I lived with my grandfather. I can't say that anyone really raised me, but if anyone did, it was him.

I'm sure my life would have been a lot different if Grandpa Abe hadn't died so suddenly. I know he would have planned things out for me if he had the chance. He was always thinking ahead, but he was always right there for me at the same time. He was great, but he didn't stay with me long.

I know every kid thinks that his grandparents are great, but I'm not talking about that. Grandpa Abe really was different, and I'm not the only one who thought so. I may be an orphan, but that doesn't mean I don't have family. I've got aunts and uncles and cousins, and I even stayed with my Aunt Joan for a while and then my Aunt Joyce when I was growing up. All of them thought my grandfather was great, and they don't say that about anyone else.

Anyone who knew him thought the same. My grandfather took me in after my parents died in a car crash when I was four. It sometimes feels bad to say, but I don't really remember my parents all that well. Grandpa Abe would always tell me that they loved me more than I could imagine. As a kid, I spent a lot of time trying to imagine that. There were lots of times later on that I felt alone as a child, but not while my grandfather was alive. I only really started feeling alone after he was gone. When we were together, I didn't know what loneliness was.

Grandpa Abe had the most incredible way of finding everything interesting and meaningful. There was a peace that seemed to surround him all the time. I never knew him to get angry, even when I thought he should. He could turn things around that seemed like such a big negative deal to me, and suddenly they would be the best thing that could have happened. How something could go from terrible to fantastic in just a few words is something I could never understand. Those *were* happy years. Too bad they didn't last longer.

I know you're supposed to be sad when someone you love dies, but I wasn't sad. I was pissed off. When Grandpa Abe had his heart attack, I was scared. The hospital was bad enough, but the look on the doctor's face made it pretty clear that things were not okay. Even a kid knows that look. That's when I realized my grandpa would never be coming back, and things would never be fine for me again.

It didn't take long for that numb feeling to give way to anger. Why did everything bad have to happen to me? Why did *I* always have to get the short end of the stick? Everyone else had parents and brothers and sisters. All they had to worry about was not getting what they wanted for Christmas or their birthday. I got to be alone and I missed my grandfather terribly. It wasn't fair.

I don't really think I let anyone into my world after that. I felt miserable, and I wanted to feel more miserable. If I was miserable and no one else really cared, then I would make them miserable too. Why should I be alone in my misery?

That's the funny thing about being fed up. You start to become very comfortable with feeling down. It's like that's just who you are, and you accept it. If you don't have anyone who cares enough about you to help you get out of it, then you actually start to believe that it's normal to be miserable and depressed.

I lived that way for so long that anger and frustration became my two best friends. That anger followed me when I got out on my own. I tried going through the motions and did what I was supposed to do, like finish high school. I even went to college for a year. I was smart and I'd learned a lot on my own, so I knew how to think.

If there's one thing that being alone teaches you, it's how to think and how to trust yourself. Maybe I trusted myself too much, because I couldn't see the point of college. They just tell you what you have to learn, and you just play the game until you graduate so you can get a job.

So I left college after a year and thought I'd just go straight to the getting-a-job part. I tried a few jobs, but they all just seemed too much like busywork. No one I worked with was going anywhere and they all seemed so thoughtlessly unaware in their own little lives. Everything felt so pointless. I always got bored pretty quickly. After a few weeks, the boss would catch on that I was just trying to get by and then I'd be out again looking for another job.

It seemed so futile. Everyone was just playing the game in order to get a paycheck so they could turn around and buy some useless toys like a new computer or a cool car. Or it might be a bigger house or a motorcycle. Whatever it was, it just meant one more thing they lorded over everyone else. In the end, everyone really wanted to be on vacation but slaved away to chase their toys, giving up all the time they had. The world seemed to think all those people were successful and I was a failure. After all, I couldn't even hold down a job. While everyone else seemed focused on building lives and careers, I was building up frustration in an indifferent world. That world didn't care for me and I didn't care for it.

I suppose it might have been different if I'd had someone to share my frustration with, but I wasn't looking for anyone's help. I never had any help and I wasn't about to ask for any now. I'd always made it on my own. I'd make it on my own now, too. At least that's what I thought in the beginning.

But moving from one failure to another was getting to be too much. It's one thing to be an idealist as a kid or when you're in college, but the world doesn't give a damn about your idealism. It just wants you to show up for work and play its game or get out of the way. Well, I sure as hell wasn't going to play the game, and this screwed-up world had no room for me.

I remember one day just sitting there contemplating my predicament. How was it possible that I was feeling better than everyone else who had it so easy, but I couldn't even make it on my own? How could I possibly be better than them when the world was tell-

4

ing me I was so much less than any of them? This world did *not* make sense to me.

I guess when your world stops making sense, you stop caring. And when you stop caring, you stop feeling. All I know is that I didn't care anymore and I was tired of feeling like a failure. I was so fed up with trying and falling flat on my face that I didn't want to try any more. I felt trapped and couldn't see any way out except one. So I decided I wouldn't have anything else to do with it. I was going to check out of this ridiculous world. Anyway, it wouldn't miss me if I were dead.

I remember that morning well. I was sitting in my apartment. It was a dark room lit by a single small lamp. I sat on my old sofa, staring at a wall that was bare except for a calendar and a single picture of my grandfather as a young man. In the photo he was standing proudly at attention in his military uniform. *He* had found a purpose in life. *I* was lost.

I had been up all night with just a faint breeze coming through a single open window for company. Through that window I could hear the city starting to come to life. The delivery trucks with their low beep-beep-beeps had stopped backing up an hour earlier. The sun had not yet risen over the skyline, and for a while all the buildings blended into the same shade of gray. Then the sun broke out from behind the clouds on the horizon and lit up the world's many fractured pieces.

I sat on my beat-up sofa, clutching the broken medallion my grandfather had given me before he died. Other than my memories, the medallion was about all I had left of him. I don't know how it broke, but that's how it was when he gave it to me. I pressed my thumb hard across its sharp broken edge and stared off into space. The other side of the medallion was smooth and perfectly curved with a small raised lip on both sides. The contrast between the two edges had a familiar feel.

I can't tell you the number of times I'd held that medallion. If there was anything that comforted me, it was the feeling of holding that piece of my grandfather's life. It was a comfortable puzzle— sharp and smooth, kind of simple yet etched with some unknown writing on one side and a sun or flower pattern on the other.

I had long ago given up on making any sense of the markings. In my childhood, I thought the medallion was some sort of special map, or maybe a clue to my grandfather's life. There were times when I was younger that I thought it might have been a medal that he earned for his bravery during the war. I could see him doing something brave.

It didn't make any difference, though. I had made up my mind. Today was the day I would clear up my affairs. Most had already been taken care of.

I packed away my few belongings and stared at the picture of my grandfather. I felt ashamed, as though he could see me and was disappointed in what I had become—or rather, what I had not become. I unhooked the wire from the nail that held the picture to the wall. As I turned, I tripped and fell, sending the picture out of my hands and crashing to the floor.

The shattered glass seemed to fly up in slow motion, each shard catching the light and sending reflections shimmering across the room. That picture had been with me as long as the medallion had! I picked it up slowly to be sure it hadn't been torn or cut. It seemed to be fine. Relieved, I started to set it down, but then my eyes grew wide. There was writing on the back!

The picture had been framed for as long as I could recall, and I never imagined there would be anything on the back of it. I stared at the writing. The words grabbed me, like a new conversation with an old friend, the kind that starts back up exactly where it had left off years earlier.

My Dearest Yosh,

My time with you has been the greatest joy. Know that you are loved beyond your ability to know. I have seen in you the qualities that make for joy and fulfillment, the like of which you deserve: curiosity, determination, honesty, sincerity, and reverence. You do not yet know the value of these things, but I know them and know that you possess them. I want you to know that you are

THE MAN IN THE MOUNTAIN

never alone, for that which resides everywhere resides with great abundance in you.

With My Love,
Grandpa Abe

I felt a tight knot in my throat as I read those words over and over again. How could this be? How could I have let him down? I was not the person he had seen—yet I longed to be that person.

I couldn't remember having cried for many years, but while sitting there alone on the floor the tears welled up and didn't end for a long time. When I finally stopped sobbing, it felt like something had changed. I was exhausted, but the heaviness I had been feeling for days and weeks was gone.

I sat there, empty but numb, staring *through* the picture as much as staring *at* it. As I slowly ran my fingers across the writing my focus changed, and I found myself looking directly at those words again. It was only then that I noticed a name, printed in Grandpa Abe's handwriting, at the bottom:

Jim Cramford
Chama, New Mexico

Why would my grandfather put someone else's name at the bottom of a note he had written to me? I had practically memorized every letter he had ever written to my folks or me, but I had never seen that name. Why would he put it there?

At first I tried to dismiss its importance. What difference did it make anyway? Jim Cramford was no one to me and I was no one to Jim Cramford! I sat there steaming in my loneliness.

Somewhere in there a thought lodged in my mind, a glimmer of hope. Maybe this 'Jim' might know something about Grandpa Abe. My grandfather was the person who had mattered the most to me, and Jim must have been pretty important to Grandpa Abe if he wrote his name there. If Jim was important to my grandfather, maybe Jim Cramford was someone to me.

My curiosity began to grow. Without intending it, I found myself picking up the phone and calling directory assistance. They were no help. The Internet turned up nothing. I looked through the few papers I had from my grandfather and found nothing there either. Instead of waning, my curiosity only grew stronger with each dead end.

Eventually, I called my Aunt Joyce. I hadn't spoken to her in a while, and she knew nothing about what I was going through. She had always tried to be there for me but had enough troubles of her own. I didn't need to burden her with any more worries.

When she answered the phone, I skipped right past the small talk and asked her if she recognized the name Jim Cramford. She thought for a while, but nothing came to mind. I kept pestering her, though. Something must have jogged her memory because she suddenly seemed to remember a 'Jim,' who might have been my grandfather's friend from his years in the Army Air Corps.

My grandfather had loved to fly and had been stationed at Brooks Airfield in Texas during World War II. Aunt Joyce said he hadn't talk-ed much about his time in the military. What she knew about that time she had heard from her mother who had said Grandpa Abe had come back from the service a changed man. Changed, but not in the way that most people are changed by war. He had changed in the opposite way. At the time I had no idea what that meant, but it would soon make sense to me in a way I could never have imagined.

It seems Grandpa Abe had written to my grandmother pretty of-ten while he was stationed in Texas. My aunt had saved her father's letters and remembered that they were packed away in a box in her attic. She went to get them while I sat on the phone imagining my grandfather as a young husband with my aunt and my father as his children, hanging on his words, just as I had done many years later.

I was still lost in my thoughts when Aunt Joyce got back on the phone and told me she had found the letters. As she went through them, she got lost in reminiscing about her childhood with her mom and dad. Eventually, she found a paragraph that finished with "My buddy Jim just had a daughter. They already have a son, so they're happy they had a little girl. They decided to name her Sharon."

At least Aunt Joyce thought it was "Sharon." It was hard for her to make out the name because it was at the end of the page and the old paper was pretty frayed. I thanked her for going through all those letters, told her I'd see her soon, and ended with an impatient "goodbye."

There were two listings for "Cramford" in Chama, New Mexico. At least that's what directory assistance had listed. Neither of them was Jim or Sharon. I called the first number and a woman answered the phone. She was curt, said she didn't know who Jim Cramford was, and hung up saying she didn't want to be bothered again.

I had a little better luck with the second listing. This time a man answered the phone. He started out sounding like he was very suspicious. After I managed to convince him that I wasn't a telemarketer or a stalker, he opened up a bit. I asked him about Sharon Cramford, and he said that the person I was probably looking for was a woman named Shuren Figueres. She was his cousin and had been known as Shuren Cramford when they were younger, before she was married.

Then I asked him about Jim Cramford, since I hadn't gotten a listing for that name. He told me that Jim Cramford, his uncle, was Shuren's father and that Jim lived nearby but didn't have a phone. I thought that was strange—but who was I to judge? I was still getting used to the name Shuren. I'd never heard it before, but then I guess not many people had heard of anyone named Yosh, either.

The cousin was kind enough to give me Shuren's phone number. I thanked him and hung up as fast as I could. As soon as I got a dial tone, I was back on the phone calling Shuren.

After the third ring, a woman answered. Her tone couldn't have been more different than either of the other Cramfords—no anger or suspicion. Her voice was practically chirpy. I thought she must be pretty oblivious to all the misery in the world to be so happy talking to a perfect stranger. There was a disarming openness to her answers that I both resented and admired.

The only time she hesitated was when I explained that I was Abe's grandson and was looking for his old friend Jim. There was a noticeable pause. I thought the line must have disconnected. Trying to reestablish contact, I met the silence with a series of "hellos."

In a suddenly measured voice, she told me that her father was the Jim Cramford I was looking for and that he did not live far away. She said he would be happy to hear from me and that I should call back in an hour, which I agreed to do.

I hung up and turned back to clean up the fortunate mess I had made. I marveled at how my plans for the day had changed so dramatically. An hour later, I was back on the phone to New Mexico.

The phone rang and a man's voice answered, "Hello."

"Is this Jim Cramford?" I asked.

"Yes, this is Jim. Are you Yosh?"

"Yes," I responded. "I'm Abe's grandson."

Jim cleared his throat. "Well, Yosh, Abe was a very good friend of mine. Even though I lost contact with him many years ago, I knew that he'd taken you in after your parents died in that terrible accident. In fact, the last time I talked with Abe he spoke very highly of you. I think you must have been about eight years old at the time. After that I lost touch with him. I had no idea what had become of you."

His voice was slow and deliberate and carried the same warmth that his daughter's words had conveyed. He sounded noble and wise.

"Actually, Grandpa Abe passed away eleven years ago when I was nine," I said. "He had a heart attack. It was all pretty sudden."

"Well, Yosh, I'm sorry to hear that Abe died so long ago. I suspected he'd passed away when I didn't hear from him. I know that you have other family, but we were unable to contact any of them. We tried for a long time."

"I'm embarrassed to say that he never told me about you," I said. "I found you kind of by accident."

"That's nothing to be embarrassed about, Yosh. You were just a child at the time and I'm sure you had your hands full. As I said, he told me a lot about you. From his description, I knew that one day you'd probably call."

I sat back in my chair, puzzled. Why would I have been likely to call Jim? My call was just a fluke. It had happened by chance.

Feeling the need to clarify, I sputtered, "I found a note to me on the back of a picture of Grandpa Abe. Before today I'd never seen it, but it had your name at the bottom. For some reason I felt like I should call you. I mean, I don't know why else he would have put your name there."

"That's fine, Yosh. I'm happy you called. I'm sure that Abe would have wanted you to contact us."

I started to get a tight feeling in my throat. It had been so long since I'd heard any words of encouragement or support. Or maybe it had been so long since I'd allowed myself to hear any. I didn't know. I got choked up, which I'm sure came across as silence.

When I finally spoke I was unable to censor my thoughts. "To be honest, it's been a little rough for me lately, and I thought it would be nice to speak with someone who knew my grandfather. Other than my Aunt Joyce, he was the closest family I had."

Now there was silence on the *other* end of the phone. Suddenly, I felt embarrassed. Maybe I'd been too personal with this stranger. At the same time I really didn't care. I just wanted to hold on tightly to this connection with my grandfather, one I had never known existed.

It was probably only a second or two of silence, but it seemed longer before Jim's voice came back on with a question I certainly wasn't expecting.

"Yosh, before Abe passed away, did he give you anything?"

"Well, the only things I have from him are his picture and a broken medallion. My Aunt Joyce has a bunch of his letters and I've got—"

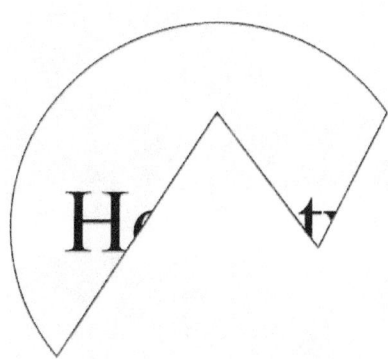

"You have the medallion?" Jim interrupted.

"Yeah, but I don't think it's worth anything. It's broken."

In an instant, his tone seemed to change from curious and surprised to urgent and concerned. What he said next was even more unexpected.

"Yosh, there's probably a great deal to discuss, but I think it would be best if we spoke in person. When can you make it down to Chama?"

THE MEDALLION

It was now *my* turn to be surprised into silence. I must have been quiet for longer than I thought, because Jim wanted to know if I was still on the phone. I managed to get out a "Yeah, I'm still here. I guess I could make it down there just about any time."

I could hear Jim whispering to Shuren before he came back on the line and asked, "Can you make it down here tomorrow?"

I was surprised that he wanted to see me as quickly as I wanted to meet him. I tried not to let that show and just said, "I suppose I could, but I don't want to impose on you."

"It's no imposition, Yosh. It's what your grandfather would have wanted."

How could he know what my grandfather would have wanted? I wondered.

I didn't question it, though. It felt good to be relevant to someone, even if it had nothing to do with me. I know how friends can be. Maybe meeting me was a way of seeing Grandpa Abe, or at least a way of sharing a part of Grandpa Abe that he missed.

I just said, "All right, I'll fly down tomorrow." I didn't have much cash, but this was something I just had to do.

"Great, Yosh. It will be a pleasure to meet you in person."

He gave me Shuren's address and told me Chama was small enough that all I needed to do was ask for directions. We said our goodbyes and he hung up.

I sat there with the phone in my hand, feeling like a drowning man who'd just been thrown a lifeline. Today was the day I was going to end my life, and suddenly I felt more hopeful than I had in a long time. It was strange to think about it so bluntly. The finality of my anticipated demise had never really sunk in until that moment.

How could one short conversation change my life so much?

But then, nothing had really changed. This would probably be just another wild goose chase. Still, there was a faint glimmer of hope in Jim's words. There was a sense of purpose in his urgency. I had failed to find purpose for myself, but maybe he could find some for me. Was that all I needed—someone to give me a purpose—or was there something else too? How could this brief conversation have awakened me to the enormity of what I had planned to do?

I put the phone down and instinctively felt for the medallion in my pocket. I rolled it around between my thumb and fingers. In some strange way, my grandfather had reached out across the years and given me hope in the form of this broken piece of metal.

With newly found purpose, I was back on the phone and onto the Web, making flight arrangements and renting a car. The first flight to Albuquerque left early in the morning, but I was packed and ready to go fifteen minutes after hanging up the phone. I sat back in my chair, lost in thought.

I hadn't traveled anywhere in a long time, and I'd never been to New Mexico or even to the southwest. I had no idea what to expect, but at least it was something to look forward to, and I wondered if this was what hope looked like.

My musings were interrupted by the realization that I would be going away for a few days, and I had quite a bit to do before I left town. I had pretty much been a recluse for the past week and really didn't care what I looked like. Now I had to get back out into the world. I got up and walked over to the bathroom.

I looked into the mirror hanging over the sink and barely recognized the gaunt face that looked back at me. It was hidden by the stubble of the past week's neglect and by my light brown mop of hair, which badly needed a trim.

I shaved and was surprised at how pale I'd become. I always tanned easily, just like Grandpa Abe had, but I'd been going outside mostly at night, and my skin had forgotten what the sun felt like. In all the pictures I'd seen of her, my mother had been fair, with beautiful, sharp features, and my father's face had seemed strong and proud. As I shaved, I could see them both in me. I was taller now than my father had been but still a couple inches short of Grandpa Abe's six feet.

He had carried his stature well, unlike me. I looked at myself slouching in the mirror and remembered how straight Grandpa Abe had stood. He had always towered over me with his high cheeks and his lips pursed in a perpetual, wry smile. He always looked like someone who had just heard a joke that everyone else had missed and was content to enjoy it by himself.

I had been in pretty good shape before I fell into this funk, but Grandpa Abe always seemed fit and never sat still. He had a solemn determination that was carved into his dark eyes and a sense of purpose when he walked. I always wondered what it was that drove him. Maybe Jim shared that with him—maybe not. I didn't want to get my hopes up, but it was already too late for that.

In nervous anticipation, I spent the rest of the day tying up loose ends. I managed to get in a phone call to Aunt Joyce that evening to let her know where I was going and told her I'd call her from Chama. Excited as I was, I was also exhausted. I lay down on my bed and was asleep as soon as my head hit the pillow.

It felt like I had just gone to sleep when my alarm jarred me awake out of my dreams. I called a cab, got dressed, then hurried downstairs. The cabbie looked like he'd been up all night and he didn't have much to say. We rode in silence through the yellow glow of the streetlights and the near-empty city streets.

We approached the airport and were greeted by the strong smell of jet fuel and the harsh rumbling of engines overhead. The usual crowd of early-morning travelers was there, mostly suited for work in distant cities and focused on their plans for the day. As I went through check-in and boarding, I realized I was no different than any of them. I was also focused on my day and the plans I'd made. I, too, was lost in my thoughts of where life was taking me.

It wasn't long before I was sitting on the plane, clearing the city, and flying south over endless farm fields barely visible in the moonlight. I kept my thoughts to myself. Mostly, I marveled at what a difference a day makes and wondered about this friend of my grandfather. As I sat there, lost in thought, I reached into my pocket to confirm that the medallion was still there.

I nodded off and woke to see the retreating darkness give way to reds and purples announcing the coming of a new day. We began our descent into Albuquerque around seven in the morning with the city still nestled in the shadow of the Sandia Mountains. We touched down and taxied to the gate. Soon, I was marching off the plane with the rest of the passengers. I picked up my rental car and hoped they wouldn't notice the one-year age difference on the fake ID I used to get into bars. The car about maxed-out my card and left me with just enough cash for gas money. Before I knew it, I was headed north on I-25 toward Santa Fe.

As I drove north, the cool air and the gentle hum of the engine lulled me into that place where my thoughts just seemed to bounce around, going off on one tangent then another, till I wondered how I had gotten to a particular thought.

I marveled at how quickly I felt alive again.

Wasn't it just yesterday that I had thought everything was going against me? How was it possible that the choice between life and death could hinge on so little and that this journey could capture me so totally?

The miles passed by, and I felt the problems of my past falling away behind me. This was country that was totally new to me. It felt like a blank slate, clean and uncluttered. I took I-84 up from Santa Fe, turned north on Highway 17, and pulled into Chama just before lunch.

At first glance, it looked just like what I pictured for a small southwestern town. It must have had a population of a little over a thousand and was tucked into a valley in the Rocky Mountains of northern New Mexico.

Looking more closely, though, I could see that there were two Chamas. Most of the town was made up of small family homes set on tree-lined roads just west of Highway 17 with a scattering of inns and bed-and-breakfasts. But the area along Highway 17, which ran right through the middle of town, was different. It was lined with galleries, restaurants, small shops, inns, and bars.

The varied architecture reflected the different faces of the town. Brick buildings with classic western facades alternated with adobe structures and wooden houses behind white picket fences.

The people were a mixture of locals and visitors who were there for the shops or to ride the narrow-gauge railroad that left from the terminal there to go up into the mountains. Taking it all in, Chama seemed like it was both stuck in the past and moving fast into the future. I knew that feeling, so I was comfortable with it.

The people were friendly enough with directions, and like Jim had said, Chama was easy to navigate. Before I knew it, I was walking up the path to Shuren's door, wondering if I was just getting my hopes up for no reason.

Shuren's house was a small, well-tended home with a couple of big elm trees framing the front porch. It had a fresh coat of light-gray paint with white shutters and a white railing around the porch. I walked up three small steps that rose to the porch and stood in front of a bright red door. There was no bell, so I knocked. I heard footsteps and then the door swung open to reveal a short woman with a broad smile.

"Hello, you must be Yosh," she said.

"Yes. I wasn't sure I was at the right house."

"You're at the right house. We were expecting you. I'm Shuren."

For some reason, I had pictured her as much taller, but her manner was every bit as warm as I'd imagined. She was probably in her late fifties and dressed in a long blue skirt with a white blouse. Shuren had just a hint of a southern accent, or maybe it was a western accent. I wasn't sure. It was her smile that made me feel more at home than her words. She held the door open and invited me in.

There were two men in the room, both dressed in work shirts and jeans. They studied me intently as I entered the house. I won-

17

dered what they thought of me in my polo shirt and khakis. Shuren introduced the older one to me as her father, Jim. The younger one was her son, Luke, who looked about thirty. A picture of confidence, he was just a little taller than me. He stepped forward and gave me a firm handshake. His hand was rough and tanned, marking him as a man who spent his days outdoors. I wondered how different his world must be from mine.

"Welcome to Chama," Luke said. "Mom told me you'd be coming down to see us, so I wanted to be here. I've heard my grandfather's stories about his friend Abe since I was a kid. So it's a pleasure to have you with us."

"Thanks," I said. "It's kind of you all to invite me down. I really had no idea that my grandfather had such a close friend until yesterday."

Jim had just stepped toward me and I shook his outstretched hand. I was surprised at what I saw. I had been expecting an elderly man, and I knew that he must be in his early eighties, but he looked like he was only sixty years old. His grip was strong and steady. Though his skin was weathered, his eyes were sharp and penetrating.

Smiling, Jim said, "Welcome to our home, Yosh."

"It's wonderful to meet you," I replied, wondering what I would say next.

As it turned out, I didn't need to think of much. Jim invited me to sit down. He had a thousand questions. I could see Luke smiling and realized he must have witnessed his grandfather's interrogations before, or maybe he'd experienced them himself.

Jim wanted to know everything about Grandpa Abe's last years—and about me and my life since my grandfather had passed away. It would have gone on like that all afternoon if Shuren hadn't interrupted.

"Dad, Yosh must be hungry. Why don't we eat before you finish talking his ear off?"

It was only when Shuren mentioned lunch that I realized how hungry I was. In my rush to get to Chama, I hadn't eaten anything all day. Soon, the house was filled with the aroma of grilled onions, fresh cornbread, and country stew. Lunch was on the table before I knew it.

I was feeling pretty much at home here. Actually, I was feeling much better than being at home.

The conversation over lunch was much lighter and mostly revolved around my questions about life in Chama and their questions about my family and my years with Grandpa Abe. I told them how my grandfather had taken me in after my parents died. I spoke about the little things we did together and the talks we had. I recall telling them that I barely remembered the detail of those talks, but I remembered how good they made me feel. Even though Grandpa Abe and I didn't go many places, I felt like I was traveling all over the world through his stories. Jim smiled knowingly. It seemed he and Grandpa Abe must have taken similar journeys together.

For my part, I learned about their family and the relatives that they had in the area as well as what it was like to grow up in a small town. As it turned out, their family was a mixture of Native American, Spanish—via Mexico from the 1600s— and European with a long history in that area of New Mexico. Shuren had married young and then divorced when Luke was in his teens. It sounded like an amicable separation because she had decided to keep his name, while Luke eventually decided to take his grandfather's name and went by Cramford.

I was beginning to understand that Shuren and Luke were pretty independent sorts, and I liked that about them. With lunch winding down, Jim ushered us all back to the living room, and it was clear that he still had a lot on his mind. I came to see that he was a man who didn't like wasting time.

Over the next few hours, Jim probably learned more about me than many of my closest friends had over years. Occasionally I'd throw in my own question, or Luke or Shuren would ask something. It became clear pretty quickly, however, that this was Jim's show and he was quick to return to his inquiry.

His questions to me weren't the superficial ones you usually get when you first meet someone. He asked a lot of *why* questions. Why had I chosen this or that? Why did I live alone? Why did I quit college? Why did I keep switching jobs? Still, it didn't feel like an interrogation. He just seemed genuinely interested.

The conversation finally got around to his friendship with my grandfather. It turned out they had met while Grandpa Abe was flying out of Brooks Airfield in Texas. But then a few minutes later Jim said that they had met in Chama. This made no sense to me since Chama, New Mexico and San Antonio, Texas (where Brooks used to be) are about eight hundred miles apart.

Before I could confront him about this, Jim asked me about Grandpa Abe's last years. I told him what a happy time that had been for me. Eventually, I explained how my grandfather had died suddenly of a heart attack, though he had seemed fine the day before. I took a deep breath and tried to keep from getting choked up. We all sat there and for a while no one said a thing.

Jim finally broke the silence and asked, "Yosh, did you bring the medallion?"

At first his question didn't register with me. I was still lost in my thoughts about Grandpa Abe. But then it shook me out of my reverie. I looked up and said, "Yes."

I felt for the medallion in my pocket, pulled it out, and held it up. Jim held out his hand. "May I see it?"

I handed it to him. For just a moment I felt suspicious. Had I come all this way just to deliver the medallion to him? I hadn't even known about Jim two days ago. Still, I felt that I could trust him. Or maybe I needed to *feel* that I could trust him. For some reason I sensed that he had no intention of keeping it. Don't ask me why.

Jim looked at the medallion like it was something precious he had lost a long time ago. He walked over to a small walnut desk at the side of the room, opened the drawer, and pulled out what looked like an old cigar box. He brought it over and handed it to me. I lifted the lid and looked inside. I could feel Jim studying my face. In the box was a piece of a broken medallion similar to mine. I held it in my hand. It felt the same as my medallion. It had the same sharp break and the same smooth edge.

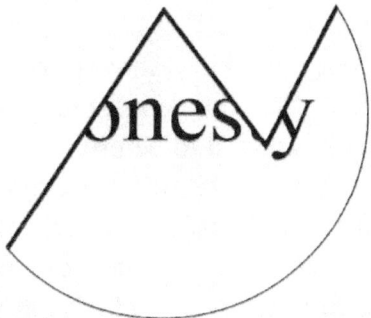

I looked up at Jim in amazement. I had never even thought that there could be another part to my medallion. Could it be that what I had was only one half of a complete medallion?

Jim handed my medallion back to me, and I reflexively brought the two pieces together. I was expecting some kind of revelation. My hands were sweating. The medallion was now whole again.

I have to tell you, my reaction was not what Jim must have been expecting.

My face fell. I was expecting something profound. I stared at it again and thought to myself, *How hokey is this? Honesty? I traveled all this way for some simplistic notion about telling the truth?* Suddenly my whole trip, like my life, began to feel like a huge waste of time. Here I was in this hick town in the middle of nowhere, talking to an old man from a time long gone, and getting Sunday school lessons about how to behave.

My disappointment must have shown on my face, because Jim stopped talking. His questions had appeared so incisive just minutes ago. Now, they suddenly seemed to be probing.

I felt the violent return of a familiar defensiveness that was never far from me. Jim must have sensed it as well because the questions stopped. He could see that I had no questions for him either. In my mind, I was right back in my apartment, sitting alone on my beat-up old couch.

Jim broke the awkward silence by telling me he needed a break and asked me if I wanted to take a siesta. I thanked him and Shuren showed me to a room. I lay down on the bed, tired, drained, and upset. I could feel the weight of all my resentment returning as I nodded off. *I guess it's not so easy to leave your past behind you. You can't just drive away from it, like I thought I could.*

I didn't realize I'd slept through the entire afternoon until I woke to the sound of someone knocking on my door. Shuren's voice came from the other side.

"Yosh, dinner's ready."

I rubbed the sleep from my eyes and answered, "I'll be right out."

I sat on the edge of the bed, collecting my thoughts, then walked to the door. I stood there for a minute with my hand on the doorknob. Then I turned it slowly and opened the door. I stepped out of my dark room into the warmly lit living room and into the spicy smell of stuffed peppers and chili con carne. I clumsily thanked Shuren and Jim for the chance to rest as my senses took in my surroundings.

As I sat down at the table next to Jim, I felt like I was still dreaming. He nodded in silent acknowledgment, studying me intently. Luke was nowhere to be seen and Shuren was in the kitchen. I glanced up at him and then looked back down at the table. I really didn't want to hurt Jim's feelings. He seemed to be such a nice old man, well meaning—though maybe a little simple.

I sat there fumbling for words and then finally spoke.

"Listen, Jim," I started slowly, "I'm glad I had a chance to meet you. I'm sure my grandfather and you were very close, and it's an honor to spend some time with you and your family. You've brought back some wonderful memories of my grandfather for me, but that was a long time ago. I appreciate your hospitality, but I don't want to take up too much of your time. I think I'll probably head out tomorrow if that's okay. Oh, and about the medallion. Seeing how it must mean a lot to you, holding on to the other half for so long, why don't you just keep both halves?"

Jim just looked at me. It was a deep look, not upset or curious, just deep, like he was looking right into me.

Finally, he spoke. "That would be fine, Yosh. I'm glad you made the trip down. I'm too old to be doing all that traveling, and it's a joy to see Abe's grandson."

I was happy to settle the whole thing without hurting his feelings. We sat together until Shuren announced that supper was ready. I got up and joined her in the kitchen to help serve the meal.

The rest of the evening was pleasant enough. We finished dinner and made some small talk. Then Jim mentioned to me that he had a box with some of my grandfather's belongings. He ceremoniously informed me that he would like to give them to me since, as he put it, "They rightfully belong to you, Yosh."

I was surprised that my grandfather had any other belongings and equally surprised that Jim would have kept anything around for that long. This guy must be a real pack rat, I thought. I wasn't much of a saver myself. If I hadn't used something in a year, I usually tossed it. I remembered hearing that people who had lived through the Depression tended to save things. Maybe that was just his way.

He left the room, disappearing down the stairs to the basement. I complimented Shuren on the meal, and she offered to teach me how to cook it. We were still chatting when Jim returned with a wooden box about two feet long, a foot-and-a-half deep, and two-feet high. He handed it to me. It was an old crate with a hinged wooden lid and a metal clasp where a padlock might go. It wasn't locked, but it was dusty enough to tell me that it hadn't been opened in a while.

I brushed off the lid and saw "Abraham L. Tsalagi" stenciled in bold block letters. People always thought our last name was hard to pronounce, but I told them it was easy. It sounded like saw-lug-hee.

I opened the lid and was greeted by the smell of mothballs. Looking inside, I found some old clothes, a pair of boots, and a large book.

"These were my grandfather's?" I asked.

"They are," said Jim. "They *were*, I mean."

"You've kept them all this time. Why did you do that?"

"Because Abe asked me to hold onto them. He also asked me to make sure that they got to whoever had the other half of the medallion. I guess that means you."

I put the dusty old clothes and the boots aside and picked up the book. It was really more of a manuscript than a book, and it didn't look like it had ever been published.

Jim continued, "The only thing Abe asked me to tell the person with the medallion was that he should finish reading the book here, or leave it here if it didn't interest him."

He added, "Since you're the rightful heir on account of Abe's intention and your relationship to him, I guess you should feel free to take it along if you'd rather. I just wanted to let you know what his wishes were. Now, as for reading it here, you can stay as long as you'd like as far as Shuren and I are concerned."

I brushed off the cover of the book to look at the title:

Unitive Awareness

"Did my grandfather write this?" I asked. For some strange reason, my heart was once again pounding with excitement.

Jim replied, "Well, yes. You could say that. It grew out of notes he had taken for years. Abe swore by that book, and he carried it with him every time he came up to Chama and went into the back country."

"Have you read it?"

"Of course I have," he said with a smile. "Much of my time with Abe was spent talking about that book and where it took us, or at least the ideas in it."

"Thanks," I said. "I'll take a look at it."

It was late by then. I offered to help clean up but Shuren would have none of it. I enjoyed their company, but to be honest, I'd had enough talking for one day and was distracted by the book. I said good night, excused myself, and returned to my room with the box.

I was wide awake now. My roller-coaster ride was on an upswing. I was thrilled to be in touch with my grandfather in this sudden and unexpected way. A book!

My feelings of sadness and disappointment again had given way to hope and expectation. I spent all night trying to decipher that book. I must have been pretty absorbed in it because I lost track of time.

The next thing I remember was sitting at the desk in my room and being startled by a knock on the door and a voice asking if I wanted breakfast. I opened the door to see Shuren staring at me in surprise. I must have looked like a mess because she asked me if I needed a cup of coffee before she mentioned breakfast again. It was only then that I realized I'd been up all night.

I followed her into the kitchen and we sat down. She poured coffee for both of us. I sat there watching the steam rise. She smiled at me, surely sensing my confusion and embarrassment but too kind to say a word about it.

Before too long, Jim joined us. He was no longer the same old man sitting in a hick town that I'd seen yesterday. I mean, he was the same guy, of course, but I just couldn't figure him. He was the man who had discussed with my grandfather the book I had tried to read last night.

My first words to him weren't *good morning*. As I remember, my first words were, "You've really read all this stuff?"

He just looked at me again with that gentle yet penetrating look of his. He didn't say a word. He just let me talk.

"I tried reading this thing, but I couldn't make head or tails out of it. It's all history, religion, and philosophy, and it just keeps bouncing around. First it's simple and repetitive, then it jumps to things I've never even heard of or thought of before. It's like there's something there, but it's hard to get through... I have no idea where it's even headed."

There was a long silence. Finally, Jim's face broke out in a smile. He half chuckled and shook his head, but he wasn't gloating. It was more like acknowledging my recognition of what simplicity truly was; how my simplicity of understanding failed to capture the depth of my grandfather's words and ideas; how I had mistaken Jim's plainness of expression for simplicity of thought. Then I understood who the simple one in the room truly was.

When he eventually spoke, Jim just graciously said, "Yosh, you can stay as long as you'd like."

We finished breakfast, and I told Jim and Shuren that I wanted to go for a walk. The fresh morning air would help me clear my head. Part of me wanted to run away and part of me wanted to give up. But part of me thought that there must be something more.

While today this was all too much, just yesterday it had been all too little. I excused myself, put on my jacket, and stepped out the front door. I didn't even know where I was going. I just started walking, lost in my thoughts again.

I must have been walking for a while, because when I looked around, I was no longer in town. Even the occasional house was not to be seen. It was quiet—so quiet I could hear the wind blowing through the trees. I could even pick out the sound of the occasional leaf drifting down to meet its siblings of the fading summer on the ground. I can't remember the last time I had been in such quiet.

I felt like there was space between the world and me, not like it was pressing down on me from all sides.

Then I did something I hadn't done in a very long time. I asked, "What should I do?" I don't know whom I asked, but I asked.

From inside me I heard an answer which was, simply: *stay*.

I don't know if it was in my head, if I just needed to give myself permission, or if I was imagining things, but that's what I heard. It's probably more accurate to say that's what I *felt*, because it wasn't like actually hearing, more like feeling the answer.

Just to make sure, I repeated it out loud. "Stay."

I turned, walked all the way back to the house, and knocked on the door. Shuren greeted me with her warm smile. I could smell lunch.

Does this woman ever stop cooking? I wondered, but I was happy she didn't. And I could tell that she was happy for that as well.

Jim was sitting in his chair, and I sat down on the edge of the fireplace next to him. He didn't say a word, so I just said, "Jim, I'd like to stay."

He looked at me, took a deep breath, and softly said, "Yosh, I was hoping you would."

That is the beginning of my story.

HONESTY

Jim, Shuren, and I sat on the porch after lunch. The faint smell of a wood fire filled the air. The branches of the elm trees swung slowly in the breeze. The sun turned the movement of the branches into a dance of shadows on the floor of the porch. I stared at the show, mesmerized by the play of light and shadow. Eventually, Jim interrupted my daydreaming.

"Yosh, why is it that you decided to stay?"

I tried to collect my thoughts. It wasn't easy to admit that I might have been too quick to judge him. How do you tell someone who actually cares what you think that your initial impulse is to trust no one but yourself? How do you explain that the first hint of disappointment feels like the beginning of the end of hope? When hope has always been a lie for you, you get tired of hoping and just don't want to get hurt again. So you run, and running becomes a way of life.

But there was something about Grandpa Abe's book that had made me stop running. For the first time, it looked like there might really be hope there. At some point during the night, it hit me that this might be my last chance. And it dawned on me that Jim had actually shared this understanding with my grandfather. How could I possibly have thought that Jim was such a simple guy? At that moment, I looked at him and saw a depth and a strength I hadn't seen before.

"I suppose I'm just tired of running, Jim. I mean I feel like I've been running my whole life. I've been running so long, I can't remember if I'm running from something or running toward something."

He let my words hang there for a while and then said, "I know what you mean, Yosh. Many people spend their entire lives in that place."

"Then how come it bothers *me*?" I asked angrily. "It doesn't seem to bother other people."

"Yosh," he said, shaking his head, "people often live their lives without inquiring very deeply into the assumptions they make. The demands of life can be so great that they simply live their lives to the best of their ability.

"When they finally get a chance to stop and look around, they don't even realize where they are in relation to where they started. And without realizing *where* they are, they can't even think about *how* they got there."

I looked at him in disbelief. "How could they not realize it?"

The answer he had given me didn't make sense. I knew plenty of people who were perfectly content just to be where they were. They were at the top and couldn't care less how they got there. My thoughts practically screamed: *They were happy. They had money. They had a family. They had a life. They didn't have all these doubts like I do.*

Jim interrupted my mounting anger. "They might not see it for any number of reasons, Yosh. They might be happy for the moment with what they're running toward. Others might be totally focused on what they're running from, yet be unaware that they are even running at all."

As he spoke, I could feel myself calming down and my brain engaging.

Jim continued, "In either case, they have created a situation for themselves in which they focus on obtaining only the desirable part of things. The *habit* of narrowing the focus onto just what is desirable imperceptibly fosters the *need* to narrow the focus. It is not long before these people create a situation in which they are *limited* to seeing only the desirable part of things. It is often this progression in thought that accounts for their perception of relative happiness."

This was a lot to think about. I asked, "So people's happiness is a lie?"

"No, I wouldn't say that. I would say that it is a result of a certain frame of mind."

"Why can't *I* have that frame of mind, then? At least I would be happy."

"Because you don't want to have that frame of mind, Yosh. If you did, you would already have it. The reason that you have the medallion is the same reason that you've decided to stay. You are seeking something greater than happiness, and you are dissatisfied with not having that greater something."

How could he know this about me? Anyway, he was wrong, I decided. Of course I wanted happiness. Everyone wants to be happy. That's why we do everything, isn't it? Ultimately, we want to be happy.

I wanted to understand his first statement, though, so I asked, "So how does a person fall into this situation of needing to see the desirable part of things and then being able to see *only* the desirable part?"

Jim continued, "People who find themselves in that situation exist in a world in which it is possible to separate the desirable from the undesirable consequences of their actions."

"But isn't that the very nature of the world? I mean, we all want what's good for us and want to avoid what's bad for us."

Jim took a deep breath, was silent for a few seconds, and then said, "The predicament that you seek to understand lies in the space between your statement and mine. Can you see what that is?"

"No," I responded, growing frustrated again. "We're saying the same thing."

"I disagree," said Jim. "The desire to seek what you would call good and avoid what you would call bad is natural, as you said. But this does not mean it is possible to separate the two consequences from any given action. It only seems to be the same when you are stuck within the frame of mind that I mentioned."

I still found this confusing, but I knew I'd just get more pissed off if I argued with him. Instead, I thought I'd just run with it. I asked, "Okay, so if someone does fall into this situation, why don't they ever get themselves out of it?"

"Some of them do, Yosh. You may not know it yet, but you are trying to get yourself out. Unfortunately, in the past, most people have not tried to get themselves out. And most people are not trying to get themselves out right now."

"Why is that?" I asked, realizing that his distinction was still lost on me.

"Mostly because they don't even realize they're in this predicament, just as you yourself don't yet see it." He was calling my bluff. He could tell that my anger was starting to well up again.

I was determined to keep calm, though, hard as it was. I repeated my question, searching for a clue. "Why wouldn't someone in this predicament be able to see that they were in it?"

"Most often, they become so attached to their *doing* that they don't stop long enough to see *what it is* that they're actually doing. Even if they happen to glimpse it, they do not stop long enough to ask whether that act of doing even has value to them. By failing to understand what they are doing or whether that doing serves them, they remain mired in a predicament they're not even aware of. The ways in which any particular person may be mired in this predicament are infinite, but there are also many reasons *why* someone might not see it."

Gradually, his words began to sink in. I replayed the countless occasions when I had behaved without understanding the predicament I was in, and suddenly my anger seemed to lose its focus.

"I think I've done a lot of things in both categories at some time or another," I said.

"Of course you have," Jim replied. "We all have. The question is not what you've done in the past. The question is why you've chosen what you are doing today."

He paused, seeming to gather his focus, then repeated his original question. "Let me ask you again, Yosh. Why did you choose to stay this morning when last night you had planned to go back home?"

Instead of answering impulsively this time, I paused for a second to think. Already I could feel a change in my actions. In a measured tone I said, "I guess I've always thought I knew what was best for me. I feel like I've always had to make my own decisions about things—

to rely on myself, you know? It's not like I had someone telling me what to do."

"So you thought that going home would be the best thing for you to do?"

"No," I said, starting to feel ambivalent. "It's not like I thought it would be best for me. I just felt like I needed to get out. I felt like I needed to get away. When I saw the word 'honesty' on the medallion, I felt like I had gotten my hopes up again, and it was just one more reason I shouldn't trust myself. Don't you understand?" I asked almost plaintively. "Trusting myself is all I've got!"

I was staring at the floor of the porch with that tight feeling in my throat. When I looked back up at Jim and Shuren, they both had such understanding looks on their faces that I allowed myself to finish my thought instead of shutting down and running. My brain said *run* but my heart said *stay with it*, so I stayed.

Regaining my voice, I said, "When I saw the pieces of the medallion come together to form such a trite word, I thought 'I'm just a loser who keeps dreaming of something better, only to be reminded that it's only a stupid dream.' That's why I'd decided to stop dreaming in the first place. I was hurt and angry and upset with myself all at the same time. That's where I was at when you gave me Grandpa Abe's book."

I was expecting Jim or Shuren to fill the silence, but I was mistaken. They just let the silence sit there… along with the three of us on the porch. Eventually I asked, "How do you possibly square something as simple as honesty with all these ideas in *Unitive Awareness*? That complex stuff and 'honesty' just don't fit together. At least I can't bring them together in my head."

Jim said, "Well, maybe there's more to honesty than you think."

"Maybe you're right," I said, still unconvinced.

"So, is that what you were thinking this morning?"

"Well, that's one thing," I said. "Then I thought that my leaving here would just be running away again… that maybe people have been trying to help me, but I just didn't want to see it because I wanted to figure it out on my own."

"Figure what out on your own?"

"Figure out what I'm doing in my life—and why I should keep going when the deck is always stacked against me. I just see myself running around doing things without any purpose. I mean, is that all there is... and then you die?"

"That's an excellent question, Yosh. It sounds like something you've been wrestling with for a while."

"I guess I have. But this morning it hit me that I haven't been able to figure it out on my own and that this might be the last time anyone offered to help me."

Jim nodded, silently. "You may not know it yet, Yosh, but you may have stayed because you have been honest enough to see that the things you are doing with your life lack purpose. The reason that Abe would have wanted you to read his book is to show you that there is a way out of your dilemma."

I stared at him. "Why didn't you just come out and say that in the beginning?"

"Yosh," Jim said, shaking his head, "you told me the answer to that question yourself. Like you told me, you wouldn't have heard me. You were dead set on doing things your way. It was your reaching inside—being honest with yourself—that allowed you to recognize the help that was being offered. By the way, you have been honest before," he teased.

"When?" I was surprised that this man had again found a redeeming aspect to my actions.

"While you may think that recognizing yourself as running from one meaningless goal to another is a common understanding, I can assure you it is not. While such a flash of recognition may occur commonly, it is not common to hold on to that thought. For most people, it's like a disturbing single frame inserted into the movie of their lives. It's a very uncomfortable flash of recognition to embrace, so our impulse is to reject it, particularly because of its brevity. We ignore it, and then it quickly gets replaced by the next frame in the movie. If we aren't paying attention, and often we are not, we may wonder if we ever saw it at all.

"For many people, the movie only slows down enough for them to see that they've been running around after meaningless things just before they're ready to walk out of the theater on their deathbed. Unfortunately, it doesn't do them much good then."

I said, "I guess there's more to honesty than I thought."

Jim continued, "Yosh, you thought so little of it that you couldn't even recognize how much you had gained for yourself through honesty. It probably just seemed quaint to you. Now I think you see that it is not quaint at all. You thought of honesty and intellectualized it. True honesty is deep enough to reveal the ignored assumptions on which grand intellectual structures are often built. This is an easy lesson to forget."

I responded, "I think I'll remember this one."

"Don't be so quick to think that you're over this problem, Yosh. It is a habit that does not die easily. When you are tempted to look superficially at a thought in the future, remind yourself about 'honesty' and you will be well served."

Just as he had brought me up out of my gloom, he now pushed me back from my readiness to congratulate myself. But he wasn't finished.

Jim continued, "You thought, 'Honesty isn't a very complicated concept. How much value can it have?' To you, honesty was about not lying to other people, or at least not telling anything worse than a little white lie. You failed to understand that honesty must first be directed at yourself."

He glanced at Shuren and then back at me. "At least you did until today, Yosh. Now you know that if you can't be honest with yourself, then all your 'honesty' with others is just another way of getting what you want."

Jim stopped, sensing I needed to absorb his words, then started again. "The disease of narrow intellectualization is probably the hardest one to cure. While the intellect confers the ability to understand, it also provides the ability to bend both truth and honesty to one's own will. It's a kind of disease. One thing is for sure, though. If you don't know you got it, there's not a damn thing you can do about it."

I liked that one and decided I would bank it. I knew how easy it was to get tripped up by my own thoughts—to lock myself into thinking a certain way and not be able to get out of it. I'd had that disease before. *If you don't know you got it, there's not a damn thing you can do about it*, I repeated to myself.

Still, Jim's criticism of the intellect troubled me. So I asked, "How can any thought be a disease? Doesn't everything we've been discussing have to do with thinking?"

Jim replied, "It isn't thinking that's the problem, Yosh. The intellect represents our capacity for rational thought. The habit of the intellect is to explore deeply a particular area of inquiry. But dysfunction can arise because of limitations in our thinking that the intellect itself is not even able to perceive. Having arrived at these erroneous 'answers,' it then seeks to apply them as absolutes."

"I'm not sure I understand what you're getting at," I said.

Jim thought for a moment. "Let me give you just one example. Take language, for instance. The intellect can be limited by language. Your specific language assumes a particular perspective. For example, your language may imply the concept of responsibility in a different way than another. You might say, 'I broke my arm,' while in another language you might say, 'My arm broke itself on me.'

"One language may be particularly adept at defining frames of mind such as the German word 'Zeitgeist' meaning 'spirit of the age.' Another language may be limited by lacking specificity for words such as love, pride, or kindness.

"The same language that lacks specific words in one area may possess them in abundance in another area such as shades of color, specialties within a profession, geographic locations within its world, or qualities of snow or ice under particular conditions.

"Still another language may allow for detailed distinctions in kin relationships and have specific names for maternal or paternal grandparents, older and younger brothers of your father, or a sister of your mother as distinct from a sister of your father. To you, probably they are all just aunts and uncles because you don't have such specific terms.

"A person using such a highly detailed language can convey information and nuances of meaning in certain domains of knowledge that you would neither be capable of conveying, nor have reason to understand. Your language, in turn, certainly possesses detailed thoughts that are not available to the speakers of some other languages. Each language will lend itself to a different depth of intellectual inquiry within certain fields of particular interest."

"That makes sense," I said, though I wasn't certain what he was getting at.

Jim continued, "The intellect can also be limited by the cultural tendency to think in a dichotomy of black and white, good or bad, friend or foe. Alternatively, it can be limited by its need to rely too heavily on shades of gray, qualifying all comments with an exception. Don't get me wrong, each habit of thought has its strengths, but each also has its weaknesses. The problem arises when the intellect fails to recognize its own limitations. This is what I mean by narrow intellectualization."

"So it's narrow because it is stuck in its way of thinking?"

"That's right, Yosh. But it may be more correct to say that intellectualization becomes narrow when it fails to account for the limitations inherent in its ability to frame a question or an area of inquiry. It is not this blindness alone that makes this a disease. The blindness is simply an unrecognized fault or shortcoming."

"So what turns that fault into a disease?"

"Intellectualization becomes a problem when a person becomes attached to his or her intellectual perception as being 'correct' or 'the truth.' First, this usually ends the inquiry. Second, this encourages applying that particular 'correct' or 'true' reasoning to other areas of inquiry that they have not investigated as fully. Since the thought leaders of a society tend to be the intellectuals, it becomes difficult for others to challenge this when it occurs. This is what makes such intellectualization narrow, and this is the tendency that allows it to become dysfunctional."

I nodded silently, letting his words sink in.

I'd had conversations with people who thought of themselves as intellectuals before, but no one had ever spoken to me like this about the intellect itself. My eyes silently thanked him for sharing his thoughts with me, but there was something else. It wasn't just the thoughts themselves. It was more that he was *taking the time* to explain them to me. He actually thought enough of me to share his thoughts with me.

"I think I'm finally beginning to understand what you were talking about when you spoke of honesty. There *is* a lot more there than I thought," I said, embarrassed by my earlier rush to judge and my hasty interpretation.

"You know, Yosh, being honest with yourself can only take you as far as you permit it to take you. If you stop short, then you never get to the bottom of the problem. Acting from the *middle* of understanding always gets you bogged down in conflicting goals later on."

He could see that he'd lost me… so he tried again. "Why do you think the medallion says 'Honesty' and not 'Truth,' or some clever saying written in an obscure language?"

Although my mind wanted to return to my romantic fantasies about the medallion, I tried to stay focused. His question, I thought, required a pretty fine distinction. Truth and honesty are really the same thing, aren't they? I thought carefully, and what came tumbling out of my mouth surprised even me.

"Well, I guess truth is something that you can search for, and honesty is something you can't."

Jim's eyes focused in on me and he asked, "So truth exists outside of you, is that what you're saying?"

I'd never thought of it that way, but I said, "Yeah, I suppose that's the way I think about it. Truth is something that simply is, like, 'We hold these truths to be self-evident,' or 'The truth, the whole truth, and nothing but the truth.'"

"Then how about honesty?" he asked.

I responded, "Well, I guess honesty is not really a thing. It's more like the way someone is, or a trait they have."

I had never given this much thought, but I could see that there was something important in this distinction. A few minutes ago, they were just two simple words that I thought meant pretty much the same thing.

I looked at Jim, but he was no longer looking at me. He was gazing off into the distance, nodding slow acknowledgment of my words. I said nothing and he was silent as well. The silence started to become uncomfortable, but I couldn't think of what I might say to prod the conversation along.

Eventually, Jim looked at me and then at Shuren. I was surprised that Shuren hadn't said a thing during the entire conversation. She didn't seem to share my discomfort with the silence but just returned Jim's gaze and smiled at him understandingly. With that, Jim stood up and said, "Well, I guess I better get out and see if Luke needs a hand out back."

Apparently, Luke had been busy with some repairs around the house. I couldn't tell if Jim really needed to go or if I had disappointed him in some way. *Either way,* I thought to myself, *he isn't going to just end our discussion, is he?*

As it turned out, that's exactly what he did. As he got up and left, I sat there staring at the floor, fuming silently, my returning frustration burning a hole into the worn planks of the porch.

Shuren and I sat there alone. I could feel myself slipping back into my habit of stewing in anger, but this time it was different. This time I could actually see it happening rather than simply getting lost in it. The brief pause allowed me, once again, to hear the sound of the birds and feel the breeze on my face as I emerged from my thoughts about myself and my expectations.

Shuren said nothing the whole time. She just sat there with me.

SHUREN

It took me a while to move from staring angrily at the floor to staring in confusion across the yard. I guess you could call that progress—but not much.

I was still sulking when Shuren finally broke the silence.

"Jim enjoys the give and take, but he can get a little impatient sometimes. I know it's hard to follow a line of thinking like that when you're not used to it."

"I wasn't trying to be disrespectful," I responded.

"Oh, I'm sure Jim didn't think you were being disrespectful. True discussion is like any other tool. It needs to be approached with a certain discipline in order for its usefulness to become fully apparent. Let's just say you were being inattentive."

"But I thought I was paying attention pretty well."

"You were, Yosh. Jim is just used to a different level of attention, and I think he was trying to prove his point about the fallibility of the intellect when faced with emotion."

"Well, I think he made that point well enough."

"Then I wouldn't concern yourself with it any further than that. Besides, Jim has other things on his mind right now."

I didn't want to probe, so I didn't ask about this. I figured she would tell me if she wanted me to know. Surprisingly, though, Shuren wanted to continue the conversation Jim had started.

"Words are funny things, aren't they?" she said.

"They can be confusing," I responded, warming to the challenge.

"Yosh, I think what Jim was trying to get at is that our words are limited in what they can express."

"Right, I understood that."

Shuren smiled softly and continued. "But Jim was also pointing to a flaw in the way in which we use these words. We often use our words without being aware of their inherent limitations. When we do that, we lose sight of the way in which our language influences what we assume to be true."

"Was that the point Jim was trying to make about honesty?"

"Yes," Shuren said. "You see, Yosh, most often we see the ability to be honest as really an ability of degrees. I mean, we think of being honest in one situation but not necessarily in another. We think of being honest to a certain degree with some people and to another degree with others. We know that we can be honest about some things with everyone, but about other things only with those we are very close to—who see the world as we do."

"So I was right when I told Jim that I think honesty is the way someone is or a trait they have?"

"You're right, Yosh. Honesty is a quality. Unlike truth, honesty does not exist outside of people and their interpretation of their world. Objects do not have honesty because they do not interpret their world. Animals possess it to the degree that they are capable of interpreting their world. Only in people is the capacity for honesty so fully possible, because only in people is the habit of self-deception so fully developed."

Her words made perfect sense. "So is that how honesty differs from the truth?" I asked. "Is honesty internal and truth external?"

"I don't really see it that way, Yosh. The way I understand it is that truth exists both *inside* of us and *outside* of us. We literally swim in the truth. Truth is the currency of our world. It's built into the very structure of our world, but we each may understand it differently.

"That doesn't mean that the truth is different for each of us—we each just *understand* it differently. Our understanding of the truth becomes our truth, and this is where honesty comes in. It's an essential quality of honesty."

"So honesty and truth are not separate," I interrupted, trying to make sure I understood what she was saying, "but honesty is an attitude toward the truth?"

"That's well put," she said. "Honesty is the expression of an individual's relationship to the truth. Honesty often exists in degrees and may vary with the situation or context. As humans, we are familiar with these aspects of honesty.

"We learn about shades of honesty on the playground when our understanding of truth starts to conflict with the way that other kids understand truth. We learn about these dimensions of truth so early that we forget that there is another dimension to honesty, and that dimension makes all the difference. It's a dimension of honesty that is rarely considered. If your stay with us ended tomorrow and I could only give you one gift to take with you, it would be the awareness of this dimension of honesty within yourself."

Her words started to swim in my head, but I tried to keep up. It was strange how both she and Jim could have me thinking about the same thing in different ways. While she was good at knowing what I was *feeling*, she differed from Jim, who seemed to understand what I was *thinking*.

I was simply amazed that they could read me so well, each in their own way. I felt like I was transparent to them even as I struggled to get my head around the curious way in which they thought.

"Thanks," I said, "but to be honest, you lost me back there."

Shuren gave me a slight smile, sighed, and resumed. "Let me explain it this way. Honesty exists in its original relationship to truth by a degree of timing. The most important dimension of the relationship is not how much, in which circumstances, or why... but *when*."

Her voice changed a bit. Almost solemnly she said, "If you ask any question before you ask 'What is the truth?' you will only be seeking to justify your position. You see, everything that we are capable of affecting in our lives is impacted by our ability to act deliberately. The things we do unconsciously—without thinking—cannot intentionally change who we are at all. Those things have no power to impact us, except to confirm to us that we are who we already thought we were. Any other change is really quite incidental."

I wasn't following her. "Why would I want to be anyone other than who I am?" I asked.

"Because you are unhappy with who you are," she responded.

I became instinctively defensive. I remembered telling Jim that I was unhappy with myself, but it sounded so different when it came out of another person's mouth. Coming from me it was an observation. Coming from Shuren it felt like an attack, and my impulse was to defend myself.

"I know I told you that I'm unhappy with who I am," I blurted out, "but what I really meant was that I'm unhappy with how the world perceives me. It's not *me* that has a problem. It's the *way the world works* that's the problem."

"Oh really?" she asked, leaning forward with a questioning look.

I was caught off balance by her challenge to my simple remark. I looked at her and she stared right back. Her smile was gone, and it was replaced by a look of intense concentration on me.

"Well, Yosh," she said, "why don't you tell me some of the world's problems?"

"Okay... there are lots of them. You can't get into a decent college without money. Then you can't get a decent job without a college degree. Even when you can find one, you can't keep it without kissing up to the boss. You can't get a good apartment without coughing up most of your pay. Most people are in it for themselves and only care about you if you can give them something they want. The economy sucks. The Middle East is blowing up. We're running out of oil and destroying our environment. How's that for a start?"

"Not bad," she said. "It does seem like there are a lot of problems in your world. When exactly did these problems start? And when did they become *your* problems? I mean, did you have these problems yesterday? How about last month? Did you have them when you were living with Abe? Were your problems there before you were born? Surely the *world* was here before you were born."

She was right. The world had been having these problems before

I was born. At some point I had made them mine. I had somehow taken ownership of them. I couldn't remember doing that—but I must have.

She saw me thinking about it. "So what made the world suddenly become a problem? You see, Yosh, it's not that the world does or doesn't have problems— it's that you *experience* them as problems. If you look at every problem you can think of, there's an 'I' there that's experiencing the problem. You already know this because you've already understood that if you remove that 'I,' your problems will cease."

My jaw dropped when I took in her words—*if you remove that 'I.'* How could she have known that I had been thinking of ending it all? I hadn't said a word about that to anyone. I wondered if Jim had been intimating the same thing earlier when he asked me what I planned to do about my frustration with trying to figure things out.

I wasn't sure, so I asked, "When you talk about removing the 'I,' are you talking literally?"

Shuren answered me with a knowing look. "Removing the 'I' from a situation you experience as a problem can be figurative, as in *running away* or *ignoring the situation.* It can also be literal in the sense of killing yourself. You tell me, Yosh—which way *should* we be speaking about it? I sense that you feel deeply hurt and are angry, but I don't know how deep those feelings go."

I felt choked up by her words. It was hard for me to speak. She didn't know for sure about my near-miss, but she suspected I'd been thinking of ending my life. At first I felt ashamed and exposed as a failure in *her* eyes, too.

For a while it was hard to look back up at her, but eventually I did, and there was no judgment or condemnation in her eyes. No pity. Only the warm, understanding smile and that steady gaze that seemed to embrace me.

Then I started looking at it another way. These people actually cared.

For everyone else, I was just a bit character in their lives. I was a responsibility or a ward or a client or a student. I was a patient or a renter or a problem. But Shuren actually thought that I mattered and that my pain was not just something to be medicated or plastered over. To her I was a person.

I hadn't felt valued for just being me in a long time. Both Shuren and Jim actually cared that I was having problems. They wanted to help me understand things, not just hide from my problems. It was disarming, and my anger couldn't find anything on which to anchor itself. They met my anger with understanding—this was new to me.

I knew that I had to be as direct with Shuren as possible. If I wasn't frank with her in that moment, any further discussion would be pointless.

In a hushed voice I said, "Before I came down here I was pretty close to calling it quits." There was silence and I wasn't sure she had heard me, so I tried again. "I mean, I had been thinking about checking out permanently." I couldn't quite bring myself to say it more bluntly than that.

Letting the words pass between us, she finally responded. "I'm sorry to hear that things have been so hard for you, Yosh. I know it's not easy to be on your own from such a young age. But you have to know that you are not alone in feeling this way. The world that we have all constructed can be a harsh place. Difficulty and pain are not distributed equally. Still, 'checking out' is not an honest response to the problem, and I think you understand that now."

"I do understand that now. I always thought that I was thinking clearly on this stuff, but now I don't know. I just assumed that I was thinking pretty objectively and that my emotions flowed from my thinking. Now, after talking with you and Jim, I'm not sure at all. Maybe it's been my emotions that have made me think the way I've been thinking. This is all very confusing. I've gone from being depressed to being confused."

"That may be progress." Shuren smiled.

"It doesn't feel like progress. It feels uncomfortable."

"Progress often does feel uncomfortable. To grow into a new way of understanding means letting go of your old way. Usually that growth is accompanied by a degree of discomfort. But that discomfort is really the combination of two emotions—the emotion of separating from your old ways, and of fearing the implications of the new way of thinking. As you said yourself, it is important to distinguish an emotional response from a cognitive response."

I felt weighed down and deflated. "I have no idea how I would do that. I never even thought about the discomfort of change as a feeling separate from my thoughts. I'm just realizing how intellectually flawed my thinking has been that I could... I could talk myself into wanting to end my life."

"Don't be so hard on yourself, Yosh."

"That seems to be another habit of mine."

"Well, it's good that you recognize it," she said. "It's easy for our minds to be drawn into some pretty dark places. Few of us are very deliberate when it comes to the construction of our internal worlds. It's amazing that so many of us choose to call such a terrible dysfunction of thought 'home.'"

"But I didn't choose my life. I was born into it."

"You were born into your circumstances. This is true. Within those circumstances, though, you are free to make choices. The choices that you make are made for emotional reasons, for rational reasons, or a combination of both."

"Okay, I kind of follow that."

"When we fail to be deliberate about our reasons for making a choice, then it is generally an emotional choice. The 'narrow intellectualization' that Jim was speaking about is the veneer that our minds place upon our emotional responses."

"But why would my mind do that?"

"So that your intellect can justify how it's constructed your internal world without doing the hard work of examining its own inconsistencies."

"All right, I can see that too. All those inconsistencies are the reason that the world is screwed up."

Shuren shook her head. "No, Yosh. These inconsistencies are *internal to us* as individuals. The problems of the world are only reflections of our own internal inconsistencies. You've already told me that your internal world is confusing. How much more confusing is the world that we all create together? The fact that we often see these problems as external is at the heart of the flaw of the intellect."

"This all seems so complicated. If most people live like this, why would I succeed in escaping this way of thinking?"

"Why? Because you've reached the end of your rope, Yosh. You've recognized that you are trapped in a dysfunctional world and you find that unacceptable."

"Right—and my response very nearly was to kill myself."

Shuren smiled, sensing that I had moved comfortably away from that decision. "Yosh, do you realize how far you have come in just a few hours?"

I did feel that I'd come a long way. It already felt like I was talking about someone else and not myself.

She thought for a bit and then continued. "Contemplating suicide is an emotional decision made by a person who can't see his or her way out. Actually, reaching the point of thinking about your frustration with life is a commendable distance to have traveled. It requires deep intro- spection, which is often the silver lining of a cloud of terrible pain and suffering. It would be a shame to lose such an opportunity."

"Opportunity!" I exclaimed. "How is depression an opportunity?"

"Depression is *not* the opportunity. The opportunity arises out of an awareness of the fundamental incongruity of the life that you may find yourself living. The *recognition of that incongruity* is the opportunity. The depression that may follow that recognition is really the frustration you feel in not being able to reconcile the conflicting elements of your reality.

"Of course, not all depression is *this* kind of depression, Yosh. When I speak of *this* depression, I am being very specific. I'm talking about the depression that is inherent to what the philosophers call existential angst. This can be as deep as any other kind of depres- sion—and just as deadly. It exists not *just* because you find yourself in the situation I described, but because you also believe you should not rationally be there—*or* that you should be able to get yourself out of it by yourself."

"But shouldn't I be able to get myself out of it? I mean, I got myself into it."

"To say that you got yourself into it is not entirely correct. You most certainly contributed to the predicament, but many other factors beyond your control were also at play. The important thing is that you now recognize the inconsistencies in your reality, and they disturb you. This is the opportunity I'm speaking of. To recognize your problem is the first step in addressing it. But if you seek to end your recognition of the problem by ending the observer, well that's neither rational nor constructive."

Shuren studied my face to see if I was still with her. I was, but I was struggling a bit. These thoughts were whipsawing my brain.

"Can you get out of this predicament by yourself?" Shuren asked rhetorically. "Yes, you can. But it means being patient with yourself as you investigate your condition. When you embrace a destructive option—such as ending your life—you are not then capable of extricating yourself from the predicament you find yourself in. If that's the case, as it was with you, then you need professional help to save the *potential* for growth, not a discussion aimed at helping you realize your *opportunities* for growth. So you tell me, Yosh, are you able to get yourself out?"

I didn't like the answer I would have given her a couple of days ago. I felt that my answer was different now. But Shuren and Jim had given me so much to think about in so little time that my thoughts were running into each other.

Shuren's look insisted on an answer. I couldn't give her the old one, and I wasn't sure about the new answer, so I didn't give her one.

"Yosh, the important thing for you to realize is that you do not need to get yourself out of the predicament *by yourself*. There is an element of pride in that sentiment that will not serve you well. True self-respect is necessary for you to escape the trap in which a defensive pride imprisons you."

"So I need to replace my pride with self-respect? How would I possibly go about doing that?"

"That self-respect is not found overnight but comes with a realization of your true nature. When you find such self-respect and establish it in yourself, then you will be able to walk out of the trap on your own."

"I really can't see how. It feels like I'm a long way from getting there."

"How long it takes is up to you, Yosh. In the meantime, help is available. If you refuse to accept that help because of your pride, then I think it would be fair to call that an intellectual temper tantrum. But it would only appear to be intellectual. In reality would be an immature response by an intellect that is mired in its own assumptions. The refusal to challenge those underlying assumptions is the intellect's pride. It reveals how flawed that thought process can be."

"So you're saying that if I can separate the recognition of my problem from my need to solve it on my own, then I'll be able to get rid of my depression?"

Shuren said, "It's not your *need* to solve it on your own, but rather your *desire* to solve it on your own. Also, I didn't say recognizing your problems means you can solve them. It only provides the opportunity to resolve them."

"So let's assume that I recognize my problem and that I'm willing to accept help in resolving it. What kind of help are we talking about? Do you mean I have to go into a program or something?"

"Yosh, there are many wonderful programs that can help, but I have none of those to offer you. If you truly wish to end your life, our conversation is of no value to you at this time, and we should take you to the hospital. Is that what you'd like?"

"What would that do? Would that cure me?"

"No, it wouldn't necessarily cure you, but it might buy you enough time to reconsider things. In that way, it might allow you to find a cure."

I could feel myself moving to a decision. My old answer was *not* the answer. I just hadn't seen any honest option. Now I realized that I wasn't even being honest in how I was deciding things. I shuddered at the thought of this intellectual cage I had made out of bars of emotion. No wonder I couldn't escape it! I couldn't even see it for what it was. My answer was becoming clear to me. I thought about it for a bit before I finally spoke.

"I know I didn't answer your question, Shuren. To be honest, I might have answered differently a couple days ago, but now I know the answer. I don't need any more time. I've already reconsidered things. Before coming here I *did* feel trapped. I can't say that things are fine now, but I do feel better just talking with you and Jim. It feels like there might be a way out of that trap, even if I can't see it yet."

"Well, that's a judgment only you can make, Yosh. But once you've decided that you will go on, then you can find the way out. Actually, there are two ways out."

"Why didn't you tell me that before?"

"Because you hadn't made a decision to go on."

"Well if there's a way out—*two* ways—then I do want to go on."

"All right then. Since you don't want to waste any time, let's not. I'm getting a bit thirsty, though, and I missed my morning coffee so it will have to wait for that."

I told her that a cup of coffee sounded great to me too.

Shuren went inside, leaving me alone on the porch with my thoughts. For some reason, I didn't mind being alone with them as much as I had the day before.

DISTRACTION

Shuren returned with two steaming cups of coffee. She set one down on the table in front of me and sat down with her own cup. I thanked her as I watched the steam rise from the cup and disappear into the cool air. I stared at the steaming liquid and we both took a sip.

Shuren continued our conversation without skipping a beat. "I believe we were speaking about ways out of the trap, and you had decided that escape was your goal."

"That's right," I responded. "You made it pretty clear that once I gave up thinking about ending things I could get on with my life, but I couldn't go anywhere before I made that decision."

"Good," Shuren replied. She took another sip of her coffee and took a deep breath, releasing it slowly before she spoke again. "Yosh, in my experience, the depression of 'existential angst' leaves a person either through distraction or true introspection. Distraction has its advantages and is much quicker. It can be effective even for an entire lifetime."

"Isn't distraction just another name for not paying attention?"

"In a way, but it's much more specific. Distraction is paying excessive attention to one thing—or one particular category of things. This disproportionate focus undermines your ability to give attention to the breadth of life."

"So 'distraction' is really about a whole lot of little distractions?"

Shuren nodded vigorously. "Right, but these distractions fall into three categories. Some distractions can be obviously *destructive,* such as drugs, alcohol, or the excitement and short-term rewards of criminal behavior. Some can appear *neutral,* such as ambition, longing, hobbies, career advancement, or infatuation with appearance or fame. Then there are distractions that appear to be *desirable* or *good,* such as love, friendship, dedication, or duty. Just about any passionate pursuit can create a blanket of distraction to cover over the angst and help you forget the dilemma."

I had experience with the first two kinds of distraction, but that last one sounded appealing. "To be honest, I'd take almost any one out of that last group. What do you mean by distraction, though? I thought you said that this was one of the solutions to my dilemma."

"I don't think I called distraction a solution, Yosh. I believe I said that this was simply one of the ways out of your predicament."

"So now I'm a little confused. Are you saying that distraction, as a way out, is nothing more than just forgetting about my dilemma? Isn't that just a way of saying I stop paying attention to the predicament or pretend that it's not there? Frankly, that sounds more intellectually narrow than not recognizing the dilemma in the first place!"

"You're not confused at all, Yosh. In a sense, distraction is a way of 'checking out' *figuratively* without 'checking out' *literally.*"

"So there's no difference, then. I mean, checking out is checking out, right?"

"No, no—that's not right at all. There's a very important difference. Whether you 'check out' figuratively or literally, you deprive yourself of the opportunity to escape from the prison of assumptions that you have accepted as your reality. That is true. But there is a critical difference. If you were to 'check out' literally—as you were tempted to do—you'd have no chance to change your mind. You would have no opportunity to choose again. That's a very important distinction, don't you think?"

"Okay, I understand that, but it doesn't change anything if I'm still stuck in my dilemma. The only thing that's changed is that now I'm just blissfully unaware I'm stuck. It sounds like what you're saying is that there is no solution. There are only ways out."

"Actually, I'm saying *just the opposite.*" Shuren was staring at me as if willing me to understand her. "I'm saying that distraction is a way out—but it is not a solution. Remember I said that there were two ways? Well, the second way out is a solution. It is both a way out *and* a solution, but it is rarely taken."

"Why wouldn't everyone take that second way—whatever it is— if it's both a solution and a way out?"

"Because it isn't easy. It's actually quite a difficult road when one looks at it from a position that is still inside the dilemma."

"I'm sorry. I don't mean to offend you but… I think I lost you there."

She smiled, letting me know she was not offended. "Let me see if I can make this clearer. Getting to the point of contemplating your own existence requires a great deal of introspection. Persisting with that inquiry, despite its apparent foolishness in the eyes of others, implies an extraordinary level of self-reliance. To arrive at the emptiness of existential angst after expending all that effort can be quite deflating. It looks like it goes nowhere."

I felt as though she was describing my life. Suddenly she had my full attention again. This was familiar territory.

"I know that place," I said. "I feel like I've been living there for a long time."

"I believe you have, Yosh. I'm pleased that you feel you can speak your mind, and I'm honored that you would share such personal issues with me. It speaks well of you that you can summon the energy to persist in this inquiry despite the frustrations that you've had. That is *honesty*. Abe would be proud of you."

"Hearing that from you means a lot to me," I said.

"Yosh, you've traveled a great distance on your own. It's not surprising that distraction appeals to you. It appeals to everyone who reaches this point of inquiry."

"But there must be something else," I said. "I can sense it, but I can't see it. It feels like it's just out of reach, and every time I get close it just melts away."

She leveled her gaze at me and broke into a big grin. If I didn't know better, I would have described that look as pride—the parental pride that basks in the reflected achievement of a child.

"You know, Yosh, you remind me of Abe in so many ways," she said. "For a second, that look on your face made me feel as if he were sitting right there in your chair."

"Thanks, but I don't think he would have been so conflicted."

"You might be surprised, Yosh. Your grandfather valued his time here with Jim, and we valued our time with Abe. But do you know why that time was so special to us?"

Shuren didn't wait for me to venture a guess.

"Yosh, your grandfather was tenacious in his inquiry, and he had one of the most active minds I've ever known. But talk about frustration! At first he would get terribly annoyed when he came to an impasse. But it would only be a matter of time and reflection before he'd arrive at an answer. It might have taken him a while to get there, but the answer would eventually give itself up to him.

"Still, he didn't sit on an answer for long. He seemed to be more interested in questions than he was in answers. For him, one answer just seemed to be a springboard for dozens of new questions."

"Questions about what?"

Shuren stared out across the yard as a gust of wind sent a few lonely leaves falling to the ground and the rest to dancing in the sunlight. Then she looked back at me. Her voice was measured now and had dropped a bit.

"Yosh, the thing that interested your grandfather the most was the exploration of the second way out of the dilemma. The thing that you sensed but couldn't quite see drew him as well."

I couldn't believe what she was saying. "How could that be? Is that what his book was all about?"

"I know you have a lot of questions, Yosh. What you need to understand is that Abe was searching for the solution that is *also* the way out of the dilemma."

"Well, did he find it?"

"Yes, Yosh, I believe he did."

I was speechless and just stared at her.

"Yosh, when I said that help was available to you, what I meant was that *this solution* is available. I know that Abe would have wanted us to offer that to you. Before I do that, though, you have to understand that our offer does not mean that this has to be your path."

I sat forward in my chair and was about to ask her what she meant when the phone rang. Shuren excused herself to answer it, leaving me alone on the porch with my thoughts. This was certainly not what I'd expected on the way down here. These people were far from being the rustic residents of small-town America that my city mind had led me to expect.

After several minutes, Shuren returned with a bowl of shelled walnuts, a plate of chocolate chip cookies, and a glass of milk. I thanked her and took a cookie, realizing I'd forgotten the questions I had for her.

"Where were we, Yosh?" Shuren asked.

"We were talking about Grandpa Abe and the solution that he'd found. I think you said that his path to finding it brought him here to Chama. Then you said something about an offer, which I don't understand. Whatever it is, though, I'm sure that Grandpa Abe's path is my path."

Shuren sat down and straightened out her dress before she spoke. "Yosh, Abe's path need not be your path. It will not speak less of you if it is not. If it *is* your path, then you should be aware that this choice will eventually draw you out of forgetfulness—and that can be a painful experience."

"But how do I know if this inquiry is my path? It feels like it is, but how would I know? Part of me has been wishing for those distractions that sounded so desirable, but another part of me sees how hollow they are. Sometimes I feel drawn to one choice and sometimes to the other. How do I really know?"

"That's a decision only you can make, Yosh. That's why honesty is the key."

"So... that's what the medallion means by honesty."

"Yes, that's its greatest meaning. Unless you are honest with yourself about seeking the solution, you will really only be seeking another distraction."

"But how do I really know that the path I choose is the path to the solution? How do I know that it's not just another path to a distraction? Honesty sounds easy, but I'm still not sure how it leads me to the path to the solution."

Shuren replied, "There is one way to know, Yosh. When you have grown weary of seeking distraction as your *primary* motivation, you will encounter an emptiness that no distraction can fill. That emptiness is not what it seems."

"But how can emptiness be the solution? That makes no sense to me."

"The path to the solution only *appears* to be this emptiness from the limited perspective with which we all initially approach it. It is the habit of returning to confront it with ever-newer eyes that allows us to see it more clearly or more fully. As the choices of self-distraction become less and less fulfilling, you come to see the emptiness as more full than the other choices that have distracted you from it."

I had no words to even begin describing my confusion. A part of me felt like a kindergartner being shown the blueprints of a skyscraper. Another part of me wondered if she was making all this stuff up. Still, there was something familiar in what she had described. I thought I'd focus on that part of it and save the rest for some other time.

"I *have* felt a certain emptiness when I've considered all my choices and thought how futile they are," I said. "It's not a place I like to be."

"That is a frightening place, because in that place we encounter the emptiness of our own assumptions. What makes it terrifying is that it feels like nothingness. It is only through honesty that we become aware of our reflexive need to avoid confronting it. It is only through honesty that we see how we've avoided that confrontation by quickly choosing another distraction. It is only through honesty that we see how our need for those distractions requires us to build upon assumptions. And it is only through honesty that we see how our assumptions create flawed realities. Once we are able to see our habit of creating flawed realities, we are finally able to make a deliberate choice—the choice of the solution."

"But all you've described is being stuck in this 'void.' Honesty is fine, but what good does it do me if it just shows me that I'm stuck in some self-defeating distraction?"

"Yosh, once you realize that you are stuck in a self-defeating reality because of your erroneous assumptions, you have the opportunity to stop making those assumptions."

"Is that the path to the solution?"

"To cease building your world upon an assumed truth is the gateway to the path to the solution. I would describe this as sitting at the threshold of the void with a quiet mind and equanimity. When you do this, you are able to see the gateway to the solution."

"So how do I go *through* that gateway and onto the path?"

"When you accept yourself as you are, without assumption or pretension, you are finally able to inquire into the truth. When you no longer seek to defend a particular version of truth, you become open to *all* truth."

"So if I have a vested interest in any particular version of the truth, I end up chasing a distraction. But when I am *not* attached to a particular version of the truth, then I become able to see the path to the solution."

"That's right, Yosh. You find it by applying the Law of Original Truth."

"Never heard of that," I said.

Shuren responded by reciting it for me in a solemn tone that I'd heard her use before. She seemed to have reserved that tone for these words:

If you ask any question before you ask "What is the Truth?" you will only be seeking to justify your position.

As I listened to her words, I suddenly realized that she was talking directly to me when she spoke about forgetting what one has just heard. She had not meant it as a generalization. Her words were directed specifically at me.

I suddenly realized she had used the same words in the beginning of our conversation on honesty and the truth. I just hadn't thought much about what they meant. I certainly didn't think of them as a 'law.' I recognized that Shuren was making a point about hearing and listening, but I wasn't going to let on that I understood.

Instead, I just said, "That sounds simple enough."

"It's actually quite difficult, Yosh. In fact, most of the complicated problems you identified earlier grow out of a failure to consider this law. Remember, this only answers your question about identifying the beginning of the path to a solution. It does not speak to actually embarking on that path. Consider it for yourself and see if you are drawn to this path. No partial or qualified honesty will suffice."

"I'll do that—but I still don't understand how this Law of Original Truth leads to a path out of my predicament."

"The Law of Original Truth is the first step on the path to the solution because it addresses the cause of the problem itself. It doesn't allow you to forget the inconsistencies of your reality. It doesn't allow you to plaster over the problem, simply to find out much later that you only ignored the difficulty and didn't resolve it."

"You keep talking about this like it's one problem. I feel like I have lots of problems, not just one."

"Yosh, what you're having trouble seeing is that most of your problems have a common foundation. In reality, there are no problems in your world, only an 'I' that is experiencing problems. What you may think is a problem in your reality, someone else may consider to be a solution in his or her reality. We began this conversation talking about how you considered 'checking out permanently,' or removing the 'I.' If removing the 'I' is rejected as an intellectual temper tantrum that doesn't serve you, then you are left with the two options we discussed.

"The first is essentially a decision to distract the 'I' from its condition. If you can remember how being in love makes all your problems seem to disappear, you will be familiar with this way out. Over an entire lifetime, it's easy to replace one such distraction with another.

"The second way out is the solution, and that involves accepting the 'I' as flawed. Choosing this option means refusing to put the blame on the environment in which the 'I' operates. This second way out involves taking full ownership of the recognition that the 'I' carries problems into the world. The reasonable thing to do, then, is to examine the 'I' for its dysfunction and seek to fix it when possible. Honesty helps you identify and resolve dysfunction in yourself once you've chosen to address it."

This finally made some sense to me. Could it be that I was really unhappy with who I was? Was my unhappiness with the world just a convenient way to ignore my ability to change things in myself? I just sat there staring off into space, letting the meaning of her words sink in. As Shuren sat back in her chair, I considered her words and told her I could use another walk.

"You go right ahead, Yosh. I love the fall as well, and the walk down the road is beautiful, especially with all the colors coming in. I've got some work to do inside, so I'll see you when you get back."

With that, we both got up.

JIM

It was sunny and cool, perfect walking weather. This time I retraced my steps into town with all these thoughts swirling around in my head. One foot after the other, my body moved through town, beyond, and back. My mind couldn't have been further away. After a couple hours, when I got back to Shuren's place, I felt recharged.

I found Shuren shelling peas at the low table on the porch. She seemed to prefer working outside when she could. I sat down next to her and she showed me how to do it.

"Just snap off both ends of the pod," Shuren instructed. "Then peel off the strip that runs down the seam. Once you do this you can just pry the seam open with your thumb. After that, it's easy to slide your thumb down the pod, opening the seam and dropping the peas into the bucket."

I got the hang of it in no time and relieved Shuren, who got up to take care of things in the house. I sat there building a pile of empty pea pods on the table and filling up the bucket with peas.

Shuren returned, first with some iced tea, then with a pile of laundry to be folded. She poured me a glass of tea and we sat there, each busy with our own tasks.

Finally, Shuren broke the silence. "I guess you'd probably like to know a little more about your grandfather."

"Sure," I said. "No one in my family seems to know much about this part of his life."

"I knew him pretty well, Yosh. When he used to come up to visit, I was just a little girl, but Abe was like a big brother. A lot of what I knew about the world outside town I learned from him."

She gazed out across the yard, beyond the trees, to the mountains in the distance. "We didn't travel a whole lot back then, and Albuquerque was a small town compared to what it is now."

"So how did Grandpa Abe end up here? This is a long way from San Antonio."

She looked at me and took a deep breath. "Abe was a trainer in the flight school at Brooks Army Airfield just outside San Antonio. This was before there even was an air force. He was a flight instructor in the army, training pilots to fly B-25 bombers in 1944. I think you know about that, though."

"Right, I knew he was down in San Antonio, but I didn't know what he was doing there."

Shuren nodded. "Anyway, he was testing the range on a new version of the B-25 when it crashed in the southern Rockies well north of here. Your family never knew about it because those flights were classified at the time—and because Abe never wanted to worry his mother, your great-grandmother."

Shuren took a sip of her tea. "As Jim tells it, your grandfather was pretty beat up but was found by..." She hesitated for a moment, then continued. "Found by a friend of Jim's who stays up there. He patched Abe up and brought him out of the mountains, but I guess they had to wait until the snow cleared the passes before they could get down.

"I only met Abe briefly that time because he was in a hurry to get back to his post. But after that he'd come up every leave he had, and he and Jim would head out into the mountains. Jim always looked forward to those visits, and so did I."

As we passed the afternoon folding laundry and shelling peas, Shuren introduced me to a grandfather I had never known, telling me stories about his countless visits. She told me about his city boy attempts to be helpful around the ranch where they lived at the time and how those attempts evolved from clumsy efforts to real capabilities.

She told me how Abe would always bring her a present when he came to Chama, and that he always greeted her with a big hug.

"He was about as loving a person as I've ever known," Shuren said.

I could tell by her voice that she missed him. She recalled how her laughter at him was always met by his laughter at himself and how her laughter had changed over the years to become profound admiration.

Jim and Shuren hadn't known about Grandpa Abe's death eleven years ago. For some reason, after he adopted me, he asked them not to call unless they needed his help. They never needed anything so they had never contacted him. But he contacted *them* as often as he could. Even after I came to live with him, Grandpa Abe still called them regularly.

They only reached out to Grandpa Abe after they hadn't heard from him in over a year. As Jim had said, they were never able to find him or any of my family. I could tell that his absence in their lives had left a big hole.

Now it was my turn to tell Shuren about the Abe that she didn't know. I told her how he had adopted me after my parents had passed away and about those five wonderful years I had with him. So that's how our afternoon went, with her telling her stories and me telling mine.

The shadows were getting long when Jim came back up the path to the house. Luke was with him now, and I could see that they were lost in their discussion. They stepped up onto the porch where Shuren and I were still chatting. Jim brushed the dust off his jacket with his well-worn hat, and Luke did the same.

I took a long look at Jim and wondered at the odd combination of qualities he contained. He looked plain and down to earth, but the thoughts he had shared with me didn't fit that image. For that matter, neither did Shuren's. From all I'd heard, Jim must have had a lot in common with Grandpa Abe. I wondered how similar they truly were. I stared at him like I was seeing him for the first time.

Jim's weathered face matched his hands. Wisps of thinning white hair had this odd effect of standing out like a gentle crown against the leather of his face. He was stooped a bit from age but still moved with a certain self-assured resolve. I marveled at how he could contain that while remaining so open and inquisitive. He had the confidence of someone who had long ago become comfortable with his opinions—opinions that had been sifted through a mind animated by endless curiosity. He tilted his head slightly, looking at me from above his glasses, and I felt the focus of his attention from behind his ancient hazel eyes.

At his age, Jim moved slowly but didn't sit still. I could tell that he and Luke had been outside most of the day. Jim sat down with a sigh, poured tea for Luke and himself, then took a long drink. Shuren told him that we had been talking about Abe.

Jim just kind of nodded. He seemed to have other things on his mind. After a few moments, he turned to me and said, "Yosh, if you're going to be staying, we'll need a hand out on the ranch. I know you probably don't have much experience with this kind of thing, but Luke will show you the ropes."

I had been so focused on Jim that I had barely noticed Luke. He seemed so quiet. At the same time, he looked the part of what I imagined a rancher would be. His words were purposeful and few. I couldn't tell if he disliked me, if he just didn't have much time for all of this, or if that was just his way. Luke looked over at me and said, "Grandpa wants me to take you out in the morning. I'll stay here tonight but we'll head out early, maybe four o'clock."

I didn't know what to say. I hadn't really thought about how long I'd stay, or about work at all. I knew nothing about farms or ranches except for Thanksgiving hayrides and school visits. I knew that work started early on a farm, but four o'clock sounded *too* early. Whether it was four in the morning or four in the afternoon, I didn't think I could be of much help. But then I really wasn't missing anything at home.

As these thoughts flashed through my mind, what came out of my mouth was, "That sounds fine with me."

Luke gave me a small, tight smile and Jim nodded.

Shuren put down her work and stood up. "We'd better get an early dinner, then," she said. "Yosh, why don't you bring those peas and give me a hand inside?"

I spent the next hour helping her in the kitchen. She made it look effortless. For her, I suppose it was. I never knew how much fun it was to cook with someone who relishes every moment of it. I don't know which I enjoyed more, helping Shuren prepare the meal or joining them all in eating it.

We finished dinner and Luke excused himself to go to bed, making sure I remembered we'd be leaving early. Shuren returned to the kitchen, leaving Jim and me alone. I sat there not knowing if Shuren had told Jim about my conversation with her that afternoon. They seemed to be so in tune with one another that they could probably finish each other's sentences.

I was about to mention the conversation with Shuren when Jim asked me if I'd given any more thought to the topic of honesty. I told him I had, and that I understood the Law of Original Truth as Shuren had explained it to me.

Jim said, "Yosh, let me ask you this. What is it that you want? What is it that you're looking for?"

Well, he certainly wasn't going to beat around the bush, was he?

I said, "Well, I came down here looking to meet you and to find out about my grandfather."

"No, that's not what I meant, Yosh. What were you looking for the day before you found out about me—the week before you knew this place existed?"

I didn't understand what he was asking. I mean, I'd been looking for a job because I'd been out of work for so long. Before that I was looking for a new apartment because my lease was coming up at the end of the month. I wanted a new car because my old one was on its last legs. There were a lot of things I wanted. There were things I was looking for, but I knew he was asking me something deeper.

He saw my confusion and clarified. "Yosh, what are you looking for out of life itself?"

I thought about it and said, "I suppose I want to be happy."

He smiled and said, "Now *that* is an honest response. That's the reason that your grandfather gave you the medallion, Yosh, and that's the real reason you've come here. You're here because, in some way, you think this trip will add to your happiness."

I was confused again. It sounded like he was just stating the obvious.

"Doesn't everyone want to be happy?" I asked rhetorically. "What's so special about that? I don't see how that sets me apart."

"I'm not talking about happiness being your goal. I'm talking about your ability to move from specifics to intangibles in your thought. The ability to move quickly from the particulars that you desire to identifying the *cause* of your desires is not common. This habit of introspection is the basis upon which structured progress can be made."

I still thought he was giving me more credit than I deserved. Besides, my discussion with Shuren had put my brain into overdrive. I doubt I would have been so quick to make this transition he pointed out if he'd asked me the day before.

"I have to tell you," I admitted, "that I think some of this comes out of the discussion I had with Shuren this afternoon."

"That's well and good—but not really relevant. If you were capable of assimilating the discussion you had with Shuren, then this knowledge is now your own. To be able to move so quickly toward identifying the common element in the specifics of your desires reflects that you've done that. If you accept this progress as your own, then we can move on and time is not relevant. If you wish to exact a toll of time in order to digest it, then be my guest. In that case, you will have chosen for time to be a factor. It's your choice, Yosh."

"I'd like to go on," I said. "I *do* believe that I've made this progress my own. It's just that…"

"Just that, *what*?" Jim asked.

"Well, it's just that a lesson like that usually gets delivered slowly, over time, like after you get done with a movie or finish a course or read a book. Things are just coming so fast that I can't even tell that I've learned something until you point it out to me."

"We can slow things down if you'd like, Yosh. After all, you probably have more time than I do." He grinned.

I smiled back. "No, I was just pointing it out. I really am thankful to you both. In fact, it makes me happy to try to keep up with you!"

I think Jim appreciated my response because he was focused again on the issue of happiness. He walked over to the desk, took out a piece of paper, and returned to the dining room table. Then he started to draw. He drew an ocean and some waves. Then he drew some more.

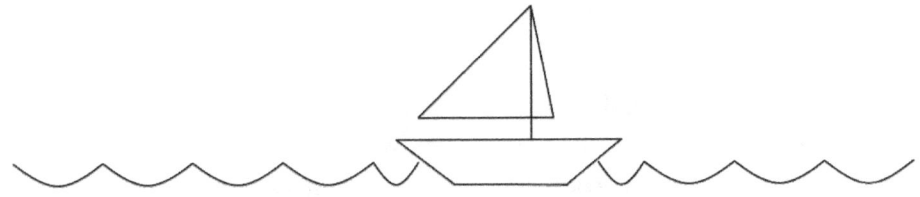

"What do you see, Yosh?"

"A sailboat on the ocean," I said.

"You see, Yosh, you've told me that your goal is to be happy. When you're happy, it's like sailing on this boat when there's just enough wind to keep your mind busy and when the waves are just big enough that the swaying motion is soothing.

"Now, *how much* wind and *what kind of* waves are perfect for any one person isn't the same as it is for another person. It's not even the same for the same person at different times in life, or even at different times of the day.

"So you see, Yosh, in order for you to be happy, the waves and the wind have to be just right. Now what's the likelihood of that? Maybe it happens once in a while."

I thought to myself, *well that's about right. That's about as often as I'm happy—once in a while.*

Jim continued. "Let's suppose that happiness for an individual exists within a range of waves and wind rather than at a certain point. I'm not suggesting that the goal of reaching that range is meaningless. It certainly is not. It is possible to increase your happiness by increasing the likelihood of having favorable weather conditions and by keeping your boat in good repair.

"Still, happiness will depend on conditions favoring it. Lose those conditions and you lose your happiness. So, if your ability to affect happiness is so limited, the question becomes this—is happiness, then, really worthy of being the ultimate goal of life?"

I'd never thought about happiness like this. All my life that's what I'd wanted, and now Jim was calling that into question.

I responded, "Of course I want happiness. What else is there? If I didn't want to be happy, then should I want to be unhappy? That makes no sense at all."

Jim kept going. "Let's look at your language, Yosh. You want to be happy—but what is happy? 'Happy' comes from an Old Norse word, 'happ,' which meant good luck or chance. The word 'happen' comes from the same root and, of course, means the occurrence of something by chance. Happenstance, haphazard, hapless, mishap— they all come from the same root.

"When you want happiness, what you are asking is for things to line up nicely for you by chance. Or you are hoping for the conditions to change that affect your happiness. You are either asking for good luck or you are asking for the means to change the conditions of your 'boat/sea' interaction. Wishing for luck is a short path to misery because it's a lousy plan. The freedom and opportunity to change your own conditions are what most people speak about when they talk of happiness, and I don't want to diminish that at all."

"Are you saying that I shouldn't want to be happy?"

"No, Yosh, that's not what I'm saying. What we're talking about is your *goal*. Aiming for happiness is not bad. I'm just suggesting that it's not necessarily the highest goal. It can be an interim step—but if it's the final goal, then it's likely to be flawed."

"How is that?" I asked.

"Well, personal happiness can be flawed in many ways," Jim responded. "It can be temporary, which means it may cause the sacrifice of long-term happiness, like missing opportunities because you're too attached to your current position, place, or friends. It can be expedient, such as when cheating, deception, or betrayal to obtain happiness plant the seeds of self-destruction. It can be selfish and impede the happiness of others by hoarding resources or opportunities so others can't benefit."

He had a point. I hadn't considered it that far ahead.

Jim must have wanted to soften it up a little because the next thing he said was, "I don't want you to think you're alone in all this, Yosh. Most folks are doing the same thing—carving out what little happiness they can by trying to make their range of conditions a little bigger. If by chance they get the opportunity to make the range a whole lot bigger, then they just continue on with their original goal.

"You see, once you set a goal, it's hard to change it because you put a lot of things together to support that goal. It's hard to remove one of those supports without having the whole thing come down on you. The best time to decide on your highest goal is before you actually begin the journey. Choosing the highest goal is critical. Once you choose the highest goal, you have the opportunity to choose interim goals that are consistent with it. That doesn't mean that any interim goals you choose will *necessarily* be consistent with your highest goal, but you'll have the opportunity to choose ones that are."

"What do you mean by 'necessarily'?" I asked. "Why wouldn't my interim goals be consistent with my highest goal?"

"Yosh, just because you've chosen the highest goal doesn't mean that you can see it clearly. That can take time. It's the very act of selecting interim goals, and then reflecting on the results of those choices, that allows the highest goal to be more clearly seen.

"Experience is the critical element. An event or interaction that appears confusing or opaque at the beginning often looks manageable and clear afterward. That's why someone once said that 'experience is something you needed the moment before you got it.' Once you have it, you do not need to repeat the lesson... unless you didn't really get it."

"So *that's* why the word 'necessarily' is relevant," I said. "The result of choosing interim goals is that I can test them for the ways they agree—or fail to agree—with the highest goal."

"Pretty much, Yosh. It's your evaluation of those results that holds the key. Evaluating the results against the highest goal lets you pick the building blocks of the *next* interim goal. As you repeat this process, your interim goals become more and more congruent with the highest goal. This is the value of experience—the value of action married to reflection."

I rolled his words around in my mind for a while and then hesitatingly said, "I didn't realize how little I'd really thought about it. I mean, I've never questioned wanting to be happy. I suppose you just grow up hearing that being happy is the goal, and it becomes part of you without even thinking about it."

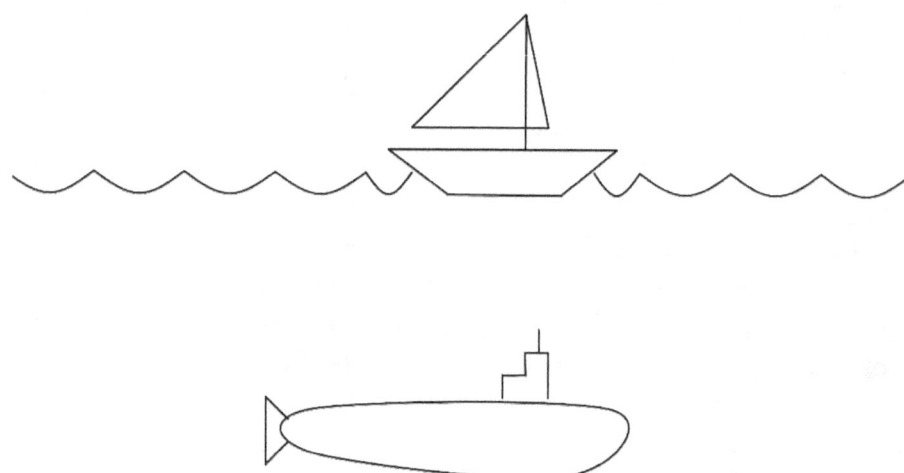

As he drew, Jim said, "Just like honesty mirrors truth and goes deeper than it, there is another word that mirrors happiness and goes deeper than *it* does. Do you know what that word is, Yosh?"

I thought for a bit and gradually it came to me. "Joy?"

"Yes," Jim said. "Joy is a word that's been with us for a long time, just like happ. But there *is* a difference. The difference between joy and happiness is that joy comes from inside of you, while happiness is dependent on the conditions around you. Joy is there whether the wind is blowing or not, whether the seas are rough or calm. Joy just cruises right along like my submarine, regardless of how stormy the ocean becomes. It's a different type of condition. Joy is a *decision* to see things as being well."

This again sounded like a simplification to me, and I objected. "I just don't see what would justify my seeing things as being well. Isn't it dishonest to base your highest goal on something that is not really justifiable?"

Jim responded with his own question. "Well, Yosh, is happiness justifiable, then? Isn't happiness, or rather the desire for happiness, also a condition? Isn't the desire for happiness just a decision that all is *not* well, or that all *will not be* well *unless* I make it well for myself or make it well for those who are important to me? I suggest that you apply intellect to both your current assumptions *and* those that might be proposed."

That made sense. Maybe there was something to joy. But I still didn't know what might justify it. But there was an odd freedom in feeling that the desire for happiness might be based on a faulty justification as well. I have to say that I was more undecided on both joy and happiness than I was sold on joy. I realized that choosing happiness as my highest goal might not be the best decision after all.

I decided not to decide—at least not yet. But joy was starting to have its appeal. Even if I did agree that joy might be a higher goal, how would I ever even approach it? It didn't seem like an easy prospect to me.

So I asked Jim, "Joy sounds like what I'd rather have, but how would I get to joy if I can't even get to happiness?"

He could see that I was still stuck, so he offered the following. "From where you're sitting, Yosh, you still see from the perspective of happiness. It's hard to get to joy from there. Flip it around. Look at it from the perspective of joy. How would you get from joy to happiness? If you were joyful, how would you move yourself to happiness?"

That was a way of thinking that had never occurred to me, so I gave it a shot. "If I were joyful, things would not affect me, and I would always be having joy, right? Then if I wanted to move to happiness, I would have to start being influenced by things that happen to me."

"Exactly," said Jim. "But this process would need to move through several steps. First you would need to have the desire to move to happiness. Then you would consciously affirm the intent to move.

69

Finally, through determination, you would assume the relationship to things that was implied by your new state of happiness. Okay, so now let's flip it around. If you wanted to move from happiness to joy, how would you do that?"

This seemed easy enough. "First I'd *want* to move. Then I would *intend* to move to joy or consciously decide that I wanted to move to it. Finally, I would work hard to assume the relationship to things implied by being joyful."

"Exactly," said Jim. "Of course that's easier said than done, but if you don't know where you're going, you aren't likely to get there. Knowing *where* you want to go or where you want to be is part of it. *How badly* you want to get there is another part of it. The fourth part is knowing *how* to navigate your way. You can get help for the fourth part, but the first three can only come from you."

He wrote down four words on the paper and asked me to tell him what they represented, assuming my goal was clear to me. The words were:

Desire

Intention

Determination

Process

I said, "Okay, let's say that my goal is joy. First I want to get there. Then, I affirm that my *intention* is to become joyful. It's not just a passing feeling then. *Determination* is just another way of saying how badly I want to move to that place or how badly I want to get there. *Process*, then, would be the way I get there or how I plan on getting there."

Next to Jim's words I wrote.

Desire *My feeling that I want to move to joy*

Intention *Consciously affirming I want to go/ be there*

Determination *How badly I want to get there*

Process *How I plan on getting there*

Jim seemed pretty happy with this. I was elated. I know I've said that before, but I really felt like I was learning for the first time in my life—really *learning*, not just getting ready to take a test or something.

I had more questions for Jim, like what about *why* and *when*? Weren't they important too? But it was getting late, and it was all I could do to try to get my head around this much. I was mentally exhausted at this point and suddenly remembered that I needed to get up early. When I thought about it, I'd spent countless more nights going to sleep at four a.m. than I had getting up at four a.m.

I thanked Jim for his explanations and said good night. Before I could turn to walk to my room, Jim said, "Yosh, I won't be going with you in the morning. I've got to take care of some business here. You go on up to the ranch with Luke. Shuren and I will meet up with you there as soon as we can."

I was surprised. I had so many more questions, and I thought we'd have time to talk up at the ranch. Then I remembered that I had suddenly jumped into the lives of these people. I was sure they had better things to do than entertain me.

"No problem," I said.

"It's good to have you with us," Jim said. "Don't worry, I'm not done with you yet. We'll have some more time together. Now go on to bed. Luke is very punctual, so you'll be up in a few hours."

Jim went to his room before I turned the lights off. In my own room, I started thinking about the upcoming day. What would I possibly do on a ranch? I really didn't know what to expect, but I knew it would be nice to be outside for a while. Besides, I could use some time to digest everything that had happened the last two days.

LUKE

The next few days were a blur of activity. I learned that Luke was rarely in town this time of year. He was usually up at the ranch that Jim and his family owned farther up in the Chama Valley. He had come down to the house to meet me but couldn't stay long because fall was a busy time.

Luke and I were up early. Jim and Shuren had gotten up early too. There was no time to sit down for breakfast. There was just enough time to wash up, get dressed, and say our goodbyes. It hadn't taken me much time to pack my few belongings the night before.

We managed to get on the road shortly after four in the morning with a couple cups of coffee, a basket of apples, and some muffins that Shuren had baked the day before. Luke hadn't said much at Shuren's house, but he must have been keeping it cooped up because we chatted all the way up to the ranch. He wasn't exactly talkative, but he wasn't quiet either. He wanted to learn more about me, but I was more interested in knowing him and his family.

Strange as it sounds, I was kind of tired of talking about me. Besides, the Cramfords weren't at all what I was expecting and I wanted to know more about them.

Eventually I won, and Luke told me about his family. I learned that they had been in northern New Mexico since the mid-1800s on his father's side and a lot longer on his mother's side. Jim was Luke's maternal grandfather, and that side of his family was a mixture of Spanish, Ute, Anglo, Hopi, and Apache. In fact, Luke still had cousins on the Jicarilla Apache reservation, not far from Chama.

I learned that both Jim and Luke had traveled around a lot when they were younger. From Luke's stories I gleaned that a certain tension between loyalty and rebellion seemed to run in their blood. Eventually, though, each had decided to return to their farm, their ranch, and their family in the area.

I could tell that Luke had been particularly defiant when he was younger. For a long time he never thought he'd come back, but then he did. I liked Luke. He was a straight shooter, every bit as interesting as his mother and grandfather. The time flew by as we drove through the dark, talking and laughing about Luke's misadventures. It felt good to laugh, and I lost myself in our conversation as the miles passed.

The pavement eventually gave way to a gravel road, and Luke's mind must have returned to the work that waited for him because he stopped talking about the past.

I asked him about the ranch and how I was supposed to be of any help to him. He smiled a bit and said we'd take it one step at a time. It was the first of October and probably the busiest time of the year for him. The small harvest was coming in, the apples hung heavy on the trees in the orchard, and the hay was ready to be cut and baled. But most important, Luke explained, they would need to start "back-riding" the summer pastures to gather their free-range cattle. "After that," he said, "the real work would begin."

I was thinking about those cows when the smell of horses and cattle started to fill the air. That smell reached us before we had reached the gate to the ranch.

It was still dark when we pulled up to the farmhouse. The light from the kitchen window glowed a warm yellow and beaconed through the darkness that outlined the house. The truck ground to a halt. We stepped into the quiet and the chill of the morning mountain air. Luke walked up the step and opened the door, announcing his return.

A voice from the kitchen answered back and Luke's wife walked out to greet us. She embraced Luke, clearly happy to have him home. Then she turned to me. "Hello, Yosh. Luke called and told me quite a bit about you. You guys must be hungry. I'll get you some breakfast."

Luke was quick to answer back. "Yosh, this is my wife, Fitra. As you can see, she'll probably feed you to death, just like Mom would."

She glanced at him, shaking her head as if dismissing his comment. I looked at her and smiled. She was a good four inches shorter than Luke but carried herself with the same confidence and sense of purpose. She had beautiful black hair tied back with a bright red ribbon and a face that radiated warmth and caring.

I answered Fitra. "Thank you very much—happy to meet you too. I hope I won't be too much trouble. Everyone I've met has been so kind to me."

Luke responded, "Don't worry, you'll be earning your keep. In fact, you might end up having to eat those words. But just in case that doesn't fill you up, I'm sure Fitra will get you squared away."

Fitra smiled and disappeared back into the kitchen. Breakfast was ready before we knew it. The three of us ate together, and then Luke led me back outside to start our work day.

As we stepped out the door, I squinted in the morning sun. The sight that greeted us left me breathless. Opening up before us was a mountain of yellow. The valley in which the farm was located was a carpet of green facing a large stand of aspen, ablaze in their fall color. The bright yellow of those trees was punctuated by the occasional green of a ponderosa pine, all of it held in the calm of the still morning air.

I thought, *what a privilege to live among such beauty.*

I was captivated by that sight, but I couldn't tell if Luke even noticed it. Maybe it was just too familiar to him. Maybe he didn't care. I don't know. All I knew was that he was now focused on getting me oriented.

He showed me around, accompanied by his dogs, Weeway and Keeley. Weeway, a male Boerboel, a South African breed I'd never heard of, was light brown with a black muzzle and dark raccoon coloration around the eyes. Keeley, a female Pyrenean mountain dog, was white with small hints of tan scattered around. They were both huge and very suspicious of me. I was glad to have Luke's company.

Luke showed me the barn and the greenhouses he had put up. That's where the peas had come from, since they're usually a spring crop. Most everything they were growing was for their own use and for the farm hands. There were a few dairy cattle, just enough for the family and some local sales. The open fields looked like corn and fodder for the animals and more vegetables. He showed me the berries that grew close by and the apple orchard farther out. It was a thorough tour of the place ending at the barn back by the house. It was more than a tour, though. Luke met with the ranch hands as he went around, introduced me, and laid out plans for the day. I got some curious looks, but everyone was polite.

We walked back to the house. The curious looks, Luke explained, were less about my presence there than about my appearance. I must have stood out like a sore thumb. Luke went back into his room and returned with some of his old clothes. They seemed to fit pretty well, though the jeans were a little long and the boots were kind of loose.

I felt much more comfortable being on the ranch now that I was dressed for the part. At least I knew that any curious looks would now be about my clumsiness and not my clothes. One of the hands who had looked curiously at me turned out to be the ranch foreman, Ahote.

Ahote was quite a character and had a fantastic sense of humor, though that wasn't always to my benefit. He was also Luke's cousin, though he had a darker complexion and a heavier build. He and his son, Takoda, who looked like him but was about my age and almost my height, had both been working on the ranch for years. They had pretty much made the ranch home, though Ahote and his wife had their own house on the grounds. Like the saying went, 'It's good to be close to family... but not too close.'

Luke's work kept him too busy to have me tag along all day, so he farmed me out to the foreman. Ahote didn't seem to mind, though. Either that, or he must have found me pretty amusing. I don't know why else he would have taken me under his wing—but he did.

To be honest, sometimes I thought Ahote must have gotten the same share of patience as Jim. Regardless of how often I screwed up, he would send me right back in to do it again, whatever it happened to be. And believe me, I screwed a lot of things up.

Ahote was directing the show, but Takoda was showing me how the work was done. He and I became inseparable. Nowhere was that more true than learning to ride a horse. I had never ridden before. I had never even been *around* a horse before. But with Takoda's encouragement, I found that riding a horse wasn't that hard. Staying on one that wants to get back to the stable—well, that's another story.

Over the next couple of weeks, I pretty much learned all the little things that go into making a ranch work—mostly sweat and attention to details. I slept better than I ever had. I had forgotten how natural it is to sleep after doing physical work all day and how restful that sleep is.

The rhythm of life on the ranch didn't feel like an imposition. It felt comfortable. In the city I made my own rhythm, and there was room for that rhythm to be accommodated. There, I had the sense that I made my own life. Here on the ranch, it was I who was accommodating myself to the rhythm, and I felt like I was a part of life.

Time didn't fly by on the ranch but seemed to pass much more deliberately. It gave me time to think about what Shuren and Jim had shared with me. And the more I thought about it, the more I came to agree that I did make a lot of assumptions. I assumed a lot of things were true that I had never questioned. I was starting to see the many ways those assumptions shaped my thoughts.

I also thought about happiness and joy, playing through all the scenarios I could think of in which my quest to be happy might keep me from having joy, or where my attempts to find happiness might make it harder for others to do the same—just as Jim had said.

I thought about these things, but that doesn't mean I knew what to do with those thoughts. If anything, it was more frustrating to have them, because now I felt like I had to do something with them. As much as I tried to put them out of my mind, they would just come right back in again through another door.

It was as if I could hear my own mind here. In the city, when I had a thought it was quickly replaced by another thought. There, my mind wanted to absorb as much information as it could. Here, sorting that information out seemed to be the priority. It was still dynamic and interesting—just in a different way.

But *now*, scrambling around just to add information on top of information seemed hollow in a way. Here on the ranch my mind actually slowed down enough for me to see that it had this habit of bouncing around from one thought to another, like a squirrel trying to get off the road to avoid a car, or a rabbit being chased by a dog, twisting this way and then that.

I thought that was strange to think of my mind as a part of me, rather than as me itself. How could I *see* myself doing this if I was the one doing it?

These were strange thoughts. They contrasted with the occasional immediacy of the work that needed to be done. The urgency of those jobs punctuated expanses of time during which my mind was free to wander.

I noticed how this staccato arrangement of time allowed me to see for the first time my habit of bouncing dissociated thoughts around. Only after I was forced to put spaces between my thoughts was I able to see them so fully. I had fewer things to think about, but I actually *thought* about them rather than just stringing them all together.

It was during one of these periods of daydreaming that I looked over at Luke. We were standing at a wooden fence, looking down at some of the cattle in the pasture. I saw that he was staring off into the distance the same way I had been doing. Luke looked like he'd stepped out of the script for a spaghetti western. He had dark blond hair that looked brown as often as not, being generally covered in the dust of the ranch. He was about ten years older than me and tough as nails, with a face that seemed to embody decisiveness.

It took me a while to learn how much ambiguity Luke was capable of containing behind that grit. He had this uncanny ability to go from barking out orders to the ranch hands to saying he had "no idea" when I asked him questions about something Jim or Shuren had said earlier.

The thing that I found strange was that he was comfortable *not* knowing. Or maybe he was comfortable just knowing what he did know and left it at that. There was an acceptance of limitation that I just didn't understand.

I usually felt okay if I didn't know about something, but once I knew about it I had to get to the bottom of it. Luke felt like it was all right not to know about something unless he had to make a decision on it. Once he knew about it, though, he only wanted to know as much as necessary to make his decision.

Luke was all about action, and he had little time to waste with thoughts he couldn't use. He still considered things deeply, but he seemed to have an end point to his thoughts. Mine kept rolling on and on. My curse, maybe.

I mentioned these thoughts to Luke one evening after a long day of riding. We were closing out the day by moving the last of the alfalfa hay into the barn. Luke thought about it for a bit, then said, "You know, Yosh, I used to spend a good deal of time thinking about these things. The truth is, I've pretty much come to terms with them. When my grandfather first spoke to me about joy and happiness, I was a teenager and it didn't mean much to me. After I got out on my own, I had some time to think about it and it made sense. I spent a lot of time thinking about it then. And I spent a lot of time thinking about other related things. But like I said, that was then—this is now.

"I've found my own place here now, and it gives me a chance to live the life I want to live. I've been down a few of the roads my mother and grandfather like to travel, but they don't seem to take me anywhere I want to go. I've got work to do and people who depend on me. I'm not really interested in a lot of talk that I'm not going to do anything with."

I looked at Luke without saying a word. He stopped working and sat down on one of the bales of hay. He stared out across the yard at the farmhouse. The light streamed out of the kitchen window like it had on the first day I arrived. He was quiet for a bit but seemed to have more to say.

"Now, as far as the ranch goes, I couldn't agree with you more," Luke said. "It *does* give me time to be with my own thoughts. Mostly, though, it gives me a chance to stay connected with life. That's a connection I never had when I was living in any city."

"But there seems to be so much more in what Jim is saying," I responded. "Maybe it's just because I never heard it put the way he puts it."

"There may be a whole lot more, Yosh. I'm not saying there isn't. You should explore it as much as you want. But I'll tell you that ultimately it won't do you any good unless you apply it. My work here just happens to be the way that I've put it to use."

"Luke, you've all made me feel right at home, and I still don't know what I've done to deserve such generosity."

"You're Abe's grandson, and from what I hear, my grandfather never had a closer friend. That makes you welcome here as long as you'd like. I'll tell you something else. Even if you weren't Abe's grandson, you'd be welcome to stay on. That has to do with who *you* are and not your grandfather. You love to look into things as much as I did when I was a bit younger, and you're not afraid to ask some tough questions."

I didn't know how to respond. Fortunately, Luke continued.

"That determination will take you a long way. It's taken me where I want to go. I'm sure it'll get you where you're headed as well. As far as all the questions, you better save those for Grandpa Jim, or Mom. They should be joining us tomorrow."

"Thanks, Luke. But just out of curiosity, when you said you've been down a few roads that Shuren and Jim like to travel… I'm not sure what you meant."

"Yosh, knowing what you want out of life is different for everyone. Some people think about it quite a bit and choose very carefully. Some people can't seem to stop thinking about it and never seem to choose at all. Most people eventually fall into doing something that seems to suit them just because that seems like the least bad thing they could do. But ultimately, if you want your thinking about it to mean anything, it has to lead to making a choice. Otherwise, as far as I'm concerned, all that thinking ain't worth squat."

"But it sounded like there was a *part* of the search that you found valuable," I objected. "Wouldn't that part be valuable to me as well?"

"The important part for me was figuring out who was doing the choosing. Not many people spend much time with that, and that's what I learned was most important. That's the road I'm talking about. It's a road I'm glad I took. To be honest, though, it's hard enough for me to just live the decisions I've made during my journey down that road. Trying to live out those decisions while not doing anyone else wrong is enough challenge for me, let alone telling anyone else what they should do. Maybe someday I'll feel differently, but I've got my hands full today just trying to live honestly."

"Well, Luke, I'd be lucky to travel as far as you have."

"Everyone has their own journey, Yosh. It's not about comparing how far we go to how far someone else might go. It's about traveling as far as it feels right for you to travel. Then it's about not doing things that keep other people from traveling as far as they might. I've done the first. It's hard enough for me to keep trying to do the second."

"I'll try to remember that."

"Well, try to remember it while you finish up with this hay," he said, leaving me to wrap up the work with Ahote.

Ahote, who had been unloading the bales of hay off the trailer, wandered over toward the end of our conversation and broke out into a grin as he heard the last words. He didn't say anything—he just kept working. He was kind enough to wait until after Luke left before he started teasing me about how slowly I worked.

Takoda was quick to defend me. He and I sent Ahote home and finished the job ourselves. We worked well together and enjoyed one another's company. The work always seemed to go faster when Takoda was there doing it with me. Before we knew it, the bales were all stacked neatly onto wooden pallets in the barn and we headed in to supper.

Missing the Mark

As usual, I got up early the next morning to start the day's work. I had been down at one of the fields and was headed back to the house after a couple of hours to grab some breakfast when I heard the dogs barking.

I arrived back at the house to find Jim and Shuren pulling up in the drive with a trailer behind their truck. It was good to see them. I had missed them both, and we spent the early morning catching up with one another.

They were anxious to hear about my experience on the ranch, and Luke painted a picture that was more flattering than true. But who was I to question it? We found out that Jim had been down in Albuquerque picking up supplies and that he and Shuren had brought them up to the ranch. The trailer seemed to be filled with enough provisions for an expedition, but I figured it wasn't easy keeping the ranch stocked for the winter.

Seeing Jim and Shuren again reminded me that my journey down to New Mexico had begun almost three weeks ago, and I started to get that odd restless feeling again. I ignored it, thinking about everything I needed to get done that day. We ate breakfast together, and after a cup of coffee, I excused myself to get back to work.

That day went pretty slowly. Mostly, I was just anxious to get back to the house and spend some time with Jim and Shuren. It wasn't until after dinner, though, that I had a chance to sit down with them.

The five of us ate together, then cleared the table and cleaned up. Luke and Fitra still had work to finish, so Shuren, Jim, and I walked outside and sat at the picnic table under the ancient oak tree that stood across from the house. We had eaten an early supper, so it was still light out but that light was beginning to fade.

Shuren was full of questions, but Jim seemed quiet. I told them about my time on the ranch and what an experience it had been for me. They were happy to hear how much I'd learned from Ahote and Takoda—from how to tend to a horse to the names of the local trees and plants, the commands for the dogs, and a hundred other things. I explained how well Fitra had taken care of me and how much I'd enjoyed my time with Luke. I thanked both Jim and Shuren for their graciousness. Then I hesitated before speaking again.

"I just want you both to know how much I appreciate the conversations that you had with me in Chama," I finally said. "I can't tell you how often I've thought back to your words. Being here at the ranch has given me time to digest those things. But I'm still trying to get my head around some of that stuff. It feels like a little bit of information has made me more confused than I was before I started thinking about all these things. Now, I can't tell if it was better to be right and confused, or wrong and sure of myself. I kind of miss being sure of myself."

Shuren looked over at Jim and then back at me. "That's not uncommon," she said. "Information that cannot be contained within a particular structure begs for either expanding or deepening that structure, or it begs to be ignored or discounted. That tension is inevitable. The feeling that goes along with it is confusion."

I thought about what she was saying, but before I could respond, Shuren said that she and Fitra had been planning to take a walk. She smiled, excused herself, got up, and walked back to the house. Jim and I sat there together, listening to the sounds of the evening, until he finally broke the silence.

"Yosh, Shuren and I didn't know how you'd fare up here at the ranch. We knew it would probably be a lot different than anything you'd done before."

"Yeah, it's pretty different, but I've enjoyed it. It feels good just to be outside working with my hands. I just can't see how that stuff meshes with what Shuren and you shared with me in Chama. What I do know is that my thoughts are a lot less pressing. That doesn't mean they're any clearer. If anything, they're actually *more* jumbled than they were before. It just seems like I've taken a vacation from my dilemma, and it's simply waiting to come back."

The fingers of Jim's right hand tapped softly on the weathered tabletop as he stared up at the tree. He took a deep breath before he replied, his fingers coming to rest.

"Yosh, there's a difference between thinking and understanding."

"I realize that," I said, thinking that this was, again, pretty obvious.

"You may realize it, but you haven't yet *done* anything with that realization, Yosh."

"What would you want me to do with it?"

He thought for a bit and then said, "What we do with a realization reveals how fundamentally we appreciate the very concept we've come to realize."

"You'll have to explain that one to me," I said.

"There is another problem that tends to short-circuit our progress in clarifying our thoughts—our habit of mistaking *knowing about* something for *understanding* the thing. It's true that they both have in common the acquisition of information, but what *knowing* and *understanding* do with that information is not the same thing."

"You've gone from too simple to too complicated again," I said.

"Well, let's break it down then. Let's look at *understanding* first. It's important because understanding goes beyond knowing about something. Understanding implies knowing something *fundamentally*, knowing it like the back of your hand. Ultimately, you can only act upon your *understanding* of things. Your actions just naturally flow out of your understanding of your world and the things that make up your world."

That sounded pretty reasonable to me.

He continued. "What do we mean when we say that we *understand* something? What that really says is that we've come to terms with it, that we believe we know how it fits into our world."

He could see the confusion that was still written on my face. "Take the dogs for instance," he continued. "When you first got here, you must have been a little frightened of them. After all, they're bred to be guard dogs. To Keeley, for example, the family and workers here are the objects that she protects. We are part of her herd. She has that as an *understanding*. When *you* first arrived here, you were not part of the *herd* for Keeley, so she was suspicious of you. Now you've become part of her herd, and she follows you around like one of the family.

"The same applies to Weeway, but he understands you to be part of his *pack* rather than his herd. Both dogs understand the need to protect. They have an understanding of who belongs in that herd or pack. And now they have a *new* understanding that includes you. You also have a new understanding. You no longer fear them. In fact, you probably think they might defend you if the need arose. And I believe they would."

"But they're dogs," I said. "I thought we were talking about how you and I understand things. Don't we have a different way of understanding ourselves and the world around us than they do?"

"Perhaps, in some ways, but I think we fool ourselves if we think that they are that different from us. Sometimes it's easier to see limitations or tendencies in others while being blind to those same limitations in ourselves. That habit applies to identification with your species as much as it applies to your identification with yourself as a member of your species. When we forget that we are animals, we cut ourselves off from countless insights that are available to us. Some of those insights can be quite useful.

"Let's look at the dogs again. They have two understandings. First, I must protect my herd or pack. Second, this new individual is in my herd-pack or outside of it. You see, the second understanding is the one that's changed. The first understanding did not change because it's a *genetic* understanding. Guarding is built into the dogs' genetic constitution. They don't think about guarding. For these dogs it's instinctive. The flexibility lies in identifying the object that is the focus of that guarding.

"Is it any less instinctive for you to want to speak, to walk upright, or be part of a social group? How you speak, how well you speak, how often you speak, to whom you speak—these are all objects within your world that are manifestations of the flexible dimension of speech.

"This awareness of the several dimensions of speech is now easier for you to understand because it parallels our discussion of guarding behavior in the dogs."

"That makes sense," I responded.

"I'm glad it helps," said Jim. "But remember... like the guard dogs, you have a whole host of instinctual aspects to your understanding that you are not even aware of. They're part of your very genetic makeup, laid down layer upon layer over millions of years in all of us as human beings—but also in a particular fashion unique to you. In many ways, you are the sum of these slight variations of instinctive tendencies. Being aware of this is both liberating and empowering."

"I can see how it might free me from a lot of ways in which I fault myself," I replied. "But I can't see how it's empowering. If anything, it seems just the opposite."

"Yosh, I know that I emphasized our similarity to the dogs. But there is also a critical difference. The dogs operate primarily on instinct, and they do not question this. A *global* understanding is largely beyond their observation. As a human being, on the other hand, you operate in the realm of a consciousness that is aware of itself. You can see yourself thinking and acting. That's why you can see the dogs' actions as they are, in a way that they can't see themselves.

"The problem for us as humans arises pretty quickly, though. Like the magician's sleight of hand, an action can happen before we even know it. We fail to appreciate the genetic and instinctual dimensions of our understanding. Failing to do that, we *assume* that our understanding is *entirely a product of rational thought*. When you mistakenly ascribe your understanding entirely to the intellect, you fail the primary test of the intellect. Unless you confront this paradox, you will be building the house of your understanding—your reality—on shaky ground."

"Okay, that kind of makes sense," I said. "But how would I confront this paradox?"

"You can confront it by going back and reconstructing your understandings while maintaining the honesty of this realization. If you can become the owner of a simple awareness, you can transform your life. That awareness can be stated in one sentence.

Thinking does not lead to true understanding
unless it also accounts for the assumptions that
thinking itself makes."

Now I was confused again. I asked Jim, "So thinking is useless because it's tied up in assumptions that we make about our world and ourselves?"

"No, Yosh. Thinking is neither inherently useful nor inherently counterproductive. Thinking simply *is*. The key lies in admitting that we possess *levels* of thought, and that each of these levels comes with its own limitations as well as its own value. To possess this awareness is to tailor your conscious intervention accordingly. This is the fullest application of will."

"You mean free will?" I asked.

"That is a useful distinction, Yosh. It is exactly what I'm talking about, if by *free* you mean amenable to conscious intervention. What I am speaking about is the degree to which any particular aspect of your will is free—or even ought to be free."

"Why wouldn't I want to apply my will? Of course I *want* free will! What use is any discussion if it doesn't end in helping me think about my actions so that I can do something to influence them?"

Jim's fingers started tapping on the picnic table again. After a minute or so, he responded. Or maybe it was just a few seconds, but it felt like longer.

"Let me give you an example of why thinking is not always useful. If you've touched a hot stove before, you don't need to think about the painful effects of a hot stove when coming upon one again. The higher levels of your mind are not engaged much when you reflexively pull your hand away from that stove.

"At an even deeper level, we possess instinctive responses that do not even require such initial conditioning. Consider the acts of blinking or putting your hand out to break your fall when you trip. You do these activities reflexively. If you had to wait for your mind to engage it would be too late. In such cases, the highest application of will would be to *not* involve the will—to take no deliberate conscious action.

"Even higher functions are not necessarily enhanced by the involvement of the deliberate mind. Look at aesthetics. When you see beauty in a thing, there is a second of recognition that is present before your intellect engages and starts laying down layers of thought.

"Knowing how much you enjoy your walks, I'll bet that's what you experienced when you saw the aspens for the first time this fall. It's one of the reasons I wanted to get you up here to the ranch. It's easy to lose touch with that part of yourself. No amount of discussion can capture that feeling."

I thought about Jim's words and started to understand what he was saying. There was a difference between the first time I saw those trees ablaze in yellow and the times I saw them in the following days. The experience of that sight had been alive in me at a level that had already become dulled. But the trees were no less bright.

I asked, "So you're saying that my thinking has all of these levels and that thinking deliberately can sometimes be a bad thing?"

"Yosh, it would be more correct to say that deliberate thought can detract from your understanding. To come to terms with this is to accept that your consciousness exists in several dimensions. Deliberate intervention can detract from some, but is critical to others. Applying universal judgments, such as a worship of free will, serves only to obscure a fuller awareness of yourself. I give this to you only as an example of ideas that we can fall into worshiping. These ideas can be as insidious as any idol.

"It is important for you to realize that the intellect exists to serve you. You do not exist to serve it. The integrity of your mind extends well beyond the intellect—but the intellect would convince you otherwise."

87

I nodded. Even if I could see his point, I didn't know how I could do what he was suggesting.

"Yosh, our ability to think is a great asset to us, but only insofar as it serves us. The human mind is very capable of accomplishing goals. It is less capable of determining *whether* they should be accomplished. By this, I mean that the human mind is less capable of deciding whether a particular goal serves us. For that matter, it has trouble even defining who the *us* is. But that's another topic entirely."

"Who the *us* is? What do you mean by that?"

"We'll get to that, but I don't know that I can do justice to the subject. The problem with discussing these ideas is that when you make a little headway, it starts to open up areas of yourself that you thought you'd already decided about. It's only then that you learn how your old definitions have been causing you problems. This means challenging your assumptions of who *you, them,* and *us* are. Right now, though, we need to stay focused on the process of thinking."

I was fine with that. I still had a lot of questions about what Jim had just shared with me, and I didn't want to open up another can of worms.

"So are you saying that thinking is simply a process?" I asked. "It's not good or bad?"

"Yes. Our ability to think and apply directed consciousness is simply a tool that can both help and cause harm. Understanding how to best use that tool is our focus right now."

"It sounds like we're thinking about *thinking*."

"Thinking about thinking is a good way to put it, Yosh."

"I kind of follow you, but doesn't that still involve the mind?"

"That's an excellent question, and we may be running into the limitation of language when we discuss this. I'll give it a shot. You see, thinking about thinking is not something the mind does very well because for the mind to think about itself, it must first admit that there is something beyond it, which allows it to *see itself operating*. That is a scary thing for the mind because the mind sees itself as the ultimate perceiver. This is the sleight of hand I was talking about a few minutes ago.

"This may be a confusing point, Yosh, so let me go back to the dogs. They have been bred as guard dogs, but between them there are differences—in breeding, for example. Weeway, the Boerboel, is bred to guard a household and its inhabitants, whom he considers his pack. He is not naturally aggressive, but *selectively* aggressive. He has been bred to the genetic boundary between protective and aggressive. Because of that innate quality, training and socialization can make him a powerful tool. The lack of those same things can cause him to become quite destructive.

"Keeley, the Pyrenees, is bred to guard a herd and can be fierce in that defense. She has more of an innate drive to establish and patrol a territory. Her breed does not require much human direction in this task. She welcomes human company within her herd but doesn't need it. Still, like Weeway, she is wary of strangers.

"There are also differences in sex. One of these dogs is male, the other female. That means one may have a little more tendency to guard a pack than a territory—but breeding can swamp this tendency so that it becomes an irrelevant difference. Each may have a little more or less of a retrieving tendency, but it is not prominent. They think in terms of guarding while other dogs may think in terms of hunting or retrieving.

"Then there are differences that are unique to each dog as an individual. Anyone who's had two different dogs of the same breed and sex can tell you just how different they can be.

"We still see them all as dogs," Jim continued. "We know that these other tendencies remain and could be bred back into them if we wanted to do that. Even though Weeway and Keeley think of themselves as guard dogs, we can see that they are actually dogs who just believe themselves to be a certain type of dog but retain the potential to be another kind of dog—even if they can't see that in themselves."

"Makes sense," I said. "But how does this apply to people?"

"This limitation in thinking may be fine for a dog because dogs are content to have their worlds defined for them," Jim replied. "That is the function of the pack. It defines a dog's world and their role within that world. As humans, we have bred dogs to accept *us* as the pack leaders. Ideally, we fulfill that role for them.

"In the same way, we as primates have intrinsic tendencies of which we may not be aware. The recognition of this type of limitation is a valuable gift that our observations about the dogs can give us. But it also points out a difference. We can see this limitation in them and infer such limitations in ourselves. On the other hand, they are unable to see these differences in us and infer them in themselves. It is this capacity for observation that separates us from them."

"That's a pretty big advantage," I said.

"Again, Yosh, it is both an advantage and a disadvantage. It depends on the way in which we make use of this awareness, or even something as simple as our failure to acknowledge it."

"I'm not sure I know what you're talking about," I said.

"Well, consider how much less there is that can go wrong in a dog's world than can go wrong in ours. Complexity brings greater potential rewards, but it also brings more opportunities for dysfunction. For instance, take the ability to *infer*, which we have just spoken about. The dogs may not be able to make inferences about the genetic basis of *our* thinking. Let's even forget about how dogs might view other species and look at how they relate to one another. We humans often project our world onto our dogs. A dog doesn't project its world onto another dog. It doesn't say, *Well, I think those retrievers should really learn to herd.*

"Dogs also don't make judgments about themselves based on their intrinsic shortcomings. A dog would never think *I may be a good herder, but I'll never amount to much as a guard dog.* A dog is content to be what it is.

"Yosh, when we are also content to be, then we are in the same state as they are in relation to our identity. We are at peace. From this example, I think you can see how our ability to infer is *not always* an advantage."

Jim was looking directly at me now, and I could tell that his example was carefully chosen. I actually understood what he was saying.

It took me a few moments to say, "So if I were to be content with who I am, I'd be at peace too?"

"Yes, Yosh—you and everyone else. But this is not our normal condition, at least not most of the time. As people, we are not content to *be*. Our gift and our curse is that we are able to project our world outside of ourselves—to conceive that there is an *outside of ourselves*.

"This can be valuable in satisfying our needs and accomplishing goals. It becomes destructive when you become so accustomed to it that you fail to see your origins and begin to associate your *self* with your *story*. You can only do this by accepting the assumptions that have gone into creating what your mind determines to be your identity."

"So, are you saying that I should simply be content to be alive? Are you saying that I shouldn't have any aspirations?"

"My goodness no, Yosh. Having aspirations is also intrinsic to who you are as a human being *at certain points in your life and to certain degrees*. When you become content just to be alive, you can recognize that *contentment* is your normal state, just as contentment is the normal state for the dogs. Then, aspirations can be added to that state—or allowed to fall away from it without threat or fear of loss. Then *discontent* becomes a tool and not a definition.

"When you recognize your intrinsic nature as contentment itself, you are able to perceive that you are already complete. Aspirations may then come and go. From that point forward, the outcome of your strivings no longer threatens you.

"When you come to see yourself fully, then you are able to stop seeing yourself as a sum of the particular events of your life. What I'm saying is that when you are tied to the story of your life you don't allow for these natural fluctuations and changes to occur. Then your energy gets dissipated and you forget who you truly are. You come to the false belief that *you* are *your strivings*—or that *you* are *the result of your aspirations*."

My mind was whirring. "So my normal state right now is contentment? I don't even feel close to being content. How could I possibly feel contentment? That would just be a lie!"

"That's an honest statement, Yosh. Failure to recognize our true nature is at the heart of our problems. That failure is at the heart of *your* problems. You correctly point out that this recognition cannot be forced upon you. That does not change the fact that you have forgotten your intrinsic nature—your original nature.

"This dilemma is the deepest meaning of *sin*—which means *missing the mark*, or *hamartia* as it is expressed in Greek. This original error we've been talking about is the *original sin*.

"In this expression, you can see the meaning it conveys as a tragic flaw in our thinking that lies at the root of the problems we experience. When we *miss the mark* on this understanding, then all our subsequent understandings become intrinsically unstable and carry with them the seeds of their own destruction."

"I have to tell you that I'm not particularly religious, Jim."

"Neither am I, Yosh. That doesn't mean I'm prepared to throw out the accumulated wisdom regarding our condition that has come down to us. Honoring our traditions doesn't mean that I just take them in without challenging them. What it does mean is that I make a commitment to inquiring into them for the value they truly hold. The same concept is expressed with different words in other traditions, but *sin* is the term I figured you'd be familiar with."

"Yes, but I haven't heard it expressed the way you did just now."

"The inquiry that you and I are discussing is an inquiry that spans place and time. If you truly seek to understand your predicament, why would you limit yourself to one place or one time? After all, limiting yourself in place and time is at the heart of the dilemma. If you wish to escape, why would you tie your hands in such a way?"

"I don't understand. How am I tying my hands?"

"You do it in two ways, Yosh. Neither is unique to you. In fact, both are quite common. The first is that you seek to understand the dilemma *only* from the perspective that your society currently condones. In doing so, you *fix the framing* of the problem in place and time. The second is that you fix *yourself* in place and time by defining yourself in such limited terms—by seeing yourself as only one particular part of one story."

"Are you saying that my decision to associate my *self* with my story kind of fixes me in time?"

"That's right, Yosh. You have fixed yourself in both time and place. But you are not alone. Most of the world does this same thing. In fact, there is a brief period in each of our lives when we make this initial decision of who we are. It is a decision that is demanded of us as a price for inclusion into our particular society, and all societies do it. That price is the acceptance of your *self* as the intellect's definition of self. This has been called the ego by many people."

"The word *ego* is pretty confusing to me." I said.

"That's because it has been used in many different ways. It is used professionally in a different way than it has been used popularly. Perhaps it would be worthwhile for us to define it for the purpose of our discussion."

"Like you said back in Chama, the way we use language is critically important. You see, I *have* been listening."

I smiled playfully and he returned my smile with a chuckle before resuming.

"As I see it, Yosh, ego has two stages. First, it is your acceptance of the limited definition of your *self* by the mind. You grow into this acceptance gradually as a child. Parts of this process have been described by psychologists such as Jean Piaget, Malcolm Slavin, and Daniel Kriegman as well as others. The bottom line is that the mind does this in order to reconcile its internal experience with its external experiences and the expectations of the society in which it happens to find itself. This first stage of ego is what I would call the ego with a *little* 'e,' the *little-e-ego*, the '*little-ego*,' or simply the *ego*.

"Now, this *little-ego* is not inherently dysfunctional. It is simply the way that we 'individuate' ourselves so that we are capable of acting within the world in which we find ourselves. This *little-ego* is honestly trying to integrate its inside world with its outside world. The *little-ego* does *not* project itself beyond a degree to which it is genetically programmed to project itself."

"Okay, I understand the little-ego, but this business of genetic programming—what is that?"

"When I talk about genetic programming, what I'm referring to is the fixed biological structure of your mind. When we talk about taking action, it's important to separate out aspects of yourself over which you have no control from those that you can affect. You can picture this aspect of the mind as existing in two parts.

"The first part is the common, shared inheritance of all humans. The second part is unique to each person and imparts individual dispositions and personality traits. You have no control over either of these aspects of yourself. They simply *are*. Both parts are necessary foundations for the *little-ego,* and without the *little-ego* you would not be able to operate in your world. We have this in common with dogs and all other consciously social creatures.

"As humans, though, we can consciously choose to emphasize or de-emphasize the tendencies within the second part of our genetic programming. In other words, we have a certain ability to influence what part of our genetic programming gets expressed. This is what separates us from any other creature as far as we know. This aspect of the little-ego *is* within your control, *if* you choose to control it."

"All right, I follow you so far about the little-ego."

"Good, then we can move on to the second stage of ego. The second stage of ego is *identification with* the first state of ego. It is identification with that definition of self which was simply accepted before. This stage of ego I call the Ego with a big 'E,' the *Big-E-Ego,* the *Big-Ego*, or simply the *Ego*.

"The little-ego that has grown to the second stage sees itself as the ultimate arbiter of reality. It is the little-ego that has become convinced that *its* reconciliation with external reality is Reality itself. Reality for the Ego is *its* reality, and it projects this reality onto the world."

"Okay, so the Big-Ego is the mind's identification with the little-ego? And the purpose of life for the Big-Ego is to justify its own reality?"

"Exactly. The purpose of life for the Big-Ego is to *justify its own reality* because that is how it justifies itself. The problem it creates for itself, however, is that it is destined to fail because it has not made allowance for the fullness of Reality—only for its local, filtered view of Reality.

"When the Big-Ego is your state of mind, then you can be sure that your world will be dysfunctional. It cannot be otherwise. The point at which we enter into identification with our little-ego and see our self as a Big-Ego is the moment at which we enter into *dysfunction*. This is the point of entry into *original sin*. This is *forgetfulness of Being*. This is becoming enmeshed in *maya*, one of many names it has been given."

"If it has so many names, how come I haven't heard of them?"

"Because you have not previously sought to understand the underpinnings of your dilemma so sincerely, Yosh. Even when you might have sought them, you did not question your assumed understandings and that has precluded further inquiry."

"So is that why this distinction between little-ego and Big-Ego is so important?"

"Yes, Yosh. Since you now understand this distinction, we can simplify our language. In the future, when we speak of the Big-Ego we will simply refer to it as the Ego. Since most of our discussion will be about the Ego, I'll simply refer to it as such. When I want to refer specifically to the little-ego, I'll identify it that way."

"Okay, I think I follow your distinction between little-ego and Ego. But is understanding the underpinnings of my dilemma, as you called it, the same as finding the way to the solution that Shuren talked to me about in Chama?"

"Yes they are, Yosh. They are different ways of saying the same thing. Both ways seek to identify the point of the original error, the error of mistaken identity. If you wish to address your dilemma, you need to understand the point at which your world became dysfunctional. That *point* is a decision that is tied to a point in time when you assumed an identity. If you can identify that point, then you will become capable of seeing your way out of the dilemma. When you do that, then you can return to a position of increased functionality and well-being. That is the path of the solution. When you arrive there, you will see that who you truly are is vastly beyond the highest imaginings of the Ego's world."

"I don't feel like I'm anywhere near what you describe."

"But you can be, Yosh. You *can be* if that is what you want above all else. That is something only you can decide—but it is not easy."

"I know," I said. "It seems impossible."

Jim smiled, "It's not impossible, Yosh. It is hard, but it's easier when you have help. When you make this decision, you join others who made the same choice before you—like Abe. It all begins with inquiring into what you know to be originally true and unchanging. It is possible to follow that question to your true identity."

I listened intently to what he was saying. This seemed to fit well with Shuren's Law of Original Truth, but I still had a lot of questions. There were so many strands of thought floating around. Just when things started to get clear, they would become confusing again.

Finally, I asked, "So, Jim, if the Ego thinks its world is the real world, then it must think the world works a particular way, right? And when things don't work out that way, then it gets frustrated, right? Doesn't that lead the Ego to understand that it was wrong and that its assumptions don't really describe the world well?"

"That's a great question," said Jim, "The Ego can change bits of itself just like the dogs learned to trust you and include you in the pack. What it has trouble doing is accepting its relation to something greater than itself. That would require it to change its underlying identity. There's a word for this. Can you think what it is?"

I thought about the emotions I had when I didn't want to admit that I was wrong about something. The words that came to mind were 'stubborn,' 'closed-minded,' 'indignant,' 'superior,' and 'special.' I tried each one out on Jim but he wasn't satisfied.

Jim put his hand to his chin like he was considering something deeply. We sat together in the fading twilight, watching the fireflies blinking on and off in the pasture. It had been a long day, and I'd been anxious to sit down with Jim when it had started. I never thought it would end with another long discussion.

It was all or nothing around this place, I thought. I felt like a car speeding from one stoplight to the next—in a hurry but getting nowhere fast.

Jim looked off into the distance. For a few seconds it looked like he was elsewhere. Then his focus returned to our conversation and he stared at me. "Yosh, we've discussed a lot today. All of your answers have merit, but there is a common thread that runs between all these words. Perhaps it would be best if we stopped here for the day. Why don't you think about it? We can continue tomorrow if you wish."

"Thank you. I'd like that," I said. "Besides, Luke's got me running around pretty good, and there's still a little more work that needs to get done today."

I excused myself and went to find Takoda. I was looking forward to getting my hands dirty. Somehow that always helped me clear my mind. Jim gave me a knowing glance.

We got up from the table together. I hurried off to the barn as he walked back to the house, following the kitchen light to the door.

I spent the rest of that evening trying to put together all of the words I had thrown at Jim and looking for the common thread that he had mentioned.

At some point later that night, I think it came to me. I looked forward to trying it out on him in the morning.

To Know

The next morning, I was up early and back to my routine. There was a lot of work to be done, and I could easily see how falling into work that you like could define your purpose. I hadn't been there at the ranch long, yet I already felt wrapped up in it, without ever having intended that to happen.

After supper, Luke grinned as he left Jim and me alone in the kitchen. "Good luck," he called back to me. "And don't keep him too long, Grandpa. He's still got work to do."

"Don't worry, Luke. He keeps tabs on himself well enough," Jim answered.

I smiled to myself, thinking of how Jim must have been in Luke's shoes many times over the years. I could even imagine the positions reversed with a young Luke sitting at the kitchen table watching Jim step out the door.

Jim was ready to get right back to our discussion and asked me where we had left off talking.

"I thought about it for a little while last night," I said. "Sometimes, I think it's easier to think while I work. When you asked why the Ego has trouble accepting its relation to something greater than itself, I realized it was because the Ego doesn't want to admit that anything is greater than itself. So maybe the word you're looking for is the word that empowers all of those other words with that same attitude—*pride*."

"Excellent, Yosh. Pride *is* the barrier that the Ego cannot cross. It's flexible enough to revise its understanding to incorporate new information. In fact, your Ego has been doing that since it first came into being. What it can't do is use new information that contradicts its fundamental structure. That kind of information is either ignored, or it bypasses the Ego's awareness to influence the mind without the mind even understanding that it's being affected."

"So how can the Ego ever change? Is it just something that we have to deal with and we can't do much about? Do we just have to suck it up and live with it?"

"Again, we have to remind ourselves of what the Ego is. Remember, the Ego is an attachment to the definition of *self*. So your question really is about how to undo the attachment to one's definition of oneself. I'd say there are several ways to do that… different ways appeal to different people.

"My choice is a logical way, so I can speak to you about that. For me, it's been a very slow and purposeful way. This has had the benefit of helping me to convey my thoughts, but it does present other limitations. Let me tell you about my way. Then you can see if anything there appeals to you. It may be that you'll need to hear it from someone else."

I said, "It's more likely that you just have a slow student. I wish this stuff came easier to me. It's just hard to organize all of these new concepts in my thinking. This stuff doesn't want to stay nailed down."

This must have reminded Jim about something because he got up from the table and went over to a room that he used when he came up to the ranch. He came back with a couple of small picture frames and sat down next to me. Each looked like it contained a single quote, though I couldn't quite make them out before he laid them down on the floor.

"I want to share these with you, Yosh. I'm a slow learner too. But I've found that it's not how fast we learn, it's whether we ever learn these things at all—*and* the depth to which we learn them.

"Let me explain. Everything you have access to in your consciousness exists either as content or as structure for that content.

There is overlap in these distinctions, however, because the very nature of organizing content is related to deciding how the content is structured.

"It might be useful for us to look at how content and structure are related. One person who has looked into this is Russell Ackhoff. He was a systems theorist who classified the content of the human mind into five categories. I believe that there is a sixth category that is relevant to our discussion, so I've added that."

He took out a piece of paper and wrote down:

Depth of Learning:
1. Data ---------------------------- symbols
2. Information -------------------- "who," "what," "where," "when"
3. Knowledge -------------------- "how"
4. Understanding --------------- "why"
5. Wisdom ----------------------- evaluated understanding
6. Awareness -------------------- integrated/consonant wisdom

"It's too much for us to discuss each of these in detail right now, but I wanted to share a framework for how content might be organized. Roughly speaking, *data* is raw symbols that have some agreed-upon meaning, such as numbers or letters.

"*Information* is the organization of data into meaningful groupings that can prove useful and can answer "who," "what," "where," and "when" questions. A word might be an example of content organized at the level of information.

"The next level is *knowledge*. Knowledge is the organization of information with the intention of making it useful. This is the first step that requires intention in the creation of structure because that is the purpose of inquiry at this level. A sentence would be an example of content organized at this level because it reflects relationships and patterns between objects. The human mind is the most powerful pattern-seeking device that we know of. It literally seeks structure in whatever draws its attention. The depth of knowledge within a mind grows out of patterns recognized in information and then accepted as valid.

"This same relationship helps us develop *understanding* based on the patterns seen during the acquisition of knowledge. *Understanding* is the organization of knowledge in meaningful ways. In our example of language, *understanding* might be a paragraph. At the *understanding* level, groupings can begin to interact with other groupings, and it is possible to begin asking questions about knowledge. These questions can lead to investigation for new knowledge at this same level or back down the organization in the quest for new information.

"The next shift up in organization to *wisdom* has a similar relationship to understanding as understanding has to knowledge. In our example *wisdom* might be a book.

"But *awareness* has qualities all its own, and you might think of it as *both* a library *and* the act of selecting books from the library."

"Wow," I said. "That's useful, but what does this have to do with the Ego?"

"Great, Yosh. Let's look at how the Ego develops in all of this. *Information* is the level at which the little-ego is born. *Knowledge* is the birthplace of the Ego. Where we go from there is more complicated than I can probably explain, but I'll give it a shot.

"The movement from *Information* to *Understanding* marks the fullness of the little-ego and the period of greatest growth of the Ego. This growth continues at the level of Understanding, but is also challenged at that level. Paradoxically, this also becomes the stage at which doubts about the unassailability of the Ego may arise.

"The next category, *Wisdom*, implies the selection of a higher goal, a goal beyond the Ego. As such, it may mark the beginning of the end of the Ego. Wisdom, itself, does not mark this ending, however, because Wisdom is still fragmented in the identity it serves. It is only when Wisdom is reconciled within the final category—*Awareness*—that the Ego finally melts away. Awareness represents the death of the Ego and the birth of something greater—consonance with a greater reality that is beyond our ability to contain within the mind."

I wanted to ask him what he meant by *greater reality,* but I sensed that Jim wanted to get this all out at one time. For that matter, I really didn't understand a lot of the details of the levels he was describing, but I was learning something important—to hold my questions. I don't think Jim cared much for interruptions in his train of thought.

As if anticipating my question, Jim continued. "It is this *greater reality* that science seeks to understand in parts. And it is this greater reality to which our religious traditions seek to point and often seek to objectify. It is this greater reality that the arts attempt to convey in essence. By its nature, it is just beyond our grasp. We can call it *Source* or *Spirit,* or we can give it even more specific names.

"You see, Yosh, the place from which we are having our discussion is between these two levels here…" He pointed to the paper. "Between Knowledge and Understanding. In order to make a constructive transition to Wisdom, our work must begin at the level of Understanding, which needs to be re-ordered to facilitate movement to a particular Wisdom.

"This is a difficult transition because, unlike the previous transitions, it is resisted rather than supported by society. If an individual can arrive at the point of wanting to move beyond Understanding to Wisdom, then he or she must challenge many of society's assumptions. Why? Because society is, by definition, an entity that exists upon a shared view of reality. To challenge that reality is to challenge everyone who accepts and projects that reality. The greatest resistance, then, comes from those who benefit disproportionately from that accepted view.

"This is why societies revere their living proponents and their dead rebels. The challenge of the dead agitator can be manipulated to water down his message. Water it down enough and you can minimize the need to make any drastic change in society's perception of reality. The collective Ego is far more tenacious than the personal Ego. What both dimensions of Ego share is a fear of doubt. What they both love is being right."

With that he showed me the first of the two framed quotes.

> *Doubt is not a pleasant condition,*
> *but certainty is absurd.*
>
> *– Voltaire*

"Yosh, if you can become comfortable with your doubts about what passes for reality, you will become capable of moving from Understanding to Wisdom. This will be possible not because you treasure your understanding, but *because you doubt it*. This is what I call The Paradox of the Intellect."

> *Wisdom can only come to those who search for understanding, but can never be attained by those who possess it.*

Jim had given me a lot to think about. At the time, though, I didn't understand how this paradox was meaningful.

"I don't understand, Jim. How is it possible to both value and dismiss our power to understand?"

"Another good question, Yosh. That is the nature of the paradox. It's not about dismissing the *value* of the intellect. It's about dismissing your *attachment* to it. The question is not whether you use the intellect, but *to what end* you use the intellect.

"If you are attached to your intellect or your understanding, then you will not let that understanding go, regardless of the contradictions you might see. You will either refuse to see those contradictions or you will justify them as exceptions or misinterpretations and seek to avoid reconciling them with your understanding."

"But how would you come to understand something unless you use the intellect?" I asked.

"You are right to question this, Yosh. The intellect is both the problem *and* the way out of the problem. I don't mean to speak in circles—but as you point out, when it comes to understanding, the intellect is all we have. The question is, does it *face inward* to serve the Ego or does it *face outward* toward wisdom and a greater reality?"

Then I understood that he was speaking about understanding in the same way that he and Shuren had spoken about the intellect that day in Chama. I was still troubled by this term *greater reality*, though. It sounded too religious, and for some reason that rubbed me the wrong way. So that's what I told him.

Jim replied, "I'm sorry, Yosh. Sometimes I forget that not every-one speaks my language. *Greater reality* is a term I use to make sure I'm being consistent with my own understanding. It may not even have meaning to anyone else. Feel free to ignore it if you wish, but I use it as shorthand for my own goal.

"The way I see it, the schools of science, religion, philosophy, and the arts each seek to extend our reach into the unknown. Part of that unknown is external and part internal. Each of these *schools* places the boundary between internal and external in different places. They even move that boundary over time."

"I'm not sure I know what you mean," I said.

Jim thought about it for a few seconds. He cleared his throat be-fore speaking again. "Let's look at just one example—the concept of the mind itself. Where is it? There was a time when science believed the mind was located in the brain. Many people still think of it this way, but how does that definition accommodate the role of hormones that are regulated and produced outside of the brain? What about the spinal cord and its intrinsic regulatory functions? How about other organs that have intrinsic activity, such as the heart?

"We truly do not know the physical extent of the mind. There is even data that suggests that aspects of the mind may reside in much more localized levels within the body. And it is possible that aspects of the mind exist beyond our physical body."

"So how do you know where to draw the line?" I asked.

"That's my point, Yosh. *Greater reality* sounds religious to you, but there are elements of it that are available to scientific inquiry. In fact, science may have more to say about some aspects of *greater reality* than religion does.

"If I wish to perceive this *greater reality*, then I do not limit my-self to certain schools of inquiry while rejecting others. If my goal is to perceive it as fully as possible, then I must be open to the advan-tages of the scientific approach. That approach may help me to know where to draw the line."

"So you define the *greater reality* by using science?" I asked skeptically.

"No, science is only one avenue of investigation... not the only one I would use. I point it out mainly because it seems to be an unlikely school of inquiry into the *greater reality*. My point is that I do not ignore it."

"So you use science because of its strength of inquiry."

"No, Yosh. That's not it at all. Every school of inquiry has its own strengths and weaknesses. If you are not aware of both the uses and limitations, then a particular school of inquiry will not serve you well."

I could tell he was getting frustrated by my frequent misunderstandings. I wanted to know about these schools of inquiry, but I knew better than to take him further off subject. I figured it would be best to get back to his example.

"So science has its limitations as well. And what you're saying is that I would need to understand both its strengths and its limitations in order to use it effectively?"

"That's exactly right, Yosh. We've spoken about the value of science, but we must balance the knowledge gained by science with the limitations of science. For example, scientific systems do not exist in a vacuum. They exist within organizations. As such, they are prone to all of the shortcomings of organizations. This includes an inertial resistance to change and the promotion of individual and group self-interest. What's more, a scientific fact may be known, but its impact and acceptance can be delayed, obscured, or minimized. Or, entire areas of scientific inquiry might be ignored because inconvenient facts might threaten political structures."

"But science is the only way we know things for sure," I said.

Jim didn't even respond to my statement at first, but then said, "I don't know if I agree with that, Yosh. What I do know is that science is the way we come to understand knowable facts. But I also know that science can frame itself out of asking certain questions and that it cannot tell us how to use those facts in a manner that best serves us. The sentiment of your statement is a good example of what we've been discussing.

"If we get married to certainty and having all the facts before we act, then we may fail to act when necessary. We might wait for facts that never come. We may ignore the reality of the other aspects of our being that request action but for which we are lacking facts.

"We end up being very deliberate about some things and entirely random about others. We make rules to contain the tiniest problems we can objectify and ignore the gargantuan issues that we cannot objectify. These are then relegated to decisions by force of political or social power. The mind that has walled itself off into scientific absolutism often waits for facts that never come.

"Keep in mind, though, that every school of inquiry has a similar progression of limitations. Again, I only use science as an example. But it can be informative to follow the progression of dysfunction through a school. It can likewise be helpful to consider the insight necessary to correct that dysfunction.

"If we continue with the example of science, this insight was summarized well by one of our greatest scientists. I believe it was Albert Einstein who reminded himself that *Not everything that counts can be counted, and not everything that can be counted counts.*"

This made sense to me. I hadn't thought about the limitations of science in that way. I always thought that anyone who attacked science was a nut-job, but maybe there was something to the argument.

My next question for Jim was, "So if science is limited in its ability to perceive this greater reality, does that mean we have to rely on religion? Or can philosophy get us there?"

"Yosh, I'm not saying that science can't *get us there.* What I'm saying is that science has its role in helping us to perceive the greater reality. Without science we would be limited in many ways. We need to honor it for the power of perception that it provides us. I'm simply saying that it is not the only tool in the toolbox.

"Religion, philosophy, and the arts are other tools. Sometimes they're even parts of the same tool. The distinction between religion and philosophy has not always been the distinction that you see today, and some religions are as much philosophy as what you may think of as religion. Art moves in and out of this space as religion and philosophy seek a way to reach beyond the cognitive to a perceptual realization of the greater reality."

"I can see that, but it doesn't answer my question. Does that mean that religion and philosophy are better at helping us perceive the greater reality?"

"This is the point that I'm making, Yosh. When we become attached to science, religion, philosophy, or the arts as *The Path* to perceiving the greater reality, we cut ourselves off from the other paths. When we become attached to a particular field within science, a particular philosophy, or a particular religion, then we are simply saying that we will perceive the greater reality *only* from this perspective.

"When we get attached to one particular viewpoint as being *right*, then that implies all others are *wrong* to one degree or another. Our efforts are then spent exploring the depths of our *right* perspective and defending ourselves against the *wrong* perspectives of others.

"Our perspective informs our concept of self. If we accept a limited perspective as our ideal one, then we close ourselves off to perceiving the greater reality in other ways."

"I think I understand it now," I said rather uncertainly.

Jim paused and then said, "You see, one of the problems with approaching this dilemma of identity from an intellectual or cognitive approach is that it's easy to get lost in details that can distract you from your goal. If you want to arrive at a certain point, you have to decide in advance where you're headed. And you need to be pretty specific."

This puzzled me. "How can I be specific about my goal when that's kind of what I'm trying to define?"

"Well, what I'm trying to say is that you have to be honest about the extent of your vision and then define your goal accordingly. You have to take it one step at a time, but you can't overreach. It's too easy to get wrapped up in speculation that can sidetrack you from real progress if you go too far down the path.

"Let me give you an example. Many people argue that there is an Ultimate or Absolute Reality—God, Spirit, The Source, Being, Allah, The Divine, Brahman, and many other names. Now it's hard for me to say that there *is* an Absolute Reality, though I don't discount that possibility. The nature of Ultimate Reality, or *Reality with a capital*

R, is not even necessary for us to discuss because the limit of what I believe *we can* discuss is the existence of a *greater reality*.

"Given our limited ability to perceive reality, I don't honestly think it's possible to describe Ultimate Reality with words, much less debate it. But I do think we can come to an awareness that we *can* participate in a reality that is greater than our ability to understand."

"Are you saying that we can be aware of this thing that we cannot understand?"

"Yes, I'm saying exactly that. If we wish to be honest, we have to admit that we can be aware of something that our guard dog minds cannot understand. If we wish to participate in a reality greater than ourselves, we cannot do that at the level of our understanding—or even at the level of wisdom. We can only do so at the level of Being.

"But whether that higher reality is simply a little beyond my ability to conceive or light years beyond my ability to perceive is purely academic. You see, because I cannot see beyond a greater reality, I refuse to speculate about that. It's enough for me to understand that *our* greater reality is more consistent with Reality than is *my* reality.

"In the end, when I seek to bring my reality into line with the *greater reality*, the direction of my goal is the same as if I chose Ultimate Reality as my goal. When I move in that direction, my Ego begins to dissipate because I see that my attachments to my concepts of reality are the things that keep me from growing in an awareness of the higher reality."

This still sounded puzzling to me, but it seemed like he knew what he was talking about. And to be honest, I was getting confused just listening to him. Jim had a way of jumping in and out of ideas that sometimes made it hard for me to follow his line of thought. Still, every time we spoke a small piece of the puzzle came together.

I realize now that part of it was just my impatience with religion. I never had given much thought to it. Most of the religious people I knew were either trying to sell you something or trying to guilt you into something. I'd only met a few who were really trying to help anyone, so it didn't seem like a high-yield proposition.

I needed a break and I was thirsty. I excused myself, went to the kitchen, and returned with two glasses of water. I offered one to Jim before taking a sip from my own.

"Thanks for taking the time to explain all that, Jim," I said after sitting back down.

"You're welcome, Yosh. I don't know if I explained it all that well. What I do know is that this is pretty important if you're looking for the path to the solution that Shuren spoke about. The tricky part is that the way out of the dilemma is not linear.

"Finding it requires a depth of overall understanding. The desire to develop that *global* understanding comes with moving from Knowledge to Understanding in many smaller parts of your life. This, in turn, raises questions that beg for answers. This is the value of giving up certainty in exchange for inquiry. It leads you to focus on building structure within your content that will support Wisdom. Then it leads you to create the conditions that support this construction. This process grows out of questioning yourself deeply and, in turn, leads back to further questioning. You need to find enough confidence to question yourself and enough independence from society to question society's assumptions."

"That makes sense," I said. "It sounds like we're back to truth and honesty."

"That's right, Yosh. This is the central role that honesty and truth play. It took me time to understand that as well. For a long time, I thought that searching for the truth would lead me to a greater appreciation of reality. But it didn't. It only led to dead ends. I came to think that the search was a waste of time. Those failed attempts caused me to become discouraged. I suppose part of that was the message I got from others who were also searching. They would tell me to search for the truth and that the truth would 'set me free.'

"Well, the truth did *not* set me free, and this upset me. The truth just kept leading me to dead ends. It was only much later, with the help of a friend and in the company of Abe, that I realized the true function of truth. I realized that the truth *would* set me free, but not in the way I thought it would. I realized that the truth came in layers, as we've discussed. I also learned that finding the truth had a lot to do with how I related to it."

My mind was thinking back to my conversation with Shuren about *the truth* and at what time in our questioning we look for *the truth*. But Jim went on.

"I had thought that the truth setting me free would be an epiphany, but that epiphany never came while I was waiting for it. As a young man, I had almost given up hope of encountering it. The epiphany did come, but many years later. I don't even know what thoughts came together to bring me to it, but suddenly I realized that all of those dead ends together *were* the truth.

"I realized that the value of seeking the truth in my reality is not that it *confirms* certain aspects as true, but more that it *denies the validity* of certain assumptions.

"As I looked at all of these denied assumptions together, I felt diminished. Indeed, my Ego was diminished. That left *me* feeling diminished because *I was my Ego*. Then I recognized this as the 'dark night of the soul' spoken of by mystics from many traditions, and I realized this was the same as the 'existential angst' of the philosophers who would follow them.

"The epiphany was that there was a way out… and only one way out. I had to reach for something greater than myself, and in that reaching I could *be* someone greater than myself. The death of the Ego is a natural consequence of seeing the Ego for what it is—a dead end. Once you see that the Ego is a dead end, then you become capable of growing beyond it."

He stopped as if he had completed his thought and had nothing to add. I thought about it for a bit and decided to try applying Shuren's explanation of her Law of Original Truth.

I asked, "You mean that by being honest with yourself you were able to see the untruth that had become part of your reality?"

"Exactly, Yosh. That's exactly right. Honesty is the key, and that honesty exists in two aspects as you may recall from the start of this conversation. The first aspect is *depth of exploration*, which we discussed just now. Do you recall the second aspect?

I thought back to the six levels of content and seemed to recall that he had said 'whether we really learn it.' So that's what I repeated back.

"Right," said Jim. "The intellect likes to play games. Like little children, it likes to try on clothes and look at itself in the mirror. It likes to play at different roles, to evaluate esoteric concepts, to debate and display its cleverness.

"The Ego will use the intellect to avoid challenging itself, and these are some of its favorite games. But wisdom is not a game, and the conflicts that mar our world because of our attachment to our Egos cause more misery than any natural disaster.

"We are truly trapped by our Egos. The structure of that trap is reflected in the six categories of content that we discussed. But the path to escape that trap is also reflected in this structure. We are only trapped when we do not see it as a trap. We free ourselves when we see our condition for what it has been. The two things necessary for this awareness are *clarity* of awareness and *depth* of awareness."

"That does help bring this together," I said.

"Good, Yosh. We have spent a lot of time on *clarity of awareness*. Do you recall the key to that aspect of awareness?"

"Yes, that would be honesty."

"Right, so what would be the key to depth of awareness?"

"Isn't this the same as 'whether we learn it,' like we just talked about?"

"Exactly. *Clarity* may be the first requirement, but it only shows you the lay of the land. Getting a detailed map of the path to the solution requires you to actually walk through the territory. This is where *depth* comes in. It requires incorporating the lessons that honesty has gathered for you. Unless that is done, honesty cannot proceed further.

"The failure to recognize this is one of the greatest tricks of the Ego. It fears that you will actually use your clarity to take action. If it can give you the appearance of action and satisfy you, then it will have won and retained you in its trap."

"I think I understand what you're saying," I replied. "It's playing games with me in order to keep me trapped. So how do I get the Ego to stop playing these games?"

"You do not get it to stop. It *will not stop*. You return the focus to yourself. *You* will *stop allowing* the Ego to trick you into playing intellectual games of cleverness when you realize that these are not games. You see, Yosh, what appears to be a game to you is death and misery for others. When you see that this is so *and* you care about it, you will stop treating the Ego with kid gloves and see it for the terribly destructive entity that it is.

"When you develop this resolve and awareness, then your inquiry will carry new weight and will become truly transformative. There is a simple way to know when this has occurred—*look to your actions*."

With those words he handed me the second framed quote that hung in his office:

To know and not to act is not to know.

– The Dictum of Wang Yangming

"When you are willing to accept that you may not be the Ego, then you stop being attached to that definition of yourself and to the story of yourself. If you can then apply the onus of action to your inquiry into the truth, you will gradually deprive your Ego of hiding places within your mind.

"Once you have closed off enough doors that lead to dead ends, the path to wisdom becomes clear. When you accept that path by rejecting the Ego, then bringing about change in yourself becomes a matter of joy and not an obligation."

He had managed to bring a lot of his different thoughts together. I felt like I finally understood much of what he was saying. At the same time, though, he had planted many new questions in my mind. Besides, who was I kidding? I didn't think I could do all those things he said were required. I barely *understood* what was required.

I didn't know what to say except, "Jim, that sounds like a pretty lonely journey. I'm not so sure I have all that in me."

"Yes, Yosh, it is a lonely journey. That's why it's a road that's not frequently traveled. You have to travel it alone because it means rejecting the self that you've been taught is so valuable. It requires feeling very comfortable with something inside you that is greater than the Ego. And it requires being deeply dissatisfied with who you happen to be. That's why such angst is important. It marks a point of decision.

"It is at this point that help can be invaluable. If such angst and depression are due to frustration over the feeling of thwarted growth, then help can be critical at this time. That's the reason that I'm sharing this message with you, because you are requesting it, even though you haven't asked."

From the way he expressed his understanding, I knew that Jim must have been in my position at one time. The example of his growing out of it meant as much to me as all the thoughts he'd shared with me that day. I felt a kinship with Jim that I hadn't fully realized until that moment.

I didn't need to think about his words for long. I knew that if I did need that help, then Jim must be the person to lead me to it. It was late by now, and he had given me a lot to think about. I looked at the clock and realized that Luke had been right to be concerned. I had missed getting the rest of my work done. I knew that Takoda had probably picked up my slack, and I promised myself I wouldn't let that happen again. I'd make it up to him tomorrow.

I thanked Jim, said good night, and returned to my room. As I lay in bed, I thought about all that he had said. His parting words had almost sounded like some kind of offer, but I was probably just imagining things. I stared up at the ceiling for a long time that night before I finally drifted off to sleep.

F arming and the small dairy operation were important for the Cramfords, but these activities were the smaller part of life on the ranch,
especially during the spring and fall. The larger part was the cattle,
and they seemed to keep coming.

I had seen cattle on farms before. They would mostly just be
standing around or sitting in pastures on a farm. But this was open-
range ranching, so not many cattle were kept on the ranch during
the summer. As Luke explained it, his operation was a spring-calving
ranch. That meant that the calves were born in the spring between
March and May. Calves and the rest of the herd spent all summer
fattening up in the high mountain pastures that were allotted by the
Bureau of Land Management.

Summer may not have been a very chaotic time on the ranch,
but fall was a different story, and October was crunch time. That was

when most of the cattle were brought in from those summer pastures.

Much of that work was done on horseback, and it continued once the cattle had been brought back to the ranch. At first, the cattle were placed into a pasture to recover from the drive. In the following days, the work of separating calves from cows and culling cattle for winter pasture was done.

I had seen the operation at the ranch during the second week I was there, with small herds of cattle being separated and then transferred to the holding pens. From there, the spring calves would be loaded onto cattle trucks to be taken to market.

Luke and his men didn't bring all the cattle down at once because it was easier to spread the work out over a few weeks. Before a herd was brought down to the valley, Luke would know roughly how many calves would be going to market and would arrange for the cattle truck to arrive at a certain time in the morning.

He sold most of his cattle through a livestock option, so they were shipped out rather than being held at the ranch longer than needed. He'd give himself a couple of days just in case the unexpected happened but tried to time the arrival of a herd pretty close to the ship date so that he didn't have to use up too much of his fodder or winter hay.

I had a front row seat to the whole show and had enough experience to be a bit player. The first two weeks of October things had been leisurely with some punctuated chaos, but by the middle of the month things were starting to pick up. Once the drives started in earnest, there was a flurry of activity with shipping day the most chaotic.

By that time, though, I was a little more prepared for the organized insanity. I could even manage a horse! I had started riding just a few days after I'd gotten to the ranch, so I wasn't totally green by the time most of the work needed to be done.

The horse that Luke put me on was a sorrel mare named Annahme. I'd never ridden before, but she was as gentle and good-natured as a horse can probably be. She was a quarter horse and seemed a natural at cutting—or separating—calves from cows and the rest of the herd. At least she seemed a natural when Luke rode her.

When *I* rode her, she seemed much clumsier. I learned quickly that it was me who was clumsy, not Annahme. As I learned to move my balance and work with her instincts, she no longer needed to shift her weight to keep me from falling off.

I had never had the experience of feeling my body adjust like that. At first, it was all I could do to just think about staying in the saddle. But once I learned to use my knees to squat in the stirrups rather than just using them to hold on, I fared a lot better. I remember the first time I did that. I did it without even thinking. But, at the time, I was too busy to mull that over. I'd already moved on to thinking how I should move—and I kept being wrong.

After about a week of constantly trying to dissect what I was doing, I just let go. I was amazed to feel my body instinctively moving its center of gravity. It was a bit like riding a bike but very different too because, unlike any bike, Annahme was moving on her own. She was anticipating and positioning herself, and as my body felt that movement, it moved on its own to match it. For the first time in my life, I felt what it was like to act without really thinking, to just act and to create out of that action.

It was good to be free of my mind and all the thoughts that had accumulated. As much as I enjoyed the conversations I'd had with Jim, Shuren, and Luke, this was an experience that went beyond even the insights they had shared with me. I could *feel* that I was something more than the collection of my thoughts. Perhaps there was something to all this talk and the ideas they had shared with me.

Over the next week, I gradually took on more of a role in the roundups. There was a pretty typical routine. The morning that the calves are supposed to ship out, the herds are in separate pastures where they spent the night. The whole herd needs to be driven from the pasture into a corral. Then you can get to the work of cutting out the calves from the cows and bulls.

The calves are then moved into a shipping pen, and the older cattle go back out to the pasture, leaving the corral open for the next herd. This step gets repeated for each herd in the pasture at the ranch until you have a shipping pen full of calves and the adults are back in the pastures.

The timing is important because Luke gets paid by the pound, and the animals are under a good deal of stress from being separated. The calves actually lose weight the longer they're in the shipping pen (something called 'shrinking'), so they need to be moved to the cattle trucks as soon as possible. It's a busy morning, but that's where most of Luke's income for the year comes from.

The next few days are spent managing the remaining herd called "dry" cows. He needs to cull out any that are too old, weak, or injured to make it through the winter, as well as the cows that were barren, which were tagged earlier. Then there's the vaccination, branding of any summer calves that are kept in the herd, and pregnancy testing.

I learned that cows have a gestation period of about nine months, just like humans, so if a cow isn't pregnant in October, she's likely to get culled. All this culling leaves a smaller herd that's kept in a winter pasture and needs to be maintained on fodder.

It was hard work but I was learning every day. It was a different kind of learning, though. I was learning with my body as well as learning with my head, the way you learn a sport. That's how much of my time at the H.R.C. Ranch went. I knew that the fall roundup was about finished when Luke asked me if I wanted to join him in bringing down the last herd. He must have thought I'd had enough riding experience by then, so I jumped at the chance.

He told me that we would leave in the morning. Knowing Luke, I understood that to mean pretty early in the morning. Fitra seemed to know exactly what I'd need to pack and helped me put it all together. I would have been lost without her. She just took everything in stride, moving to take care of problems or changes as they came up.

I thought about how much she came at life the same way I'd learned to come at riding.

True to form, Luke had us on the trail just after sunup. At first, it was like all the other days I'd spent riding. But riding into the high country was different than riding on the ranch or in the pasture.

When we began, it was all I could do to stay focused on the trail. Riding up or down a slope means working with your horse in a different way. I was happy to be riding Annahme, who made up for most of my inexperience.

It took me a while to feel comfortable enough to just ride. When my hill riding finally moved from *thinking* to *feeling*, I was able to look up and see the world I was riding through. I had been so focused on the challenge of the ride that I hadn't stopped to think about the trip itself. Now, looking up, I took it all in. I felt it more than I saw it. And it felt like nothing I'd ever imagined. I finally understood what it means to "see the forest for the trees." But the forest was only part of it.

The best reward was the autumn mountains in all their splendor. It felt like a dream. Riding the trail meant focusing on the dirt path gradually making its way upward through the forest, then suddenly hitting a rise and looking up to see patches of deep blue sky through the rustling of bright yellow leaves. Clearing the rise, a high mountain valley would open up in front of us, and then, heading down, we'd break back into the white pillars of birch forest pierced by the autumn red of a smooth sumac. And so it went, from one magnificent vista to the next.

The allotment that Luke led us to was in just such a valley, broken up by a few lodgepole pines and spotted with gambel oaks. It was covered with low grass and inhabited by a few hundred head of cattle. A couple men had already made it up ahead of us to set up camp. We dismounted and watered the horses.

I'd never been big on camping. I guess I just thought of it as a hassle. A lot changed for me that day, though. Maybe part of it was that much of the work of setting up camp had already been done. Mostly, though, it was the way the camp settled down at dusk and the warmth of the fire in the chilly October air.

I sat chatting with Luke and the ranch hands with Keeley lying next to my feet. The two border collies who called the ranch home had joined us on the ride and lay curled up nearby. They seemed to sense the pace of the day in a much deeper way.

It grew gradually quiet as dusk fell. As the smoke from the fire rose up, my eyes followed a few stray sparks into the dark night sky.

The sparks faded quickly and I found myself staring into the expanse. As my eyes adjusted, the dark seemed to explode with countless stars.

What a marvelous thing to have something appear so empty one moment and then so full the next.

Lying down in my sleeping bag that night, I could feel the strain of the ride flowing out of me into the ground. I stared up at the stars. The occasional spark glowed as it rose then blinked off to join the dark. I drifted off to sleep.

Waking up the next day meant breaking camp and getting ready to drive the cattle back down to the H.R.C. It was a challenge, and I have to admit I had little to do with it. Mostly it was the experienced hands, Luke, and the dogs. I did have a chance to help out, and it was fun letting Annahme take the lead, cutting off renegades that tried to break free from the herd or stragglers that wanted to stop moving forward.

I had little time to let my mind wander as I had on the way up. Now, there was work to be done and it required concentration, not daydreaming. Eventually, we moved the herd back down into the valley and into the pasture. I was exhausted and I hadn't even done much.

It was only after the last cow had entered the enclosure that I looked up to see Shuren, Jim, and Fitra standing at the fence. They, too, were admiring the last herd brought down for the year. They waved and we headed over to them.

A lot of questions were thrown my way. Luke answered most of them for me with inflated commentary about my horsemanship. I could only chuckle.

Was this feeling of being a part of things happiness or joy?

The conversation was still going on around me when I realized I had started to have this strange dialogue going on in my head, like I was talking to myself.

I don't remember doing that before, I thought.

I only snapped out of it when Luke reminded me that we needed to tend to the horses. I looked over at him like he'd woken me from a dream. He must have known my thoughts had drifted, but I guess that was nothing new. Now that I was back, though, I realized how hungry

I was. We tended to the horses before we fed our growling stomachs, but I have to admit I rushed through it.

Fitra did not disappoint us. The food was waiting outside on the picnic table. To Luke and me, it looked like a feast. Supper was lively with questions about my ride and Luke's continued exaggeration of my abilities. It felt good to belong, and I realized how much I missed that feeling.

We finished eating together and laughed at stories of Luke's first ride up to the summer pastures as a kid. That's when Jim and Shuren took Luke aside to speak with him in private. I knew there must be a great deal to plan for the following day. After they had left, I found myself sitting at the table with Fitra, who brought me up to speed on all the goings on while Luke and I were away.

It was great to see Fitra again. She sat there in her blue, checkered scarf and her always simple but tasteful blouse and jeans. I thought how much I had misjudged her when we first met. She was far from my preconceptions of a simple farm wife. She was comfortable in her role but far from simple.

Fitra was a woman in constant motion. She managed the chore-ography of the ranch and the farm with an ability that I found unimag-inable. She could carry on several discussions at once and not skip a beat in juggling all that she was doing. I learned that she and Luke had met when Luke had been traveling after college. She had moved back with him when they'd decided to get married. She had never lived outside a city, let alone on a farm or ranch. I thought about all that she must have gone through to adjust to this life and of how capably she had managed it.

She had made this life her own. Still, Fitra seemed to be as much at home behind the desk managing the accounts as she was out on the farm, directing the harvest, or in the kitchen fixing one of her wonder-ful meals. She was an accomplished rider herself and helped out when an extra hand was needed, but that didn't happen too often.

She was truly the heart of the whole ranch. From the way she was regarded by the ranch hands and their families, you would have thought it was she who had grown up there and not Luke.

Sitting with Fitra, my thoughts kept jumping back and forth between the life that I'd also left behind and the experience I was having here in New Mexico with this wonderfully gracious family.

How different my life might have been if I'd met them sooner.

I realized that it had been almost a month since I'd come down to Chama. Before this, I hadn't really thought about the time, but now I started thinking that I probably should leave soon—that I might be wearing out my welcome.

Whatever 'help' I might have given to Luke felt more like time he had generously given to me. I didn't want to abuse that consideration. As much as I had enjoyed my time, I was thinking it might be best to get back to the city and pick up the pieces of my life. Perhaps Jim, Shuren, and Luke were having similar thoughts. Maybe that's why they needed to talk.

Whatever they had in mind, they seemed to be having a serious discussion. I didn't want to pry, so I kept my nose out of their business. When Fitra and I were done chatting, we cleared the picnic table and brought the dishes and remaining food back inside. We were still in the kitchen when we heard the front door open and the screen door slam shut. I walked out of the kitchen to find Jim, Shuren, and Luke standing by the dining room table. Jim motioned for me to have a seat. We all sat down.

"Yosh," Jim said, "we'd like to talk with you about your stay here with us."

I leaned forward, intending to tell Jim that I had decided I should be leaving and would appreciate a ride back to Chama when they finished up here at the ranch.

Before I could say anything, though, Jim said, "Yosh, you should understand that we did not expect to hear from you. We knew that Abe had a grandson, but we had no idea that you would contact us at this time."

I interrupted him, anticipating his next comment.

"I know, Jim. I've been thinking about that as well. I'm sure my being here is a lot of work for you all. You've been very kind, but I was thinking I should be getting back."

They looked at each other with a little surprise and a little amusement.

Jim continued, "Yosh, I think you misunderstand. What I was trying to say was that we had no idea that you would contact us at *this time*… instead of *any other* time of the year."

Now I was really confused. I knew it was a busy time for them, but why would they rather have me here at some other time of the year?

Jim continued. "Yosh, what I mean is, we didn't know that Abe felt so highly of you that he would give you the other half of the medallion. If we had known, we would have tried harder to get in touch with you a long time ago. We would've arranged for you to come down earlier in the year."

"I'm confused," I confessed. "What does the medallion have to do with it?"

Luke picked up where Jim had left off. "I don't think you understand what Jim is saying. The truth is we enjoy having you here. It's just that we weren't expecting you *at this time of year*. That's one of the reasons that we've had to take turns sharing your company.

"Fall is a busy time, as you know, so we usually try to make trips to the mountains during the summer. We would have had you wait until next year, but there was an urgency in your voice when you called, and we felt that we shouldn't wait. We tend to listen to that voice in ourselves—and try to hear it when it comes from someone else. I think we were right to listen to it, but that leaves us with a problem."

I was more confused now. "But I haven't asked to go to the mountains, and to my mind you all have been the most considerate and generous people I've ever known. The last thing I want to do is make any more problems for you."

Jim smiled, looked me in the eyes, and said, "Yosh, the medallion your grandfather gave you was not meant as a way for us to know that you were his grandson. It was meant to help us recognize you as the person Abe wanted us to share a particular knowledge with."

"But you have shared so much with me already. I'm so changed because of the learning you've given me."

"What you don't know is that there is so much *more* that Abe intended for you to know. You see, we are each limited in our ability to teach you this. The book that Abe wanted you to have is a condensation of that knowledge, but *it* is not that knowledge. If you had been able to receive that knowledge from the book, you already would have done so."

"I wish I *were* able to absorb it, and I feel bad that I can't," I said. "There are concepts in there that sound appealing but just don't make sense to me."

Shuren cleared her throat and said, "Why fault yourself for not understanding? You recognized that the message of the book was not accessible to you. That was an honest assessment. It meant that the distance you need to travel to receive that knowledge is too great for the book to impart today."

"I suppose you're right," I said.

She continued, "Your decision to stay was a kind of intuitive recognition of this, as well as your request for help. Without requesting help, help cannot be received, even if it is offered. I believe that you understand this now."

I nodded. I did understand that. I was grateful to them for holding out their hands and offering their assistance, and I was grateful to myself for having beaten back my pride and having the humility to ask for help.

It had not been easy for me to seek help. And I knew that it hadn't been easy for them to see my masked request for help as the request that it was—not simply as me being stubborn or dismissive.

Luke spoke up. "What Abe intended for you, Yosh, is available to you, but you need to decide quickly if you want to pursue it. Ordinarily we would've wanted to help you with this in the spring or summer, and it could be done in pieces, but that's not possible now. You could wait until next year, but Mom and Grandpa feel that you're ready for it now."

What they were saying was a bit cryptic, but I'd already learned so much from them and I wanted to learn more. Besides, it wasn't like I had anything pressing going on at home. But I wasn't entirely sure what he was asking me to decide. With some hesitation I said, "If you all think it's best for me to do it now, okay. You probably know better than I do."

Jim and Shuren gave each other a look as if I'd just given the green light to proceed with something they had already planned.

Jim spoke next. "You know about your grandfather's visits with us in the years after we first met him, right?"

"Yeah," I said. "Shuren mentioned it when I was with you all in Chama."

"Well, Shuren may have told you a great deal, but there's another part of the story. You see, Abe wasn't so much coming up from San Antonio to see me as he was to see a friend of ours. Of course, I know he enjoyed our time together, as we all did, but that wasn't his primary goal."

I hadn't heard the Cramfords speak about any other friend of my grandfather's. As far as I knew, Jim was the only friend that Grandpa Abe had around here.

"You may remember Shuren telling you how Abe ended up in these parts... that his plane had crashed and he was rescued."

"I remember that."

"Well," Jim said, "the person who rescued him became his friend—the friend your grandfather returned so often to see."

"Okay. I remember Shuren saying that my grandfather would go into the back country whenever he was here on leave from Brooks."

"That's right, Yosh. Abe came to see his friend, and I'd often go with him. I knew this friend of his because that person was my friend as well. In fact, he was the one who brought Abe to me after he had found him in the wreckage of his plane the previous fall and patched him up that winter."

"Does this friend have a name?" I asked. "And how do *you* know him?"

"His name is Mideol, and he's more of a mentor to me than a friend. I knew him because my father knew his father, and my mother's family had known his grandfather. We actually don't know how far back the relationship goes."

"So it was Mideol who saved Grandpa Abe?"

"Yes, but not just once. He saved him twice."

"Twice? I know about the plane crash. How else did he save my grandfather?"

Jim replied with a question. "Has your family ever told you about your grandfather's character when he was younger?"

"I've never heard anyone in my family have anything but glowing words for him."

"So he was *always* the wonderful person that you knew?"

"Yeah, that's right."

"Think hard, Yosh. Was that always who Abe had been?"

I remembered asking my aunts about his time in the war and whether he had been a hero. They had said he'd been changed by the war—but not in the way that most people are changed by war. I hadn't given it much thought at the time, but I remembered it now and told Jim about it.

Jim said, "That's pretty accurate, Yosh. Most people who go to war voluntarily go idealistic and hopeful, dreaming of glory and adventure. They often return dispirited, cynical, and closed to the world. Of course, that doesn't happen all the time, but that's what your aunts were speaking about."

"It didn't happen to Grandpa Abe," I said. "Was that because he never fought in the war? Why wasn't he affected by it that way?"

"Well, to be honest with you, Abe *was* profoundly affected. He saw quite a bit of action in the 8th Army Air Force flying bombers over Europe in 1942 and 1943 before there was much fighter support. He was wounded several times and lost many friends in the war. He ended up going through a period of guilt at having survived while so many of his friends died. He managed to keep it pretty bottled up, though. That was a different time. He was expected to just move past it.

"But Abe couldn't. He eventually fell into a deep depression and gradually withdrew from everyone. Like you, Yosh, Abe found himself living in a world that no longer made any sense to him. So he cut himself off from the world, including his family. Your family knew nothing about this time in his life because he didn't want them to know about it. But he confided in me. He needed to tell someone, and I was the closest friend he had—well, other than Mideol."

A little defensively, I said, "I've never heard these things before."

Jim continued. "I want to share them with you because I think you need to know about this part of your grandfather's life—about his journey—because it's not unlike your own."

"I don't think his journey could be anything like mine."

I didn't want to believe this about my grandfather. How could he have been like me? I was a mess.

Jim wasn't put off by my defensiveness. "You may not want to hear this, Yosh, but the Abe who enlisted before the war even began was willful, cocky, and self-destructive. He was also fearless and confident. He was a skilled pilot and a quick learner. He had all the qualities that go into making an ideal warrior.

I was so confused. "I could see him being confident and fearless and being a great pilot—but I couldn't see Grandpa Abe being self-destructive."

"Sometimes it's a thin line that separates acceptance of risk and the possibility of harm from apathy about one's welfare and the invitation of harm. Sometimes, Yosh, the only difference is the way in which you regard yourself. When your definition of self is narrow, then it's easy to lose that self when the world challenges your definition. At the time of the war, Abe defined himself narrowly as a soldier and a pilot."

"I knew he must have been an excellent pilot. He was good at everything."

"Oh, he was good at what he did. There's no doubt about that," Jim said. "Abe loved the fight, Yosh, but he quickly learned that fighting is different than killing. Glory is a great idea, but war is really about blood and body parts, pain and loss.

"During his first two years in the service, Abe lost many of the illusions that had sustained him. By 1944 the war had taken a great toll on your grandfather. Even though he had lost a part of himself, he doggedly maintained a singular focus on his mission. His commanding officer respected him and saw the risks that Abe's apathy was leading him to take toward himself. He made sure that Abe was relieved of combat duty. That's one of the reasons that he was reassigned to training.

"But that reassignment didn't end his pain or his depression. He still felt great emptiness and tried to fill that emptiness by taking other risky assignments, even though he was removed from the war. Maybe he took those assignments *because* he was removed from it."

"How do you know that he was as lost and empty as you say?" I asked.

"He told me so," Jim replied. "When Abe thought back on the months before his plane crashed, he admitted to me how stubborn and self-destructive he had been at that time."

"Are you saying that my grandfather crashed the plane on purpose?"

"No—Abe was too concerned with duty to intentionally crash his plane. There are other ways to kill yourself, though. Not all of them require you to be deliberate in the attempt."

"Yeah," I responded, almost in a whisper. "I'm familiar with those thoughts."

Jim nodded. "Abe was ambivalent about his life in the final year of the war. He'd come to a point where he saw the world as cruel and incongruous with its much-vaunted ideals. He told me how insane he thought it was. He saw how some people have a lot and spend their lives trying to convince everyone that they deserve even more, while others have almost nothing and become convinced they deserve so little. He saw a world in which people kill one another for the smallest slight yet ignore the largest injustices."

My grandfather, it seemed, had shared a lot of my own issues with the world.

"Abe was tortured by the ironies he had seen and lived through," Jim said. "He once mentioned to me how often he'd seen people develop some clarity or sanity only in the moments before they died. He loathed hypocrisy whether it was personal or societal. He was bitter and tired of war, as well as the failure and waste that war represented."

"I had no idea that Grandpa Abe had been so down," I said.

"Yes, Abe was very despondent. Like I said, he was ambivalent about life in general, and his own life. At the time of the crash he was at Brooks as a trainer, not as a test pilot. Still, he volunteered for the dangerous task of testing new bombers, not caring much if he lived or died. While flying bombers over Europe, he had learned that the range on the B-25 could be extended if he changed the pitch of the plane slightly. In the fall of 1944, he set out from Brooks with his co-pilot and navigator to test the range on the new B-25J that had just come out. The Army Air Corps wanted to know if the 25J had this same idiosyncrasy."

"So that's why he'd come all the way up here," I said.

Jim nodded as Shuren and Luke looked on. Fitra had now joined us at the table, anxious to hear the story as well.

"Right," Jim responded. "They were on their test flight when they hit turbulence over the southern Rockies, just after turning toward their landing field in Kansas. The plane just went down. His co-pilot and navigator were killed, and Abe was pretty badly injured. He was lucky to survive the crash, but he had lost a lot of blood and was in a state of shock."

"Is that when your friend Mideol found him?"

"Yes, Mideol was up in the mountains and heard the crash. He rode out to the crash site, found your grandfather, and brought him back to his camp."

"So that's when Mideol saved my grandfather the first time. So how did he save Grandpa Abe the second time."

"Actually, I said that Mideol saved him twice, yes, but I didn't mean he saved Abe on two occasions. I meant he saved Abe in two ways. First, physically—because Abe would have died in the mountains without Mideol's help. But Mideol also saved your grandfather from himself. He helped Abe to get off the path of self-destruction and find a way to live again without the cynicism of thwarted pride or in the denial of clutching at naiveté. Mideol showed him how it was possible to live more fully than he had ever imagined."

"So that's what Aunt Joyce and Aunt Joan were talking about when they said he was changed?"

"Yes, the Abe who returned to your family was the *opposite* of the brash, self-centered, willful young man who had gone to war. He had been jaded and cynical and reckless, but your family no longer saw that in him after he returned home. His time with Mideol allowed him to see himself more fully. It allowed him to see his world more clearly and come to terms with his bitterness.

"Rather than returning shell-shocked and devoid of life, Abe came out of the mountains seeing his untarnished potential and the potential of everyone around him. He returned with hope. This was not the wishful hope of a child who needs to see the world as he wants it to be. It was the mature hope of a person who sees the world in a way that the world is yet incapable of seeing itself to be."

"So you're telling me that this Mideol person changed him?"

"No, I'm *not* saying Mideol changed him. I'm telling you that what Abe found with Mideol allowed Abe to change himself. Saving Abe from the plane wreck was something Mideol did, and without that Abe would surely have died. But saving Abe from himself was something Abe did. And without it he would likely never have lived.

"It was Mideol, of course, who helped Abe *learn* to live, not just continue on. Still, it was ultimately Abe who accepted that help. I know we're all grateful to him for doing that—just as we are grateful to Mideol for offering it."

Jim's words echoed the sentiments I had just been feeling toward the Cramfords. I realized again how defensive I had become at the thought of anyone finding fault with my grandfather, and how I had ignored any suggestion of faultfinding my entire life. I was wandering off into these thoughts when Luke dragged me back to where I was.

"Yosh, when Jim was talking about what Abe intended for you— *this* is what he intended. He wanted you to meet Mideol."

"Sounds great to me," I said.

"It's not as easy as that, though," Luke replied. "We can't just go over and meet him. Mideol still lives way up in the high country. It's a three-day ride up there—*if* the weather is good. Then there's the matter of staying out in the mountains this time of year. Once the snows set in, there's no getting down till spring. We'll take our chances with you on the trip, but we can't stay, and we'll have to turn back right away. As it is, I pushed the fall roundup ahead by a week to make sure we'd have a shot of making the journey, if you're up to it. You've had enough riding experience now to make the trip."

Suddenly, it became clear to me that Luke and Jim had sacrificed a lot to give me this opportunity. Rounding up the calves while they still could have gained some weight had cost them plenty. Babysitting me through my awkwardness on the farm must have taken no small amount of patience.

The 'help' around the ranch, the lessons on cutting cows, and the high-pasture roundup, were all carefully planned to get me ready for this trip… if I wanted to make it. They either respected my grandfather a whole lot or they thought the world of Mideol. Perhaps both. Still, it seemed like a lot of trouble to go through.

"I'm confused," I said. "Why would we go through all this trouble to just turn around and come right back to the ranch?"

They exchanged glances before Luke answered my question. "Yosh, when I said we would have to turn back right away, I was talking about whoever rides up there with you. I wasn't talking about you. You would stay there with Mideol."

That sounded strange, and I wasn't sure I'd heard him right. I must have had a pretty quizzical look on my face, based on Luke's response. "Why don't you sleep on it. I've got the cattle trucks coming in the morning, and we've both had a long day. Tomorrow's going to be busy, but the boys can handle it after that. So if we do head up there, we'll leave the following day."

I thanked them all for their planning and for going to all of the trouble just so I would have this opportunity, but it seemed like a lot to bite off. Just to make sure I wasn't mistaken, I asked Luke, "Let me get this straight. What you're saying is that my grandfather wanted me to meet this friend of his, Mideol. And the reason you know this is that he gave me the medallion. But are you saying that meeting him *now* would mean that I would spend the entire winter up there in the mountains alone with him?"

"That's right," Luke said "That's what I'm saying."

"But I don't even know the guy. That could be a very uncomfortable few months." There was more than a little concern in my voice.

"That's possible, I suppose," Jim said. "All I can tell you is that Abe spent the winter up there, and he seemed to find something that he valued his entire life. Without encountering that, Abe would probably have remained much as he was when he took off on that test flight. We're simply offering you a choice to receive *by intention* what Abe received *by accident*."

That made some sense to me, but it was still a lot to think about. I thanked them for the offer, told them I'd need to sleep on it, said good night, and went to my room. I thought I'd be up for a long time thinking, but I was so tired from the day's riding that I couldn't even remember falling asleep.

***

The next thing I remember was waking up to the smell of hotcakes and sausages. The day was already old for a ranch day. Luke and Fitra hadn't bothered to wake me, figuring I'd need my rest. I stood in the dining area of the kitchen, staring out the window to see the cattle trucks being loaded. I could see Luke orchestrating the entire process while Ahote handled the details and Jim looked on.

My thoughts drifted. *Is this some kind of dream? How did I ever end up here?*

Fitra and Shuren joined me in the dining area. They brought me breakfast and sat down, drinking their morning coffee. While I ate, I listened to their stories about the ranch and this Mideol character. I enjoyed their company, but I felt guilty about not carrying my weight, so I finished eating and headed out to see if there was any work left for me to do. There was, and Takoda was happy to share it.

I was so wrapped up in working that it wasn't till lunch that I actually had a chance to speak with Luke and Jim. The talk was mostly about the cattle and the work that would need to be done as soon as they had been shipped out or placed in winter pasture. Over lunch, no one said anything about our conversation the night before, so I thought I should be the one to break the silence.

"I thought about what you all said last night, and I've decided that I'd like to make the trip—if you're still willing to take me."

Luke acknowledged my comment with a nod, before glancing at Fitra and Shuren. "We'd be happy to take you up," Luke said, "but we'll have no time to lose."

It was like a switch had flipped. Luke was all business now, and I could see that he was already thinking about the specifics of the trip. They all seemed like a well-functioning team. Fitra, Jim, and Shuren were already deep in discussion before Luke even headed out the door to oversee the rest of the day's work. They seemed to consider my decision urgent because the talk quickly changed to preparations and what would need to be taken care of before leaving.

While they made plans for the trip, I called Aunt Joyce and asked her to collect the few belongings I had in my apartment and tell my landlord I wouldn't need to renew the lease. I told her I'd be staying in New Mexico for the winter and probably wouldn't be in touch again before springtime.

"Yosh, are you all right?" she asked. "I was getting worried about you."

"To be honest, Aunt Joyce, I haven't felt this well in a long time. They're taking real good care of me."

"Well, I'm glad. I know you're a pretty independent sort, but I still like to keep tabs on you. Why springtime? Did you find a job?"

"No, I'll be spending some time with an old friend of Grandpa Abe's, but he doesn't have a phone. I'll be okay, though. I'll call you as soon as I can, maybe in May."

I guess she'd gotten used to my being out of touch, so she accepted this without too many questions. I asked her to put my car in storage or to let my cousin use it. At any rate, I had nothing holding me back now but my own reservations about the trip.

Luke stayed busy the rest of the day arranging for everything that would need to be done over the week or so that we would be gone. The women were a blur of activity and I would soon learn why.

Jim seemed to have the least to do. He and I spent the day together. He told me Shuren would be joining Luke and me on the ride and that she had as much experience in the mountains as any of them.

As I was reminiscing about our last conversation, Jim must have been doing the same because he asked me, "Yosh, do you remember our discussion about desire, intention, determination, and process?"

"Yes, I do," I said. With that, I pulled out the folded piece of paper I had kept.

Desire *My feeling that I want to move to joy*

Intention *Consciously affirming I want to go/be there*

Determination *How badly I want to get there*

Process *How I plan on getting there*

He looked at it, surprised that I carried it with me. He said, "You're a lot more like Abe than you know. Have you thought any more about these four parts of the journey to a goal?"

"I understand what you're getting at, but these things don't seem to line up for me. I mean, I can't really say that being conscious of my *desires* always leads me to *intentions*, that then move to *desire* and then on to a *process*."

"That's a good point. You're right. This is not a linear movement. Each element interacts with the others to define itself more clearly. For this to occur requires both action and reflection upon the results of that action.

"Let me give you an example. You may have a goal, which is your *'intention.'* When you seek that goal, the degree of your effort and the way in which you employ that effort will reflect those other two elements, desire and process. Evaluating the results of your efforts in both dimensions will ultimately help you to define your goal more clearly."

That made sense in light of all the talk about the dead ends that Jim had spoken about earlier. *Weren't all of those failed explorations really just clarifications of intention?*

I told Jim, "If anything, I've seen a lot of places I don't want to go… or be."

"That's what I'm talking about," Jim said. "You've already refined your intention. As it gets clearer and more defined, your journey will get more focused. Our discussions and your talks with Shuren have all helped you define your intention with some degree of clarity. Of course, as we've seen, that work isn't finished.

"We haven't devoted very much time to issues of desire and process until now. With regard to *desire,* there is not much to be discussed in the positive sense. The intervention necessary in the element of desire is a negative one. By this, I mean it's concerned with the removal of obstructions and impediments to your intrinsic desire. You've made progress in that regard without even knowing it."

"I have?"

"The progress you've made regarding *desire* is reflected in your decision to make this trip. It's real progress, but much work remains to be done."

"Well I guess that leaves *process* to discuss."

"Yosh, process is a large area that requires more than I'm capable of discussing with you. Mideol is the best guide in process that I know of."

"Then I'm looking forward to meeting him even more."

Jim hesitated before speaking again. "There are three things I ask you to take with you on this trip. The first, I know you already possess. First, 'never accept any thought that you have *not* made your own.' The second thing is 'never fail to act on any thought that you *have* made your own.' The third is 'respect.' I know that you're a respectful and polite person, but there is a level of respect rarely discussed or given in our society.

"This third consideration that I am asking you to take with you— respect—is essential if you want to move toward the solution of the dilemma… a requirement for making progress in the area of process. Previously, when we spoke of process, we spoke of it in regards to self-directed inquiry. That is a process of your own design and choosing and will always remain relevant."

"Right. We talked about process being subject to change as it was tested."

"That's correct, Yosh. There is another type of process, though, that is shared with you by someone who has already engaged in the area of inquiry in which you are seeking guidance."

"Like a teacher?" I asked.

"Yes—for you it would be like a student in relation to a teacher, or like an apprentice encountering the master of a trade he wishes to enter into. Such respect goes to the issue of trust. Of course, I'm not saying that you should trust anyone without filtering it through your own evaluation.

"What I *am* saying is that you will likely reach a point where you must decide for yourself whom to trust without having a basis to make that judgment—except for your intuition. Remember this discussion when that time comes. The ability to trust your intuition is a valuable skill, which develops only by applying it."

I didn't understand his last point, but I listened. Intuition always seemed to me like a crutch for people who were too lazy to think things through. But I didn't want to argue with him before leaving, so I kept my mouth shut.

I thanked Jim for his advice and told him I would do my best to carry those three things with me. I excused myself to find Takoda. I needed to get to work. But as much as I worked that whole last day at the H.R.C., the upcoming trip was never far from my mind, as was the thought of how highly they all regarded this Mideol person. I had never even heard them speak about him until yesterday. One question kept running through all these thoughts—who is this Mideol that he commands so much respect from them all?

THE HIGH COUNTRY

The next morning I didn't have the luxury of sleeping in. Shuren woke me before sunup. Even though there was a fire in the hearth, it was chilly. Luke had no work waiting for me. I had great anticipation for what lay ahead.

I sat down at the kitchen table, still rubbing the sleep from my eyes. Shuren brought me a glass of water and a cup of coffee. It was then that I saw all the stuff laid out on the couch and the floor in the family room. Shuren knew I hadn't planned on being in New Mexico very long, so she had already given me some clothes, a pair of boots, and a hat. But all this stuff in the family room was much more.

She had bought me winter clothes, snow boots, gloves, a canteen, and a hatchet. There was also a Stetson befitting my new role, and a ski mask—or *balaclava*—that didn't look like it fit my role. There were also countless other small items that she thought I might need over the next few months.

"So you knew I was going to choose to make the trip," I suggested.

She smiled and mentioned something about saving the receipts. I could tell, though, that in many ways she probably knew me better than I knew myself. I thanked her and she gave me a hug. Right there, I knew why I had chosen to make the trip. They all believed so much in me that it was hard for me not to believe in myself. I'll never forget that lesson. What gift could be of greater value than seeing someone else for who they can be, especially when they can't see it in themselves?

Fitra joined us in packing everything up. There was no less activity outside the house. I went over to the barn and there were already four trucks waiting to be loaded with gear. I hadn't thought of all the work that would go into making this trip. Luke was busy making sure his checklist was complete, and Jim looked like he was enjoying the show.

Most of the gear was still in the barn and was what I expected, but some of it was surprising. There were a couple of double-pane windows, several solar panels, and wire. There were two grain grinders—or mills—and several large ceramic jars with plastic liners filled with wheat flour. There were glass jars filled with fruit that had been put up by Fitra, as well as bags of beans and protein powder. Luke and Shuren each carried a rifle and a sidearm for protection in bear country, but Luke was also looking forward to getting an elk, weather permitting, on the trip back. I lent a hand getting things stowed onto the trucks.

Ordinarily, Luke would have had several of the ranch hands helping out, but today it was only Ahote and Takoda. The four of us finished loading the trucks and then covered each bed with a tarp. Then we hitched a two-horse trailer behind each truck. We all had a quick breakfast and finally loaded Shuren's and Luke's horses along with Annahme onto the horse trailers. The other five stalls were loaded with mules.

Coffee in hand, all seven of us headed out the gates of the H.R.C. just as dawn was breaking. We drove through the retreating darkness, back onto the paved road, and then onto the gravel farther up the Chama River valley. Before long, Luke told me that we had left New Mexico and were traveling into southern Colorado.

By the time the dirt road finally ran out, we sat facing a mountain valley covered in low green grass with blades outlined in frost. The meadow was scattered with small clusters of foot-high bushes, their leaves already brown.

The valley stretched on to mid-range chaparral in shades of rust and gray. Pines flanked the sides of two low mountains that came together in a V marking the path of the river as it snaked its way back up into the mountains in the direction we would be heading.

Looking up, I could see stone outcroppings breaking through the pine cover, exposing the thin soil that held the massive trees to the slopes. With the trucks now silent, I could hear the chirping of the birds melding with the soft murmur of the river.

We let the animals out of the trailer. They moved restlessly around the trucks, breathing clouds into the chill mountain air. Keeley, who'd slept through the ride, surveyed the area as we tethered the horses and began loading gear onto the mules.

I thanked Jim for all his advice and his generosity as he prepared to go back. Meeting him had been like getting to know my grandfather all over again. I never imagined I'd have such an opportunity. Getting ready to leave Jim was like losing Grandpa Abe all over again, but I reminded myself it was only temporary.

Jim, never at a loss for words, was unusually quiet. He shook my hand and told me that he'd see me in the spring. I told him that I'd remember his words and the insights he had shared with me. Then I turned to say goodbye to Fitra.

Sometime over the past four weeks she had become the big sister I'd never had. She didn't need any words to say goodbye. The look in her eyes was enough. I thanked her for taking me in and for all her help with the preparations for the trip. I hugged her for a long time.

I shook Ahote's calloused hand and he smiled back, dismissing any talk of parting with a firm, "See you in a few months, kid." He then placed something in my hand. I looked down to see that it was his knife in its sheath. I had seen him wear it on his belt. I tried to object but he stopped me. "Yosh, it's always done well by me. Keep it clean, keep it sharp, and keep it with you."

I nodded and thanked him.

Finally, I said goodbye to my friend Takoda. I had gotten so used to being with him these past weeks that I felt torn in leaving him. We talked for a bit, but there wasn't much to say. I knew that we'd be sharing chores with one another before too long. Who knows, I thought, I might even be of some use to him by then.

How strange—leaving all of these people who'd come into my

life. I felt emptier now than I had when I was truly alone. The only difference was that now I was moving toward something.

We mounted up and I glanced back. Then Shuren, Luke, and I headed off on the three horses with the five mules and the gear in tow. We moved up the trail in single file to the steady sound of hoofbeats on packed dirt. Behind us, I could hear the truck doors shut as the vehicles prepared to head back the way we had come.

We continued up the trail until we were completely out of sight of the road. It wasn't long till the sound of the trucks faded into forest sounds. The breathing of the horses and the noisy chaos of Keeley running through the bushes mixed with the hoofbeats—the soundtrack of our departure.

We steadily gained altitude, with the trail moving past the mostly naked oak forests with scattered stands of juniper. My companions told me it wasn't unusual to have snow on the ground by this time of year, so I was happy we only had to contend with some frost. But even the frost seemed to come and go as we moved from the chill of the forests to the warmth of the sun in the meadows.

I was grateful to have had so much experience riding with Luke. It only took a few minutes for me to get into the rhythm of the ride and adjust to the pace of my horse. Amazing, I thought, how the pace of a horse can set your expectations for the pace of your day.

It was easy to forget about everything except for the ride. As I concentrated on every turn and switchback, I felt completely alive. Later, we stopped to rest the animals and eat lunch. It was only then that my mind was free to wander again. I wondered at how strange it was that the need to concentrate on the little things during the day left me feeling so full of life. But when I thought about things in a big way, I felt so small.

In a peculiar way, getting less done felt like living more. Maybe it was all the attention that I had to pay to get those little things done. Moving back and forth between the demands of the ride and my endless stream of wandering thoughts, one day rolled easily into the next.

Now, each day was set apart not by time but by new sights. The lower valleys with beaver dams and meadows gave way to hilltops with a few scattered aspen groves. These were now just naked, gray-white trunks opening to views of snow-covered mountains ahead.

The trail dropped down into a narrow mountain valley just big enough for the river, with pine trees hugging the banks and towering cliffs on either side. We picked our way across the boulder- and rock-strewn riverbed until the trail again wound through the greenery of a pine forest, unfolding ferns covering the stony floor.

The end of each day on the trail had its own comfortable routine: unpacking the mules and untacking the horses; seeing to their grazing and water before tethering them for the night; setting up the camp and starting the fire to cook meals before bedding down.

However uncomfortable the ground, it was rarely more uncomfortable than sitting in the saddle all day, so sleep was not a problem. Each morning, any memory of discomfort was lost in the anticipation of a new day and the sights it would bring.

The days passed in this steady rhythm, and I was amply rewarded for my effort. I think the rest of the party would have agreed because there were no complaints. Gradually, the sounds of the forest became comfortable to me—the song of the birds, the scampering of squirrels, the tapping of woodpeckers, the buzzing of flies, and the bugling of elk.

As I became more comfortable in the saddle, I grew even more thankful that Luke had given me the gift of Annahme to ride. She carried me over the uneven rock of the riverbeds and managed with ease the odd root or fallen branch. She had become accustomed to me and I to her. The first day had been a novelty. The second was an adjustment. By the third day on the trail I wasn't tired, owing much of that to Annahme.

It wasn't long into that third day that we approached a rise like many we had crossed before. Then we descended on a path along the face of a cliff that overlooked a high valley facing south and slightly to the east. The entrance to the path was a twisting route that I hadn't seen even when we were right on top of it.

To our left was the cliff wall. To our right, facing southeast, the river snaked along the valley floor below. Its blue alternated with flashes of silver reflecting the mid-day sun, its banks outlined in the green of fir and Englemann spruce.

Riding behind Shuren and Luke, I noticed the path along the cliff face open up to a large flat shelf. Luke dismounted ahead of me. I wasn't prepared for the sight that greeted me around the bend. I dismounted and stared upward in awe.

Before me was a vast opening in the cliff wall, but unlike most caves I'd seen, the mouth of this one was covered with glass below a large overhang. It must have been fifty feet from the shelf we were standing on to the overhang above. The glass extended all the way from the top of the cave's mouth to about thirteen feet from the bottom. That's where it met a stone wall on which it seemed to rest.

The glass wall seemed to slope back slightly reflecting the same minimal slope as the stone wall below it. There was little more than a two-inch step-off in the transition from glass to stone.

The reflection of the sun off the glass should have lit up the rock overhang, but I saw that the rock had been darkened. I couldn't tell whether the bottom of the overhang had been smudged by fire or paint. Whichever it was, I hadn't noticed anything but cliff face when I'd looked up from the valley below.

On either side of the glass and stone wall was another wall built of logs stacked on top of each other and tapering in length as each wall rose. These twin wooden walls stood at both ends of the mouth of the cave. They framed the glass and the stone wall between them, slanting back at the same angle.

Each of these walls was about twelve feet wide at the bottom and tapered to about three feet wide at the top. Each followed the contours on its side of the cave but ran straight up and down along the edge of the glass and stone wall, which they supported. Both walls blended in with the cliff face, being about the same gray-brown color as the surrounding rock and the stone wall.

All of this rested on top of a granite foundation that rose about seven inches above the level of the ledge on which we stood. Just above this foundation, built into each of the log walls, was a sturdy wooden door. Each of the two doors stood right at the edge of the stone wall, one in the northeast wall and one in the southwest wall. Altogether, it was an imposing structure and one I never expected to see way up here in the mountains.

I looked away from the cave, back to the trail and to the cliff wall that rose just above it. Set into the cliff face, on either side of the cave, were two dark metal railings. We hitched the horses and mules to these railings. Next to each of these was a long trough carved out of the rock above the level of the path.

What a strange place to put a trough, I thought. Who was going to haul water way up here to the edge of a cliff?

Farther east, the ledge turned into another trail that seemed to travel along the face of the cliff and around a bend. There I saw a small wooden structure up against the cliff—a structure I *did* recognize. It looked like one of the outhouses I'd occasionally seen on the remote farms we passed on the road.

Shuren finished hitching the last of the mules while I stared at the structure of stone, glass, and wood. She walked up to the door on the right side of the cave and knocked. There was no response. There was no doorknob that I could see, either. I didn't see how the door could possibly be opened.

While I wondered, Shuren found a lever on the back of the door and pushed. A small circular hole about two inches wide opened on the edge of the door. She put her thumb into the hole, pushed a latch, and the door swung open. I was struck by the stark contrast between the rough logs of the wall and the elegant mechanism of the latch.

Shuren stepped through the doorway and announced her presence. There was no response. She called again, but louder. Still there was no response. Through the open door, I could see a small stone landing and beyond that a flight of stone steps. Shuren walked up the stairs into the cave and repeated her announcement. Still getting no response, she returned.

"No one's here," she said.

"Is this the place?" I asked, already knowing the answer.

"Yup," replied Luke who had just joined us. "I could use a drink."

It was mid-day now and the chill was gone. I took a deep breath and stretched. Keeley sat panting next to me. I could tell she was thirsty too.

"Well, let's get inside then," Shuren said.

As we entered, I noticed the door swung outward, away from the stone wall. I imagined the door in the other wooden wall probably swung open in the opposite direction. The design was practical because even if a snowdrift blocked one door during the winter, the other door would likely still open.

Lost in these thoughts, I ascended the stairway behind Luke. From the platform, the steps rose between two stone walls. The one on my left was set with an antique brass handrail. The stone wall on my right rose all the way to the ceiling of the cave, inclining slightly outward. At the top of the stairs light streamed through the glass wall.

If the outside was impressive, the inside was both puzzling and magnificent. It was a huge space—just one single room that ended in two spaces about the same size separated by a solid rock wall about fifteen feet wide. This rock partition was actually part of the wall at the back of the cave that projected forward into the cave like a giant pillar, separating the two spaces into 'rooms' at the far end.

The marvelous thing was that over this projection of the back wall flowed a constant stream of water. It wasn't a fast stream—just a constant trickle.

A huge stone basin had been placed on the floor, catching the water as it fell down this part of the wall and holding it there. Excess water flowed over the top of the basin, down its sides, and through the floor, which was open a couple of inches along the base of the wall permitting the water to drop into a lower cavern that emptied into the river below.

I marveled at the sound that the water made as it coursed its way down the rock wall into the basin. The cave amplified the gurgling sound, which filled the space without being obtrusive.

My eyes were drawn to the wet rock face that caught the sunlight streaming through the glass wall. The reflection of the light off the water painted the ceiling of the room in liquid motion. Four large paintings hung on the walls, which were otherwise bare, an effect that made the paintings stand out that much more. As I looked facing into the cave, the painting on the wall to my left looked like this:

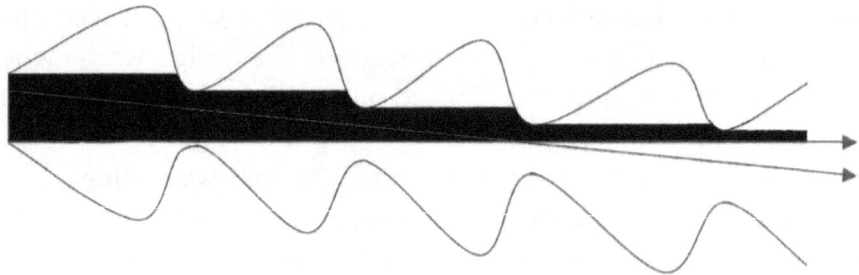

The painting at the back of the wall to the left of the 'waterfall' looked like some kind of flowchart:

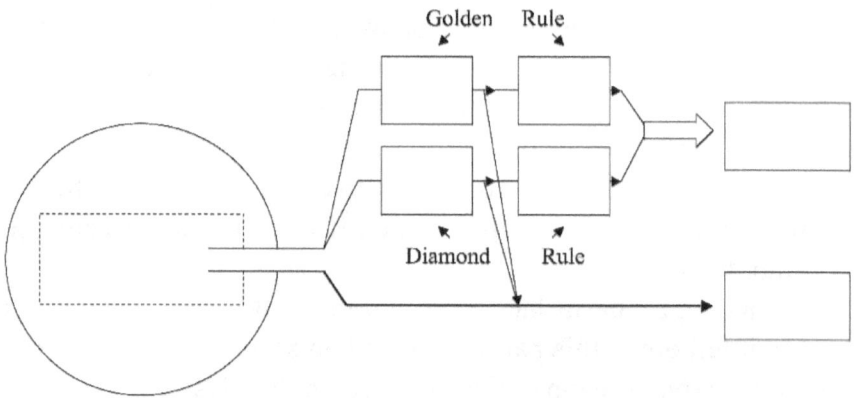

To the right of the waterfall was a painting that looked like a styl-ized version of the waterfall itself:

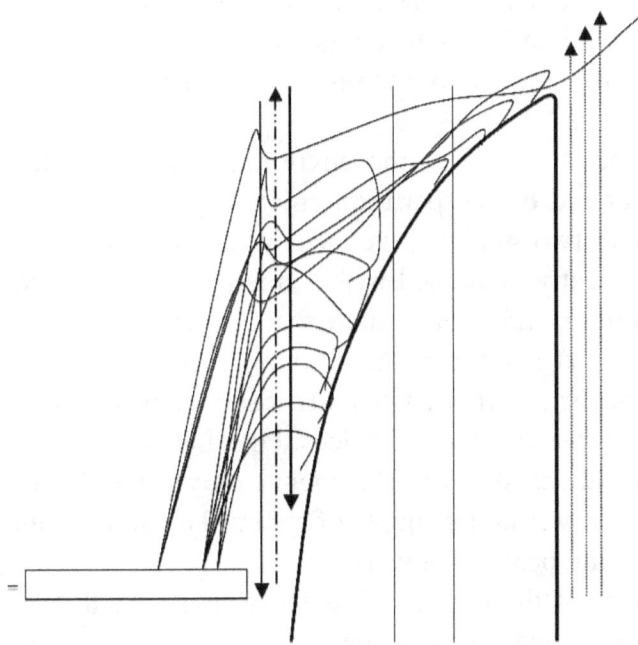

Finally, on the wall to my right was a painting that looked like this:

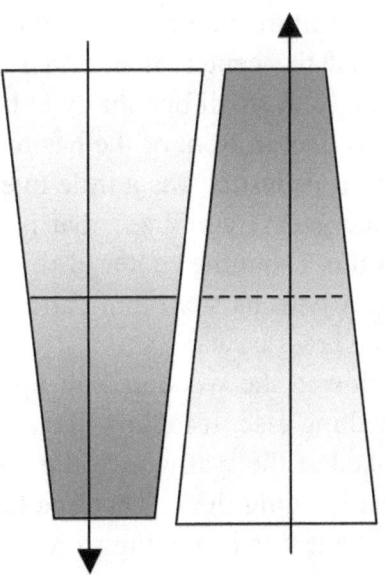

It was the strangest collection of art I had ever seen. It had a combination of rigid and fluid elements that echoed the cave itself. It was all the more remarkable for the setting in which I found it—so far out in the wilderness.

I continued to survey the environment and saw how the two rooms, separated by the partition created by the back wall, had the appearance of two smaller caves within the larger one. In each room there was a neatly made bed with a small nightstand, a low wooden chest, a painting, and a heavy stove that vented through the back wall, which contained a wooden door. Along either side of the partition wall was attached a wooden beam that served as a shelf holding jars of something, perhaps tea and spices. Pots and pans hung from hooks screwed into those shelves. The room to my right also held a small table with a drawer and a couple of chairs. The other room contained an armchair and nearby bookshelf.

The floor of these rooms was the actual rock floor of the cave and extended several feet into the main room, visually connecting the rooms to each other.

The floor of the main room was made of honey-colored oak that extended all the way to the glass wall at the mouth of the cave.

There was little furniture on the wood floor, but a beautiful, large Persian carpet covered the center of it, and several cushions were scattered on it invitingly. A small but sturdy cylindrical platform had been placed about five feet in front of the basin on the partition wall. This stone platform, or pedestal, was a little over three feet high and about two feet in diameter. I could see that it held a shallow brass bowl full of clear water. From the center of this pedestal emerged an upright red maple leaf with its stem in a narrow glass tube that rose from the center of the brass bowl.

As my eyes followed the wooden wall up above the east stairwell, I noticed something else. It looked like an *ornate frame with a blank canvas*. I looked at the wall above the west stairwell and noticed a similar object hanging there. That one looked like it was just a *blank* canvas. Maybe it was just being stored there until it could be put to use.

It looks like a strange place to hang art supplies, I thought.

But neither of those things held my attention for long because I was quickly in awe at the centerpiece, which dominated the view. Toward the front of the cave, my eyes fixed upon the massive glass wall. The sunlight streamed through it, lighting up the entire space. As I moved toward it, my focus shifted *through* the glass to the scene beyond it.

The view was breathtaking. The whole valley was spread out before us. The nearest part of the valley was obscured because the floor of the cavern rose to meet the stone wall at the entrance. With the glass wall resting upon the stone wall, it gave the effect of floating above the valley, though we were inside the cave. *What a magnificent view. I feel like I'm flying over the valley, like I'm part of it.*

Luke interrupted my daydreaming. "Well, drink up, Yosh. We need to be getting the gear off the mules."

I suddenly remembered how thirsty I was. I walked back over to the water basin where Shuren and Luke were standing. Metal cups hung from hooks on each side of the rock pillar. Shuren took the closest cup, dipped it into the basin, took a sip, and handed it to me. I took a drink and handed it to Luke. The water was cool and fresh.

Having finished drinking, Shuren turned a knob at each side of the basin. The water emptied through two pipes at the bottom of the basin. When the basin had emptied, Shuren closed both valves and the basin began to slowly fill again.

We walked out of the cave, and I was surprised to see the horses and mules drinking from the troughs on either side of the cave, which were now filled with water from the basin inside. As they drank, we pulled off all the supplies and carried them back up the stairs to the door at the back of the east room. It was a dark space, lit only by the light streaming through the door. At least it was dark until Luke hit the light switch.

Light switch?

I was surprised that there was electricity here. Now I saw that there were shelves of food and supplies all along the walls of this storage area. We added our contributions.

Back in the main room, I discovered that Luke had rolled back the carpet and removed a circular plug in the floor, revealing a large metal ring. He lifted this hinged section of the floor exposing a stairway leading down to another large storage area. This large space extended from the stone wall at the entrance of the cave to a natural platform that formed the floor of the rooms at the back. There was no food down there—just replacement parts, supplies, paint, empty picture frames, and rolled canvases.

We were making good progress moving our heavier supplies into this lower storage area when we heard Keeley barking and Shuren saying something. We walked out of the cave and saw a man about Jim's age coming toward us.

Luke broke into a big smile as he greeted our host. The elderly man had a full head of white hair and a long, well-groomed white beard. He wore a simple tan cotton shirt, a weathered buckskin vest, well-worn jeans, and calf-length boots the same color as his vest. In his left hand was an old cowboy hat. He had a darker complexion and was quite a bit shorter than Luke, who bent down to greet him with a hug. It wasn't the half hug of informal acknowledgment. It was the warm greeting of friends who had been apart for longer than they wished.

Shuren made introductions. "Mideol, I would like you to meet Yosh."

The older man studied me intently, then took my hand and shook it firmly. His eyes were dark brown, and his unblinking gaze seemed to encompass me. There was something oddly familiar about that gaze.

He smiled and his face lit up. "Welcome, Yosh. I understand that you are Abe's grandson. I can see the resemblance. I've looked forward to our meeting for some time but didn't know if it would ever come to pass."

With that he slowly released my hand and motioned us all inside. Keeley wouldn't leave Mideol's side. They must have been old friends too.

Luke and I finished unloading the last of the supplies while Mideol made some aromatic tea, and Shuren organized the supplies in the lower storage area. We cleaned up all the dirt we'd managed to bring in, closed the trap door to the lower storage area, and replaced the carpet. Finally, we all sat together sipping tea. From that time on we made sure to remove our boots whenever we entered the cave.

It had taken us the better part of the afternoon to finish stowing all of the supplies. I was exhausted. The sun was dropping fast, and I spent the evening listening to the three old friends laughing and reminiscing. I didn't feel like I had a whole lot to add, so mostly I just listened. Of course, as soon as I had some downtime, my thoughts pretty quickly turned to food.

Shuren had brought up some milk, yogurt, cheese, and fresh vegetables that Mideol liked but only ate on these rare visits. She and Mideol cooked dinner together while Luke answered Mideol's questions about the ranch and the new crops they were trying out. Mideol had a few questions for me, but I knew we would have plenty of time together after Shuren and Luke headed back. There were even more questions about Jim and Ahote but especially about Takoda. I had no idea that Mideol even knew Takoda, though I guess that shouldn't have surprised me.

After dinner I lay down on the carpet listening to more conversation. It was like watching a movie. I imagined Grandpa Abe up here in the mountains with this man. He looked ancient, but I tried to picture him as a young man—the young man who had saved my grandfather's life. They had probably stayed together in this very cave. I owed this old man a lot, but when I thought about it, I really didn't even know him.

My thoughts meandered and started to lose cohesion. Before I knew it, I had fallen asleep.

MIDEOL

I woke to find the sun lighting up the room. Shuren must have thrown a blanket over me, trail clothes and all. It was only when I heard Luke outside with the horses that I remembered I had forgotten all about them. I pulled on my boots and rushed down the stairs, not even bothering to grab my jacket.

"Sorry, Luke. I completely forgot about the horses," I said.

"No problem. I was up late, so I just got them settled last night. Shuren gave me a hand with them this morning so don't sweat it. Besides, it's nice to have only one thing to worry about. Ahote's got the ranch to look after. Why don't we eat breakfast? We can finish up with the horses after that."

I followed Luke back up the stairs.

Where had he kept the horses and mules all night, I wondered? How had he gotten them fodder up here on the cliff? I had questions, but I just kept my mouth shut and followed him back inside.

Mideol was nowhere to be seen, but Shuren had both stoves going and was filling the cave with the smell of pancakes, hash browns, and sautéed veggies—along with something she'd brought up for Mideol called *tempeh*, which soaked up flavor and tasted wonderful.

Mideol finally came in with some fresh scallions and complimented Shuren on the wonderful aromas that had led him back to the cave. Shuren smiled as Mideol cleaned the scallions, sliced them up, and threw them into the frying pan followed by a few eggs.

I was looking forward to the day, but I also knew that Shuren and Luke would be leaving soon. I just didn't know how soon.

After breakfast, Shuren informed me that she and Luke would be leaving that very day. There was already a dusting of snow on the ground, and snow in the mountains was very unpredictable. They couldn't risk waiting much longer.

I was having some misgivings about my decision to spend the winter here in the mountains with someone I'd never met before, and it would have been nice to have had their company for a couple of days. Shuren must have seen the concern on my face. She told me that we still had some time together that morning, and I could help her prepare for their journey home while Luke spent some time with Mideol. I didn't quite understand that but was ready to do what was needed. Besides, I owed Luke for having dropped the ball on getting the horses settled for the night.

It was a hectic morning. Shuren and I replaced one of the panels in the glass wall that had lost its seal and another that had cracked due to a shifting cave wall. Then Shuren showed me some old caulk that needed to be stripped and replaced over the next couple of days.

After repairing the glass wall, Shuren and I climbed to the top of the mountain with one of the mules and the two solar panels. We assembled these on an east-facing ledge next to some other panels that had been previously installed.

Next we ran cable through an existing metal conduit that ran down along the face of the cliff to where it entered the cave at the top of the eastern wooden wall. I learned that a similar grouping of solar panels was placed on a western ledge, with conduit running through the top of the other wooden wall.

Other than the waterfall and the outhouse, this pattern of redundancy seemed to permeate the place. That duplication made sense since there were no hardware stores to provide parts for a quick fix.

We were finished by lunch and rejoined Mideol and Luke. They had been gone all morning but were now seated at the table having a serious discussion. It was clear by the look on Luke's face that he was deep in thought.

I honestly had no appetite and didn't want to interrupt them, so I skipped lunch. While the three of them ate and talked, I saddled the horses and started loading the mules for the journey back to the ranch. Luke and Shuren joined me when they were finished eating.

I was surprised to see all the material that was going back down. I expected to see empty jars and non-perishable garbage. What I didn't expect were the endless rolled-up canvasses. Till then, no one had bothered to tell me that Mideol was a painter. Of course, I didn't have a chance to admire any of his art because it was already wrapped, packed, and ready for loading.

I learned later that Mideol reserved much of the west rear storage area for his completed works. I hadn't gone into that storage area until I was helping to retrieve the paintings and noticed a computer, portable hard drives, and a large bookshelf packed to overflowing. In the corner was an array of batteries. These were connected to wires coming from conduit above and probably received power from the solar panels on top of the mountain. It was an odd sight—the latest technology powered by solar panels in the most rustic and remote setting.

We finished loading the mules, leaving Shuren and Luke plenty of daylight for traveling. Suddenly, a feeling of apprehension washed over me and my palms began to sweat.

They're actually leaving, I thought. Suddenly this plan doesn't seem to be so sane. How can I possibly be feeling claustrophobic standing in the middle of this expanse of wilderness?

I thought I might change my mind. Part of me was anxious to leave with my friends. Shuren must have sensed this because she took me aside while Mideol and Luke spoke privately again. She told me they'd be back once the snow had melted and the passes had opened up.

Of course, that might not be until the end of May. This was the first week of November, so that meant about *seven months*.

Mideol knew the mountains better than anyone, she said, and despite his age he was perfectly capable of managing on his own. She then informed me that she'd left her rifle and sidearm in the east storage area behind what was to be my 'room.'

My vision blurred as tears welled up in my eyes. I told myself it was just the cold wind, but I knew that wasn't true. Luke didn't help much when he turned to say goodbye to me with a firm handshake and said Keeley would be staying with me. I was happy she'd be here in the mountains with me.

I was pretty sure that he'd leave my horse too. But Luke went on to say that Annahme would need too much fodder to leave her here and wouldn't be of much use anyway.

I thought, *how the hell do you get so close to a horse that you feel like you're going to lose your composure?* I have got to control myself.

I thanked them both, and then Mideol and I watched them disappear around the side of the cliff with Annahme and the mules trailing behind them. We stayed on the path until the sound of hoofbeats faded away and only the sound of the wind and the birds remained. I called Keeley and we all went back inside.

As I sat collecting my thoughts, Mideol brewed some warm tea. We sat together on the carpet looking out at the valley beyond the glass.

Finally, he spoke. "Yosh, I know we didn't have much time to speak earlier, but these visits are pretty important to Luke, and you and I will have a lot of time together."

"I understand." I said, "I figured you had a lot to catch up on. Besides, I enjoy spending time with Shuren. She's probably one of the wisest people I've ever met."

"That she is," Mideol said. "She also told me a good bit about you and the conversations you've had with her."

I was a little surprised by this since I thought that our conversations had been personal, but I didn't say anything. It hadn't been easy for me to open up with Shuren, but I did trust her and she obviously trusted Mideol. Still, it was strange to think that he knew a lot about me while I knew almost nothing about him.

"Thanks for opening your home to me," I said. "I know that they all consider you to be quite special."

"Just as I consider them to be quite special," Mideol replied.

Neither of us said much for a bit. Then I asked him, "Don't you get lonely up here alone? I mean, there's not much to do here, is there?"

He thought about it for a moment. "Actually, there is quite a bit to do, but I thought we would take today off and just get to know one another. We can start tomorrow if you'd like."

"That would be great."

"Well, since we're connected by our relationship with Abraham Lincoln Tsalagi, perhaps I should tell you about how your grandfather and I met."

Mideol explained to me how he had found my grandfather after hearing his plane go down. Mideol was a young man himself at the time, only about twenty years old, and lived here in the mountains with his father.

I found it strange that Mideol was a little younger than Grandpa Abe. When Jim had told me about him, I'd pictured him as being older than my grandfather.

Mideol went on to tell me how he had traveled out to the crash site in October, 1944, and had brought Grandpa Abe back here to the cave. He went into great detail about their journey across some pretty tough terrain and how there was no way to get word out because the snows came early that year. Over that fall and winter, he and his father gradually nursed Abe back to health. It sounded like it wasn't easy for any of them.

What I heard from Mideol over the next few hours confirmed the impression that Jim had given me about my grandfather. Mideol explained how Grandpa Abe blamed himself for the crash and the death of his co-pilot and navigator. They wouldn't find out until many years later that the crash was probably due to a structural failure that the crew could not have solved.

Grandpa Abe's self-loathing was much deeper than I had thought. Mideol recalled that it was his father who helped Abe come to terms with his situation and allowed his spirit to be healed along with his body. I learned a great deal about my grandfather that day. Not all of it I wanted to hear.

Mideol and Abe had become friends that winter, and Abe had come to regard Mideol as a more-seasoned fellow traveler on a journey toward what they called "the examined life." Mideol may have been younger than Abe, but he had started the journey as a child under the guidance of his father.

Once Abe had recovered enough physically, he had grown to enjoy the conversations with Mideol and Mideol's father. Mideol told me how he had taken Abe down to Jim at the H.R.C. Ranch in the spring of 1945. Jim had told me the rest of the story, but it was interesting to hear it from Mideol as well. Grandpa Abe would return every spring or summer to renew their friendship and resume their shared journey.

That afternoon, Mideol told me about the deepening friendship he shared with Jim and Abe over the next thirty years. Mideol's father died in 1961, and he had lived here alone since then. This seemed to make him appreciate my grandfather's visits even more. Grandpa Abe had continued those visits until the time I moved in with him.

After that, they mostly communicated through Jim and through letters that the Cramfords would shuttle back and forth. Mideol asked me about my years with Grandpa Abe and smiled contentedly as I spoke.

By the time we were done exchanging stories, Mideol no longer felt like a stranger to me. We were both tired of talking, though. We sat silently for some time, and then Mideol brought out his easel and painted while I looked through the books on his bookshelf. They were mostly about history, philosophy, and religion, with a smattering of scientific journals and texts. I realized then why he and my grandfather must have gotten along—but none of these books were interesting to me.

Mideol could see me going through his books but said nothing. He just kept painting. As it began to get dark, he cooked a simple dinner and we ate in silence with only the sound of the fire providing company.

He seemed to have no problem speaking this afternoon, I thought. It felt awkward to sit through a whole meal in silence. I hadn't yet learned that this was his habit and not an exception.

After dinner Mideol was again his engaging self. We sat together at the table, and I asked about living alone in the mountains. Mideol was full of stories, most of them pretty entertaining. We chatted for a long while. Eventually, he informed me that he preferred to go to bed not long after the sun went down.

Before going to sleep, he sat on the carpet facing the glass wall. At first he sat in silence. Then he chanted softly before doing some stretching exercises. Finally, he returned to sitting cross-legged on the carpet in silence.

I sat in the glow of the fire just watching him. It was a routine that Mideol would repeat every night. As soon as he was done with his routine he said "goodnight," drank a glass of water, brushed his teeth, washed up, and went to bed in the west room.

The east room was my room. I sat there for a while next to the stove trying to read but soon got bored. Since there was nothing else to do, I decided to follow Mideol's example and go to bed. I didn't feel very sleepy, though. It was way too early for me. I just lay there staring at the ceiling.

This did not look good. I'd only been alone with him for half a day, and I was already bored stiff. How did I get myself into this? I've got to find something to do, I thought, or I'll go crazy.

Eventually I drifted off to sleep, misgivings and all.

When I woke at sunrise, I found Mideol seated cross-legged on the carpet, facing the glass wall. I sat on the edge of the bed and blinked a few times just to make sure I was still there.

I was.

Mideol must have heard me get up. He asked, "Do you want something to eat?"

"Sure," I said.

We talked as he fixed breakfast and then ate in silence again.

We sat together after breakfast. He sipped a cup of tea, still saying nothing.

This was starting to get boring real fast, I thought. *I need to do something.*

I broke the uncomfortable silence and asked, "Well, what work needs to be done?"

He took another sip, thought for a minute, nodded an acknowledgment, and asked, "Would you like to chop some wood? We can use it to heat the cave over the winter."

That sounded like a good use of my time. "Sounds great."

We bundled up and stepped out the door with an axe. Mideol, carrying a small pack, took me up the slope to a stand of pines. Several had already been chopped down. He set the pack down and opened it, then handed me a thermos of water and some food packed in a metal container for lunch. He said he'd be gathering some roots and herbs for the winter and would be gone most of the day. I could stop chopping wood any time I wanted and return to the cave.

I chopped wood all day, stopping only to eat and rest, or to stare out over the valley. It *was* a beautiful place to be. When I got tired, I'd rest or have a bite to eat, then start up again. There was even a second outhouse that Mideol kept along the eastern path that led down to the valley. I preferred using this one over the one on the cliff path, not that it was any more comfortable.

Strange as it is to talk about outhouses, they become pretty important when you don't have running water or plumbing. This one along the eastern path dropped into a pit like most do. It could be relocated when needed. The one on the cliff path by the cave was convenient, of course, but it had to be emptied and cleaned every day that it was used, so I preferred to use this one whenever I could.

I sat there on top of the rise at the edge of the stand of trees, thinking how much I'd taken for granted living in the city. Even something as simple as plumbing or toilets came with a cost of time or effort. My thoughts drifted. There was a cost, but that cost was also a gift. These chores had forced me to slow down. It was only then, when the pace of life had slowed down, that I had started to truly appreciate the depth of life.

I didn't realize how long I was lost in my daydreams before I remembered how much work was left to be done. It wasn't long before I was cutting and stacking again.

Later that afternoon, Mideol returned and saw the pile of wood I had chopped. He looked pleased and we hauled it back to the cave. There he took me into the east rear storage area. He showed me a door, which I hadn't noticed before. It was just east of the door we had entered, built into the same wall. That stone wall formed the front wall of the storage area and projected to meet the natural outer wall of the cave. Like all the other walls, it was inclined slightly. From inside the storage areas, though, the wall was inclined *toward* you and toward the natural rock wall of the cave. I stepped through the door and down a flight of stairs to a space between the east wall of the living space and the natural eastern wall of the cave. He turned on a light and I could see that it was a huge space.

Both sides of this east side storage area were lined with rows of shelves. These were filled with large metal and ceramic containers like the ones we had brought up with us from the ranch. I saw that they were filled with corn, wheat, and something called quinoa.

There were other containers as well. These held flax seed, beans, protein powder, and powdered milk. Glass jars filled with vegetables, berries, and fruit lined smaller shelves above the large containers. The wall at the far end of this storage area was the wooden wall that framed the mouth of the cave.

As we walked toward the far wall, Mideol took a rope off of a hook. He pulled it and a massive door, hinged at the top, opened outward. The huge storage space was instantly flooded with sunlight.

He propped the door open with a large beam that was hinged at the bottom and swung up to meet the open door. As my eyes adjusted to the light, I could see that the door was made of the same heavy logs as the front wall but had opened almost effortlessly with the pulley above.

Inside the door were racks waiting to receive the wood I had chopped. I stepped across the granite foundation that served as the threshold, picked up the wood, and placed it on the racks.

What an ingenious design, I thought. The wood could be collected and stored from the outside, remain dry, and then be easily accessible from inside during the winter months. The whole arrangement was so well considered and, true to form, it was duplicated on the west side.

So that's how November passed. Every day I would chop and collect wood. Mideol had warned me to avoid cutting in patches since the snow pack might become unstable during the winter or spring months. And the snow that he spoke about had already started to fall.

Even when it started to snow more heavily, the work of chopping made it feel pretty comfortable. I had Keeley's company, and the play of light on the mountains and meadow created an ever-changing landscape. Mideol started to make shorter forays outside and spent more time painting. We had plenty of time together in the evenings. I expected that Mideol would have more to say, but he never did.

By the end of the first week of November, I started getting a little bored. By the end of the second week, my reservations about my time here had returned. By the end of the third week, I'd had enough, but I still bit my tongue. As the fourth week wound down, my frustration came to a boil. By this time, I had more than filled all the racks in both the east and west side storage areas. I was now piling wood high on the ground. I'd had enough.

The next morning, after breakfast, I couldn't contain my anger any longer. The thought of mindlessly cutting down trees and stacking logs without end was maddening!

"Why the hell am I chopping all this wood?" I spouted.

There was no answer.

I tried again. "I really don't feel like being used as free labor, you know. I'm bored out of my skull chopping wood! I really don't know what the hell I'm even doing here."

My outburst was met with silence. Part of me just wanted to get up, walk out the door, and start cutting down trees to spite myself. Instead, I just looked at him. He was neither upset with me nor apologetic. He just looked right at me, like he was meeting me for the first time.

It was strange—and it opened up a space in my anger. I don't know how else to put it. That space was just large enough for me to take a deep breath and see my anger. I took another deep breath and tried to calm myself. As slowly and deliberately as I could manage, I asked again.

"Just how much wood do we need?"

He finally spoke, but his answer both infuriated and puzzled me.

"We don't need any of it."

"We don't need any of it?" I asked in disbelief.

"Yes, that's right."

"Then why the hell have I been chopping for the last month?"

"Because you wanted to," Mideol answered.

"I didn't want to!" I yelled. "You told me to do it."

He calmly responded, "Didn't you want to do it? Do you remember what you asked me that first day we were here alone after we had breakfast?"

I couldn't recall having said anything significant.

He waited for me. Then he repeated my words back to me. "You asked me, 'What work needs to be done?'"

I sat there utterly confused.

"Okay, maybe I did ask you what work needed to be done, but that didn't mean I wanted to chop wood all month long."

"How was I to know?" he responded.

"Would you have let me chop wood all winter long?"

"Of course."

"You would have let me waste my entire winter chopping wood?"

"Yes."

"I don't understand!" I said, exasperated.

"That is perhaps the greatest insight a person can have," he said. "Now why don't you return to chopping some more wood?"

I was fuming. Was the old man trying to egg me on? I didn't care if he was my grandfather's friend or if everyone in the whole state respected him. He could chop his own damn wood. I put on my jacket, hat, and boots, and stormed out the door. It was cold and dark, but I couldn't have cared less.

I walked through the dark with a tight knot in my throat. I felt profoundly sorry for myself. All my life I had been deserted. All my life I had been alone. Now, for the first time, I had found a place where I felt that I belonged, and the person who everyone looked up to had nothing for me but wood to chop.

The tears welled up. This time they didn't stop. I walked till I was tired of walking, then dropped to the ground and cried till I was too tired to cry. Finally, I lay back on the snow, my eyes closed. After the tears had passed, I opened my eyes and looked up.

For the first time since my night in the camp, I looked up and I saw the stars. I mean—I've seen stars before, but this time I *saw* the stars. They seemed to stretch on forever, and I felt so small. They were beautiful, and there was no light anywhere to hide them from me. There were no clouds either, and the moon was only a thin sliver of light.

To move from tears to wonder in a single night was too much. I felt totally washed out. I couldn't help wondering why the feeling of being small when looking at the stars was almost comforting, while the feeling of being small in all that I had gone through made me feel so empty.

I didn't know… and right then I didn't care. I trudged back to the cave, opened the door, took off my jacket, boots, and hat, walked past Mideol, and went to bed.

* * *

I woke up the next day feeling strangely new. Something had changed, but it certainly wasn't Mideol. I found him sitting on the carpet facing the valley like he did every morning. Finally, he stood up and asked me if I wanted any breakfast.

I just nodded.

He brought over some biscuits with beans and some apricot preserves. He didn't say much else. I finished my meal in silence and then went to my room and sat on my bed.

So this is it, I thought. I'll just sit here till the snow melts. What a waste of time.

I resolved not to speak.

Of course, that lasted about two hours. I was bored stiff, and the thought of sitting in that cave was driving me nuts, so I opened my mouth and spoke. "So I'm just supposed to sit here for the next five months?"

There was no response.

After a few minutes I repeated myself.

This time Mideol answered, "If you wish."

"What do you mean, *if I wish*? Isn't there some kind of program or something that you're supposed to give me? I mean, what am I here for anyway?"

"I don't know what you're here for, Yosh. How could I possibly know that?"

"Well, didn't Shuren tell you?"

"No, how could *she* know what you're here for?" he asked.

"Why do you keep answering all of my questions with more questions? Is this some kind of game or something? Do you just bring people up here to torture them?"

He smiled gently. "It's certainly not my intention to torture anyone, least of all you. Asking questions is simply my habit, in the same way that failing to answer questions appears to be your habit."

His smile disappeared, and he took on a look of intense concentration, but he looked straight at me. His stare wasn't one of goading. It wasn't malicious. It was just... *open*. He looked at me like a scientist might study an experiment.

My initial impulse was to be offended again, but his look stopped me cold. Instead of taking offense this time, I asked, "What do you mean my habit is to not answer your questions? I think I've answered every question you've asked."

He nodded. "Yes, you've answered my questions. But that's not what I'm speaking about, Yosh. The questions you continuously fail to answer are your own."

I was baffled by this comment. How could I fail to answer my own questions? *Of course* I answered my own questions.

"What do you mean, I don't answer my own questions?" I asked. "Give me one example of a question that I've failed to answer. Just one example."

"Very well—how about the question of *how much wood should I chop?* Or the question of *why am I chopping so much wood?* How about the question of *now that I know that chopping wood is not my purpose, what would be best for me to do?*"

I had asked for one example and he had given me three. I thought about his statements. Were these really questions I had asked myself? I guess they were. As I sat there thinking about it, I realized that he was right. I had either ignored these questions—figuring he would answer them for me when the time was right—or I had reacted emotionally and had completely forgotten the question in the last case. I looked down, embarrassed.

I am pathetic, I thought to myself.

Mideol, who up till now had always spoken in a soft voice, interrupted my self-flagellation. He practically yelled. "Feeling sorry for yourself will not help you!"

I looked up almost fearfully.

He continued, "How long will you allow yourself to be led around by your emotions? One moment you're on top of the world and the next you want to crawl under a rock. You're either too good for anything to waste your precious time on it, or too impoverished to spend your time well on yourself. Which are you, Yosh? Who exactly *are* you?"

I was feeling backed into a corner and didn't like it. I tried to tell him who I was, but no words came out. The more I thought about it, the more I couldn't tell him.

"What do you mean?" I asked, stalling for time.

"It's not a difficult question," Mideol responded. "Who *are* you?"

I had no answer, and he seemed perfectly happy to let the conversation end right there. He picked up the dishes from our breakfast and began washing them.

I just sat at the table trying to think through everything. It must have been five minutes before I finally answered his question about who I was.

"I'm Yosh," I said. "That's all—just Yosh."

At first I got no response. Then he put away the last of the dishes, wiped his hands dry, hung up the towel, and sat down across from me. Only then did he speak. "Remember this day, Yosh. It is the day you stopped running away from yourself. What you could not accomplish in a month starting four weeks ago—and what you could not accomplish in a day just yesterday—you have accomplished in five minutes today.

"You have confronted your *self,* and you have not sought distraction from that confrontation. Remember the question I asked you yesterday. 'That is perhaps the greatest insight a person can have—now why don't you return to chopping some more wood?' You answered by running away angrily. Were you angry at me or angry at yourself?"

"I suppose I was angry at you for duping me… and angry at myself for allowing myself to be duped."

"How were you duped?"

"By tricking me into chopping all that wood."

"Do you really think I tricked you? I don't need that wood. Don't you think I can chop wood for myself? After all, who do you think does it when you're not here? First, though, let's finish with the issue of feeling duped. What was the function of your anger?"

I had never thought about anger having a function. My anger had no function, I thought. I was simply angry. And why wouldn't I be angry?

Mideol saw me struggling and rephrased his question.

"What was the *result* of your anger?"

"I guess it forced me to stop chopping wood."

"Did your anger force you to stop chopping wood, or was it your realization that the wood was not needed that led you to stop chopping?"

"I guess you're right. Realizing that the chopped wood was not necessary caused me to stop chopping it."

"Well, then, what was the function of your anger? What changed after you got angry? Think about it. What was present *after* the anger that was not present *before* the anger?"

I thought about it for a while. Then it dawned on me.

"The decision," I said. "It was the *decision*. The decision to stop chopping was not present before I got angry."

"That's right. The decision to stop was not present beforehand. In order to stop chopping wood, you needed approval to exercise your reason. Your anger gave you that permission. You knew the action that needed to be taken—to stop chopping wood—but you didn't allow yourself to do that until you could justify it with an emotion.

"You see, Yosh, you seem to have decided that without an emotional response you aren't justified in taking action. You think that you're reasonable—that you are driven by reason—but you are not. *Emotions* are your driving force. They provide you with the energy to act. Without your emotions, you believe that you are *empty* because you feel empty. Your mood waxes and wanes with your emotions, and you wonder why you have such highs and lows. Essentially, Yosh, you have *defined yourself as your emotions*."

Could he be right? Was I just a pawn of my emotions?

"Yosh, you have defined yourself as your emotions *so fundamentally* that you don't even question your emotions. They simply are. When a particular emotion has accomplished its task and then exhausted itself, you don't feel the need to inquire further into it. By that time, your assumption of yourself as your emotions has led you on to the next distraction, and you have lost any opportunity you might have had to learn about yourself and the world in which you live."

I had to admit that I recognized myself in his observation... if only a little. His comment about distractions sounded a lot like what Shuren had mentioned, but not exactly the same.

"Shuren had mentioned 'distraction' as a way out of the dilemma of identity, but I thought she was talking about being distracted by concepts of self—not distracted by my emotions."

"Shuren was correct to identify distraction as a flawed resolution of the dilemma of the self. In order to make full use of this observation, though, you must understand the nature of the self."

"I thought that I had inquired into that with the Cramfords."

"If that were the case, then we wouldn't be having this conversation."

"So what *is* the nature of the self, then? I'm confused. I thought I'd covered this. If I don't understand that, then I'm not sure what I understand."

"Yosh, it is never wrong to return to the beginning when we recognize that we may be on the wrong path. That recognition is progress, not failure. To continue on while ignoring the recognition—that is failure."

"But how can you say that I define myself by my emotions?"

Mideol replied, "This is why I asked 'Why don't you return to chopping some more wood?' You did not understand my question, but for you that was not a realization so much as a cause to *stop questioning and resort to the emotion of anger*. From the perspective of your emotions, understanding is not necessary. If you cannot understand something, then it is easier to respond with emotions. In fact, responding emotionally reinforces an emotional perspective.

"What for me is the portal to wisdom is for you a thing to be ignored. To not understand something can be either an admission of failure… or an invitation to knowing yourself more fully. The difference lies only in who you know yourself to be. You see, it returns to the question of who you are. But it begs a deeper question—do you *want* to know who you are?"

"Of course I do!"

"Your identification with your emotional responses would suggest otherwise."

"Are you telling me that I shouldn't be emotional? Are you saying that I should be some kind of robot? How would that help me in defining my self?"

"Once again, your emotions seek to shield you from the light of reality. If your capacity for honesty is truly what Abe felt it was, then you would be well served by not allowing yourself to fall prey to such sarcastic reductionism."

Suddenly, I felt kind of naked. I had mistaken his deliberate instruction for pondering thought, and he had already anticipated my emotional defense.

I really am my emotions, aren't I? Why else would I respond so defensively?

But Mideol was determined to drive a stake through my delusions. He followed his reprimand with blunt words.

"This is not a superficially intellectual pursuit, Yosh. Simplistic definitions of self as either cognition or emotion will only leave you mired in your dilemma. If you wish to escape from this delusion, then you will need to accept that both thought and emotion are intrinsic to your being. To deny the role of either dimension of your self is to leave the path to the solution obscured.

"If I were to tell you that you are both thought *and* emotion, and also that you are *neither*, it would sound like so much double-talk to you. So I will not tell you that. You can only learn it to be true for yourself.

"I *will* tell you, however, that identifying yourself with your cognition will obscure certain distractions, and identifying yourself with your emotions will obscure *other* distractions. If you wish to escape from the dilemma of delusion, you must become increasingly aware of *both* categories of distraction and *both* aspects of your being… and deny *neither*."

I was humbled. I had not even considered the dimension of emotion as part of the problem. I assumed that I was my thoughts, but it was clear that I had been responding emotionally for as long as I could remember. How could I have been so blind and so arrogant?

"I'm sorry," I said in a hushed voice.

"I do not want your apologies," Mideol said. "They are of no use to me, and they are of no benefit to you. It would be well for you not to dwell upon your mistakes. The true expression of appreciation for a lesson is in the learning of the lesson. I place little value in expressions of remorse. We will see if your actions reflect a deeper awareness."

I was silent, but I had never been more attentive in my entire life, and this seemed to be the best response I could have made.

Mideol took a deep breath and continued. "To accept and be aware of both aspects of your being—thought and emotion—is what it means to live a truly examined life. Accepting this is the gateway to the journey your grandfather and I shared. It is only the first step in living an awakened life, but it is the most important one because it is the first.

"It is not enough, though, to see the gateway. To walk through the door requires that you surrender the false identifications that you have created, or allowed to be created, in yourself. Honesty is the key to this door, but as you've seen it is no simple key. The crafting of this key requires that you accept no assumption of truth but that you inquire into truth before all else."

"Is this the same as Shuren's Law of Original Truth?" I asked. "I believe she said that you will only be trying to justify your position if you ask any question before you ask *What is the Truth?*"

"Yes, Yosh, it *is* the Law of Original Truth as applied to yourself, *not* as a hypothetical consideration."

"I don't understand. What do you mean hypothetical?" I asked.

"The way in which you have stated the Law of Original Truth implies its use as an item of philosophy, not as a tool for your personal use and benefit. Only in its specific form does this law carry any real value. Would you care to rephrase it?"

I thought about what he was trying to get me to see, then replied, "I believe Shuren said that *I* would only be trying to justify *my* position if *I* asked any question before *I* asked *What is the Truth?*"

"Excellent, Yosh. You have understood correctly."

I smiled at my small achievement, but many of the things he had said still confused me. I began to ask Mideol another question, but he interrupted.

"You have many questions, Yosh, and your habit of inquiry is admirable. Still, it is not *my* purpose to answer your questions. I will give you a word of advice, however. The reason that you are at an impasse is that you are unable to formulate the essential next question. Let me ask you—*why is this*?"

"I guess I just haven't tried hard enough to find the right question," I replied.

"Trying harder is not the key. Seeing the parts of the question for what they are is the key. You want to escape from a dilemma that you believe you have, but you have not asked yourself who it is that wishes to escape. You believed that you were your thoughts. So you wondered how your thoughts had created your dilemma of dissatisfaction.

"Now you have come to understand that you are your emotions as well as your thoughts. This helps to explain why you have *felt* the dilemma but have not been able to *define* it. Your predicament looks unclear because it has as much to do with your emotional self as with your thinking self."

"That makes sense, kind of," I replied. "I can feel it, but I can't get my hands around it. It just feels frustrating, like there's some way out... and like I need to get out but I'm stuck. I don't *want* to go back and do all those things that seem so pointless... and I *can't go forward.*"

"*Who* can't go forward?"

"*Me*. I can't go forward. I'm stuck."

"An excellent observation, Yosh. Let's look into it a little further. I believe that the way out of your dilemma is located in this observation. Once you examine it, you will be able to define your dilemma more clearly. Once you can define the dilemma with greater clarity, I believe you will see your way out. It begins with defining the 'I' that cannot go forward."

"But I thought that's what we just did when you showed me that I'm both an emotional and a thinking self."

"No, Yosh—I did not show you anything. I held your attention long enough for *you to see* that you are both emotion and cognition. Emotion is only one dimension of your being that you had not seen. In the same way that the emotional dimension had been obscured to you, there is yet another dimension that you haven't seen... and it's the cause for your being stuck in your dilemma."

"I'm really not sure what you're talking about," I said. "I just came to terms with being my emotion *and* my thought... and now you're telling me that there's another piece?"

"Not just *another* piece, Yosh—the *largest* piece. This largest dimension of *you* is constrained by your own definition of 'I.' That definition of 'I' creates the very walls of your dilemma. Understanding this process of creation of the 'I' is also the key to moving past your dilemma. The act of defining the 'I' defines the prison of your reality in ways you cannot even conceive *until* you have confronted it. But this process is hidden from you."

"Why would it be hidden?"

"It is hidden from you because of assumptions of reality that you have chosen to make. Those assumptions have come to define your reality. If you wish to move past your dilemma, you must define the 'I' in its many dimensions. Then you will have the opportunity to move out of *your* reality and into a *higher* reality."

Reality

W̶e were still sitting at the table in the east room with the morning sun streaming through the glass wall. Mideol and I sat in silence. I wasn't sure if he had finished his thought or if there was more. There was only the sound of the wood crackling in the stove and the steady dripping of water into the basin. Then he broke the silence.

"Yosh, I'd like you to look above the doors on either side. Tell me, what do you see hanging there?"

"They look like art supplies," I said, looking at the canvas and the picture frame.

"Can you be more detailed in your description?"

I said, "Well, the object on the left, over the eastern door, is a frame with a blank canvas in it. The one on the right, over the western door, is a blank canvas itself."

"An interesting observation," he said, "and a fitting representation of the dilemma in which you find yourself."

"I don't understand. Isn't that what they are? Okay, maybe they're supposed to represent the emotional part of me and the cognitive part."

Mideol smiled and shook his head. "No, Yosh, they represent the other dimension of the 'I' that I was referring to. You see, both of those objects are blank canvases. The fact that one is framed does not change that fact. They are essentially the same thing... but your mind is drawn to the presence of a frame or the lack of a frame, not to the *essence* of the thing."

Mideol continued, "You called it a frame with something in it rather than something with a frame around it. Why is that?"

"Well, because there's nothing on the canvas. If there was something on it, I would have said that it was a framed picture. But since there's nothing on it, the obvious thing was the frame."

"*This* is the habit of mind that frames your dilemma, so to speak. That which you cannot see *does not exist for you*, even though it may be the most essential part of you. That which is concrete and perceptible to your mind comes to define you, but you fail to ask how it became concrete in the first place. Who built the frame?"

"I don't understand."

"Let me ask you a question, Yosh. Are you a different person now than you were before you came to Chama in the fall?"

I had to think pretty hard about that one. I wanted to tell him how much I had changed, but to be honest, I was still me.

"I can't say I'm a different person," I said. "I know that I'm thinking differently than I was before. I think of my 'self' differently, but I feel like I'm the same person."

"And how long have you been this person?"

"All my life, I guess."

"So if you are the same person and that doesn't change, but you are also thought and emotion that is constantly changing... what does that mean?"

This was a paradox I hadn't considered. How could I be changing and unchanging at the same time? That was impossible, but he was right—I could see that a part of me was standing outside of my life looking at me as I'd changed over the past month.

That same part of me could see me as a kid with Grandpa Abe, alone in my apartment, then at the ranch, and now here. That part of me seemed to watch the other part of me as it went through my life.

I hadn't really looked at that part of me, but it was obviously there. When I looked at it, I had the odd feeling that it was looking back at me. How is that possible?

"It must mean that I'm both. "

"Both what?"

"Both changing and unchanging," I replied.

"How is it possible to be both changing and unchanging?" he asked.

I thought about it and eventually said, "I must have two parts of me. That's the only way I can conceive of being both. There must be a part that changes and a part that stays the same."

"Excellent," said Mideol. "You have discovered a great truth. If you follow this truth fearlessly, then it will be a *transformative* truth. This is the realization that has the potential to release you from your dilemma… *if* you can see it clearly and make it your own. You have encountered your 'changeless self.' And when you encounter it, you become able to see yourself as you are."

"But how does this relate to the emotional self and the cognitive self? I've got too many 'selfs' floating around here."

"Okay, so let's organize them."

With that, Mideol reached under the kitchen table, which doubled as his desk, and pulled out a piece of paper and a pencil. He wrote something down and handed it to me:

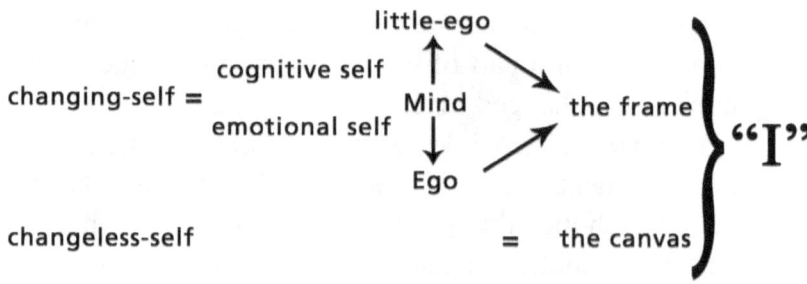

"You see, the frame of the picture is the *changing self.* It is composed of both the emotional and cognitive, or rational, aspects of mind. Together, both of these elements form the mind. As you have seen, that mind then manifests as both the little-ego and the Ego. Together, these two 'egos' make up the frame. The canvas represents the *changeless self.* As you've experienced, this *changeless self* acts *through* the mind but exists *beyond* the mind as well. Together, the changing self and the changeless self make up the 'I,' or what you call 'me.'"

"That straightens things out a lot, but I still don't understand how this helps me out of my dilemma."

"It helps you out because it defines 'you' in relation to your world. Once you admit that your reality is a world of your own making, then you become free to *remake* your world. Then you see that there truly is *no dilemma* after all."

"So you want me to just pretend that there's no dilemma?"

"No, I don't want you to pretend anything. Pretending will do you no good. I want you to see it… and only when you see it will the dilemma cease to be."

"At least I understand what you mean by all of these 'selfs' now."

Mideol got up and stretched. Then he asked me to help him bring out some paintings from the rear storage area. We placed each of them on the floor leaning up against the glass wall. After we were done, we sat on the carpet facing them.

They were all blank canvases, each with a different frame:

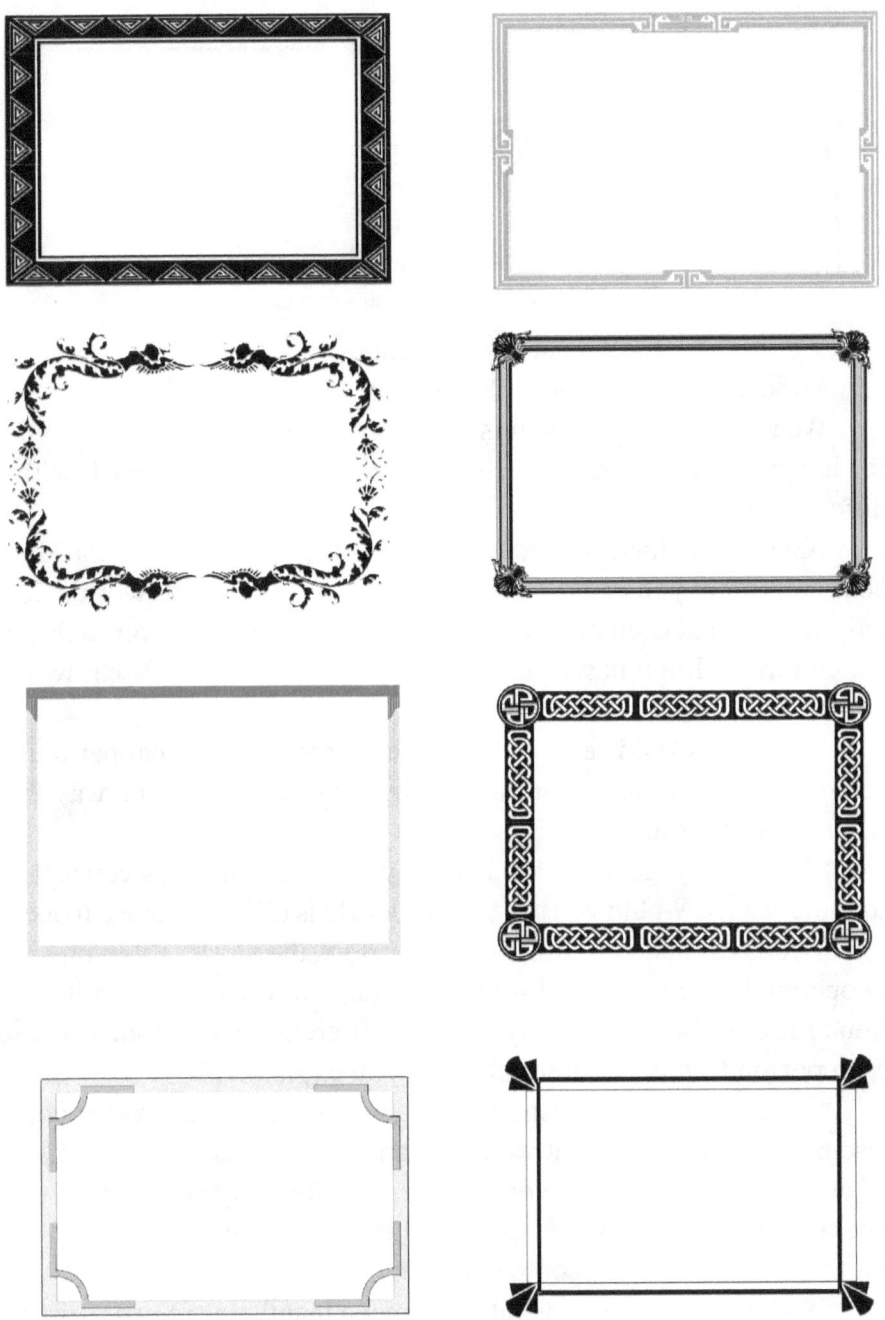

We sat there looking at his collection.

Mideol asked me, "Well, Yosh, what do you see?"

We had already played this game once, and I wasn't going to fall for it again. So I told him, "I see several blank canvases, each with a different frame."

"Good. We have already seen how the object above the door could represent you and the way in which you frame your world. Now let's assume that each item here represents a different person, a different culture, a different religion, or school of philosophy. What would you have to say about each one then?"

"I guess I would say that each one represents how that particular person, culture, religion, or philosophy sees its world—the way that it *frames* its world."

"That's very good, Yosh. I think you understand this concept of framing reality. Would you say that the world is different for each one?"

"Well, yes and no. I mean—the world is the world. Everyone has to operate in the world and we can't change it a whole lot, so it's the same for everyone in that way. But it's different for everyone because each person frames it differently, like you explained."

"That's excellent, Yosh. Would you say that 'the world' could also be called reality? That would mean reality actually exists outside of everyone, but that everyone frames it differently so that they can operate within a reality they can handle. Is that right?"

"Yeah, I guess you could say that."

"So let me ask you… would that mean that there are *two* realities, one outside of people and one of their own making?"

"I suppose that's right. I never thought of it that way," I said. "I never thought about it as making our own reality, but I guess that's what we do. I mean, I never thought that *I* created *my* own reality… but I suppose that's what I've done."

"That's an important realization, Yosh. It's such an important realization that I believe we need to distinguish these two versions of reality in our discussions going forward. How would you suggest we refer to them?"

"Well, we could call them 'reality' with a little 'r,' and 'Reality' with a big 'R,'" I replied. "That way, 'Reality' would mean the way that the world works, and 'reality' would mean the way that I *think* the world works. In other words, my 'reality' is the way I frame the world so that I can make the world useful in my life. We could even call this reality my 'personal reality.'"

"Very well, then," said Mideol. "Let's use the term *personal reality* when we wish to refer to 'reality with a little r' and simply use the term *Reality* when we wish to refer to 'Reality with a big R.'"

"That makes it more understandable," I said. "At least it should help me keep things straight."

Mideol nodded before directing my attention back to the objects sitting on the floor. "So each object here would represent a separate reality, or a *personal reality*, but each one is really just a framing of Reality itself. The formula would look like this," he said.

With that he picked up the pencil and wrote this below the diagram he had drawn earlier:

personal reality = frame + *part of* Reality

"Let's get the full value of the metaphor, shall we? Picture the blank canvas extending beyond the frame in all directions to infinity. That could be thought of as Reality. Now each picture frame simply attempts to capture Reality, but what it really does is create a *personal reality* by seeking to contain Reality within itself."

"That's an interesting way of looking at it."

"It gets better," Mideol replied. "When a particular person, culture, religion, or philosophy defines itself by its own framing of Reality, it cuts itself off from Reality. To the degree that it does this, it locks itself into the delusion that *personal reality* is *Reality* itself.

"When an individual or a tradition is stuck inside of its own frame of reference—*that* is the dilemma. This dilemma echoes the dilemma of the 'I' as the *changing self* and *changeless self* that we just discussed.

"The bottom line is that there are two ways of perceiving Reality. The first way is to be stuck inside a dense frame and believe your *personal reality* is *Reality* itself. The second way is to see that you participate in *a part* of Reality while you remain connected to *all* of Reality. In the first case, your focus is on the frame. In the second case your focus is upon the infinite canvas. Can you see the parallel?"

His model of Reality and his model of the 'I' sounded similar. In a way, it seemed like they were the same dilemmas. As I thought about them, though, I realized that one was talking about the *inner* experience of me, and the other was talking about the *outward* expression of me. In a sense, they were both talking about this 'I' but paralleled one another too.

"I do see how similar they are," I said, "but would that mean that the *changeless self* is like Reality in the other model? It seems like one formula is me looking in at myself, and the other one is me looking out at my world."

"Very perceptive, Yosh. Both speak to the same process but face in different directions, as you've observed. There is another feature they have in common. It might be helpful to look at them together to appreciate this."

Mideol motioned for the page he had given me. I handed it back to him. Below his previous writing, he wrote a second formula, or "construction" as he called it:

personal reality = frame + *part of* Reality

I = changing self + *part of* changeless self

"I see that the phrase 'part of' is in both formulas," I said. "I guess that makes sense, because the frame was cutting off just part of Reality and making that part into its reality."

"Excellent, Yosh."

"But I don't understand—how can 'part of Reality' be cut off from Reality? Isn't that 'part of Reality' still Reality?"

"Yosh, you amaze me," he said. "This question has been asked down through the ages and has been a stumbling block for many seekers over thousands of years. To arrive at *this* question so quickly means that you have truly understood the conversation.

"I cannot explain this concept better than one of the greatest seekers of this wisdom, so I will give you his words. After that, I will ask that you reflect on all that we have spoken about. When you've come to the awareness suggested by these words, then we can proceed with this part of our discussion."

All know that the drop merges into the ocean,
But few know that the ocean merges into the drop.

– Kabir

SELF

I didn't sleep well that night. It wasn't the December cold—the twin stoves kept the cave warm, and God knows there was enough wood to burn. It also wasn't hunger or thirst, and I wasn't in any physical pain, but my mind kept racing with all the thoughts Mideol had thrown at me.

I can't remember actually falling asleep, but I vaguely recalled my final waking thoughts—churning oceans crashing against cliffs in giant waves and then slowly retreating. Through half-closed eyes, the ocean calmed to an unbroken sheet of glass. A single drop of rain fell from the sky, sending ripples across the endless expanse of tranquil water.

I woke to find Mideol sitting in his morning spot on the carpet.

"Would you like some breakfast?"

"Yes, please," I replied.

I sat on the edge of the bed. I didn't feel rested and my mind was still reeling. I felt dazed. I had gone from mindlessly chopping wood to mindfully chopping up my world in a single day.

I wanted to get back to our discussion, but I also wanted to let his concepts sink in. Part of me also wanted to just shelve it and think about something else… or not think at all. Mostly, I wanted to be back outside.

Mideol didn't seem like he was in a hurry, either. He was happy to just be outside, so that's where we spent the next few days. We walked through the forest with Keeley running up and down the trail ahead of us or off to the side. Mideol would point out a sound and quiz me on its source or point out a plant peeking through the snow and tell me all of its useful qualities.

Our trips outside still involved a type of learning. He was now teaching me about the physical world, which I knew very little about. Still, the world I wanted to know more about was the one I carried with me all the time. He had started that discussion. As the days went by I grew more anxious to return to it.

Almost a week had passed since we had spoken about the *self* and he had shared his metaphor of the picture frames. I was reminded of our discussion every time I looked at the framed empty canvas over the east door or happened to see the blank canvas over the west door.

He was right. These two objects were constantly in my vision whenever I looked out of my room. Whenever I looked up from my reading or moved outside myself to gaze out the window and connect with the world outside the cave, there they were. They were a constant reminder of a task left undone.

I lay in bed that night thinking about the events of my first month here and particularly the past week. I realized that it was I who had dropped the ball, not Mideol. It was I who had not pursued the conversation further. My faltering interest had been the story of my life. I had always exhibited just enough introspection to question my personal reality, but only when I had a big problem. As soon as the problem was no longer staring me in the face, my introspection disappeared and I became distracted.

Eventually, though, I would have to confront the same contradiction. The only difference was that the next time it would be the same issue wearing different clothing. Those clothes were just different enough that I could avoid owning my distraction—hiding from myself behind this illusion.

My life had been a series of such moments, I thought—moments of introspection and then distraction.

As I lay in bed that night, I projected this habit into the future and had the disturbing realization that my entire life might pass by this same way. Seeing my life unfold, repeating the same pointless issues with different faces, made me feel like running… like there was no rhyme or reason to things… that none of this made any sense… that I couldn't handle this. I just needed to escape, get out, and get far away from here!

I don't know why, but this time I recognized the impulse for what it was. It was the first time I remember experiencing an emotion and then just examining it without responding to it. As I watched the emotion move through me, I had an epiphany.

All of my running has been just running in place. Running away was nothing more than sitting still. Needing to escape was the opposite of doing something intentionally. It was just a way of avoiding the question, of falling back into the dream without admitting that I was going back to a life of sleepwalking.

As I observed part of me squirm in discomfort, another part of me became very calm. In that moment, I realized that I could stop running around madly and unintentionally.

From that quiet place, I could decide where I wanted to go. I could choose it deliberately. Even more amazing, I could feel strong enough to get there. Suddenly, I understood the *changeless self* that Mideol had spoken about the previous week.

So, this is what tranquility must feel like, I thought.

I went to sleep and slept well.

* * *

I woke refreshed and found Mideol again sitting in his spot on the carpet—the valley behind him hidden by dense clouds.

"Would you like some breakfast?" Mideol asked.

"Yes, please."

We sat, and I ate with Mideol at the table in the east room, facing the glass wall. I looked at the snow falling outside and at the framed canvas over the door.

"If it's okay with you," I said, "I'd like to finish our conversation from last week."

"Have you had enough time to think about things?"

"Actually, I had enough time a few days ago, but…"

It was hard for me to finish my sentence, but eventually I told him about my thoughts the night before and how I was tired of running. I told him how, out of that experience, I had realized the way in which the two models were connected.

"Well, why don't you continue where we left off, then?" he asked. "Why don't you tell me how the two models parallel one another?"

"All right," I said, reaching into the desk drawer for the piece of paper containing his sketch of the two models. I sat staring at the page, thinking where to begin.

$$\text{personal reality} = \text{frame} + \textit{part of}\ \text{Reality}$$

$$\text{I} = \text{changing self} + \textit{part of}\ \text{changeless-self}$$

"I think that we had left off with you comparing the two models," I said. "What I couldn't understand was how *part of Reality* could be cut off from Reality. Then, I thought about that quote from Kabir and realized that *part of Reality* is like the drop… and *Reality* is like the ocean.

"That would mean that, like the ocean merging into the drop, every part of Reality is *all* of Reality! I have to say this was kind of disturbing. It was incredible, but it was also uncomfortable."

"Why would it be disturbing or uncomfortable?" Mideol asked. "It sounds like you understood Kabir's meaning very well."

"It was disturbing because it meant that when I try to frame a *part of Reality* into my personal reality, I'm really trying to own something that I'm not big enough to own. It's hard to explain, but that's just how it felt."

"All right, I can understand that," Mideol said, "but your realization about the nature of Reality and part of Reality is still an incredible realization. How did this affect your understanding about the 'I' and the 'part of the changeless self'? I believe you said that you now understood how the two models paralleled each other."

"Right. I figured that the same relationship that exists for the *part of Reality* and *Reality* externally must exist *internally* between the *part of changeless self* and the *changeless self* that is its ocean. I suppose if we wanted to be honest, then we would have to call the changeless self the *Changeless Self* with capitals just to be consistent."

Mideol sat there looking at me with an expression of disbelief— and also, I think, gratitude. But I wondered why he would be grateful to me? If anything, it was I who should be grateful to him.

Then Mideol did something I never expected. He got out of his chair, turned toward me, kneeled down, and bowed with his head touching the ground. Then he stood up and gave me a hug. I could see tears in his eyes but had no idea why.

After sitting down again, he finally spoke. "I did not bow to you, Yosh. I bowed to that in you that you have recognized in yourself. That which you have recognized as the *Changeless Self* is simply *The Self* that participates in *all* selves. As you correctly identified, *The Self* resides in you, in the fullness of Being, as this *Changeless Self*.

"The reason for the exercise is to allow you to understand fundamentally that this aspect of 'I' is distinct from the *Changing Self*. You, as a personal reality, are *not* the *Changeless Self*. But that within you that is changeless participates in *The Self* beyond time, place, and circumstance *to the extent that you allow that participation*. It is the existence of this relationship that allows you access to *Reality*."

"I had no idea."

"Yes, you did not realize that this was what you had discovered. This discovery is the gateway out of the dilemma of being imprisoned within your framing of reality. That act of framing reality is what had cut you off from Reality in the first place. It is the discovery of the intrinsic connection with Reality and The Self that now frees you from your illusory prison."

"Are you saying that this 'Self' is God?"

"It is God, if by that term you mean the Singular Spirit that animates all of creation and which is at once the Creator apart from creation, and the Creative Element intrinsic to all of creation."

I gave him a look suggesting I didn't really understand.

"This Source of all things," he explained, "has been known by many names. It is The One Spirit, The Source or simply 'Source,' The

Divine, Waheguru, God, Bhagwan, Paramatma, Teotl, Yahweh, Brahman, The Infinite, I Am, Ar-Rahman, Tian, Alláh-u-Abhá, The Tao, The Beloved, The Ultimate Reality, or any of dozens of other names. It is one and the same, and *It* is the highest goal.

"Because the mind cannot contain *It*, there is no point in discussing *It's* nature beyond a simple understanding. It is the font of life and its foundation. As such, *It* is the creative and sustaining principle. If anything can be called good, it is *The Source* that is good. The structure that allows us to reason and allows you to journey toward joy derives from The Source. There is nothing that exists outside of it.

"Whether The Source is benevolent toward us as individuals at any particular time or is benevolent toward all creation, it is not possible for me to say, so I refer to it in both senses. I may call it Source or Spirit. I may address *It* as Lord, Father, or The Beloved. The difference reflects this ambiguity in my ability to comprehend *It* and in my inability to contain the fullness of *It* in word or thought."

"If we can't comprehend *It*, then how will we discuss *It*?" I asked.

"We will not discuss *It* beyond this reference. We may speak of *Its* manifestations in our world, our journey toward *It*, or our relationship to *It*, but we cannot define *It* further. To accept the limitations of our thought while valuing the depth of our capacity for thought is an ancient wisdom.

"If you feel that your tradition has not adequately expressed comfort with this inherent limitation of ours, then I refer you to the Jain concept of 'syadvada,' or the inability of any singular expression to convey the fullness of Reality. The overlying concept of 'anekanta-vada' captures these concepts even more fully and may be worthy of your attention."

I replied, "I've never heard of those. I've never even heard of Jains before."

"Well, you've heard the story of the blind men and the elephant, right?"

"Yeah, I know that one," I said. "That's where each one of the blind men feels a different part of the elephant, and then they each in turn tell how the elephant is hard as ivory, as flexible as the trunk, or as hairy as the tail."

"Exactly. That is a Jain story, and this concept is at least 2,500 years old. The story demonstrates an-eka-anta-vada, or 'not-one-attri-bute-philosophy,' the Jain concept that accepts that no single human point of view can contain the whole of truth regardless of how much we may desire to project that personal reality onto Reality."

"Okay, I get that, but isn't that the opposite of what you were just talking about with The Spirit and Source? Isn't Reality a reflection of the one Source, as you were saying?"

"That is excellent, Yosh! You are correct to see this apparent con-flict. It is a conflict that people have perceived for over 5,000 years, and it has manifested in many ways during that time. Our discussion is nothing less than an effort to reconcile these apparently conflicting positions. You have much to learn before we can return to this discus-sion, but you might want to begin here."

I thanked him and told him I would study it. It was hard to be-lieve that people were having these discussions in 500 B.C., let alone 2,500 years before that!

Mideol interrupted my trip into the past by clearing his throat before speaking again. "Yosh, it is important to maintain a constant recognition of our limitations in understanding Source, The Spirit, The Lord, The Beloved, or whichever name you may choose.

"Some traditions accomplish this by using a diffusion of names, as I do. Others, such as the Jewish tradition, accomplish this recogni-tion by choosing not to give a name to The Creator. In that tradition, The Creator, when asked His name in the book of Exodus in the To-rah, simply states, *Ehyeh asher ehyeh,* or 'I am that I am.'

"It is a simple, yet powerful statement of the manifestation of Source as the cause of all things in our world. This statement neither limits *It* nor allows ownership of *It*."

"So, is one way better than the other?" I asked. "Is it better to leave *It* nameless or more useful to use a number of names?"

Mideol replied, "Whichever of the two methods you choose, the important thing is to recognize your limitations when discussing The

Spirit. You can accomplish this by using many different names or no name at all. It is the admission of your limitations that matters.

"The recognition of these limitations is the reason that I simply say that Source is the highest goal, without needing to qualify *It* beyond that recognition. Without needing to contain *It* with the limited ability of my intellect, I can still see *It* as the source of joy."

"But if you can't describe *It*, then how can you know *It*?" I asked.

"Ah—I may not be able to see *It*, but I can see the *manifestations* of *It* all around me, Yosh. Those manifestations *are* the workings of Source writ large within the very fabric of our world. Just as I know the sun by its life-giving rays, so I know The Spirit by its manifestations. In the same way that standing on the sun would detract from my understanding of it, the unrealistic desire to understand The Source would impair my ability to appreciate *Its* presence in my life and my world."

"*You* may be able to see those manifestations," I replied. "But I can't."

"That's not true, Yosh. It might be more correct to say that you have not yet learned to identify them for what they are. But you have done the more important work. You have recognized the paradox in your relationship to The Spirit that allows growth in perception of *It*. This is something that is generally not perceived until much later. Do you know what I am referring to when I say this?"

"No, not really. I'm amazed that I even understand this much."

"You said that you were disturbed by the realization that 'every part of Reality is Reality itself,' because you felt that you were not big enough to contain Reality. I believe you said that it was hard to explain."

"Yes, I remember that. I still feel it's true."

"Well, there is a diagram that helps to illustrate this awareness you have expressed. I wish to share it with you so that you may understand the paradox in the relationship between the 'I' and The Spirit."

Mideol took out a new piece of paper and drew this:

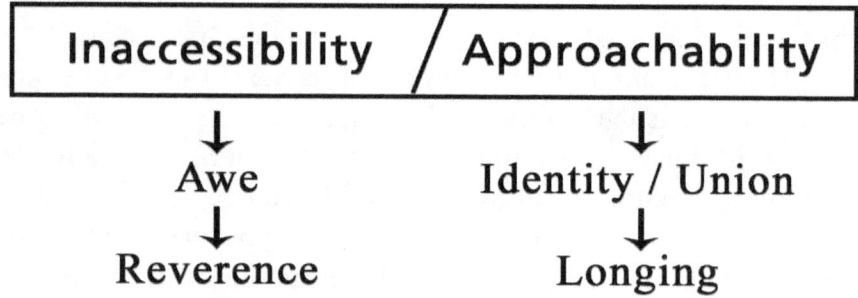

I could feel that Mideol was close to completing his thought. He shifted a bit in his chair, and there was a certain finality in his voice.

"Yosh, however you may choose to address Source, the attitude that allows you to approach *It* is one of reverence combined with longing. The paradox is this—without an honest *recognition* of your limitations in understanding The Spirit, you will waste your time in seeking it.

"A truly *abiding acceptance* of those limitations reflects the honesty of an intellect large enough to examine itself. In that examination, such an intellect becomes capable of allowing the 'I' to escape its prison, which you now understand is the frame that it has created for itself. Knowing The Spirit as inaccessible to the intellect, the intellect allows something greater, something within the 'I,' to approach The Spirit and participate in *It*. That something is the *Changeless Self* that you identified.

"This paradox itself manifests in reverence before longing can be fulfilled. I will leave you to consider this diagram as a model of the process. The ability to recognize this apparent contradiction is your recognition of the door that opens to the path of the solution. But *identifying* this paradox is not the same as *resolving* it.

"Still, you've made great progress in defining your goal with greater clarity. It may be helpful to inquire further into the process of that journey before you're capable of resolving this paradox."

I sat there, staring at the diagram Mideol had written out. I *did* feel like I'd traveled a long way. I was in awe. Maybe it wasn't the same awe that he was talking about, but it was still *wonder* at all the territory we'd covered. And something else, too—a sense of freedom I couldn't put my finger on. And gratitude.

This was guidance I'd yearned for my entire life. Just a couple of weeks ago I'd thought Mideol was going to let me down, like I'd been disappointed so often before. How wrong I had been. Now, with Mideol's help, the clarity of the goal felt palpable, and since I had arrived at it myself, I owned the knowledge. I had no idea where it would take me, but I was ready to get started.

THE JOURNEY

Over the next couple of weeks, Mideol and I spent a great deal of time talking about The Self. He introduced me to the various traditions that had spoken about The Self and the individuals within those traditions who had sought to inquire into *It*. It wasn't a formal study, just more of a familiarization.

During those middle two weeks of December, Mideol led me through an overview of Christianity, Judaism, Sikhism, Vedanta, the Sufi, Baha'i, Jain and Nath teachings, Buddhism, Taoism, indigenous inquiry from the Americas, Polynesia and Australia, and Chinese thought from Confucius (who I learned was called "K'ung-fu-tzu") to Mencius ("Meng Tzu") and on to someone I had never heard of named Mozi ("Mo Di," or "Mo Ti").

When we weren't inside talking or studying, we were outside walking in the deepening snow, clearing snow off the solar panels, or making repairs.

Every morning I would wake up to see him sitting cross-legged on the carpet facing the glass wall doing his exercises or chanting. I had never been very interested in any routine. I preferred spontaneity, and given the choice I would rather get up late.

Usually I would be getting up just as he was finishing, but I always watched him, and the more I did, the more I was drawn to his routine. There was a comforting rhythm to it, but it was still too rigid for me. Our morning greeting, though, *had* become a tradition with us, without my even noticing it.

"Would you like some breakfast?" he would ask.

"Yes, please," I would respond.

He cooked and we chatted. It was usually nothing serious, but sometimes I would ask him about the prior day's discussion. It never went far because I knew we would speak more about it later. We would eat our silent breakfast and then I'd clean up the kitchen.

While I cleaned, Mideol sat at the small kitchen table sipping a glass of warm tea. When I was finished, I'd sit down across from him. I was starting to grow fond of tea. The kind he brewed seemed to vary during the day. His morning cup, though, was always the same. It smelled of cloves, cardamom, cinnamon, and ginger, and was sweetened with honey. That smell would fill the whole cave each morning. It was a constant during our time together.

Most of our discussion would take place in the morning after breakfast, unless there was a storm outside. In that case we'd talk on and off all day. It was on just such an afternoon, toward the end of December, that we moved the table and chairs over to the west room. Mideol had an interesting habit of rearranging the furniture every lunar month. On the day of the new moon, we'd switch the side in which we would cook, eat, and chat. The armchair and the bookshelf, which sat in the main room, would likewise be moved to the opposite side. This always left the view from the new eating area open to the glass wall. So on that particular afternoon we sat together at the table after rearranging the furniture.

I sat there thinking that for some reason we had skipped making this move in November. I remember how strangely disconcerting it was for me the first time we moved things around. It had become easier, but every time we did it I felt like we were shaking things up.

In contrast, our discussion of a couple of weeks earlier had stalled. I felt like I wasn't getting anywhere. I was swimming in information, but it was all just sitting around like papers and files in a cluttered office. Changing our routine somehow pushed me over the edge, and I just had to mention it.

"I appreciate all the literature you've been sharing with me. It's much more interesting than I thought it would be. But it doesn't feel like we're going anywhere with it."

"Where would you like to go?" Mideol asked.

"That's the thing. I thought that when I finally found the way out of the dilemma I'd be fine—you know, satisfied."

"But you're not satisfied?"

"Well, maybe I just need to get back out into the world and apply what I've learned here."

"That would be great. What would happen if you did that?"

"I don't know. I'd see things more clearly, I suppose, and maybe learn how to navigate through life in a way that would serve me better because I know who I am now."

"How long would this take you?"

"I guess I'd probably learn some things pretty quickly, and some things would take a long time. There might be some things I'd never learn because I can't see them."

"Well, there is still a lot of literature for you here, and we can discuss things as you find them of interest," Mideol said.

I had this strange feeling like we were repeating the chopping-wood discussion. It was eerily similar, and I knew right away that I wasn't asking the right question. He would never lead me to it. Even during the past two weeks he seemed to let me drift. He'd say it was because that's what I'd wanted to do.

The truth is, I *had* wanted to drift. It was my old habit. I decided right then that I was going to change that habit. I was not going to drift through this. If I could anticipate doing things intentionally later on, why not do them intentionally *now*?

"Is there anything that we can do that's more structured?"

"Absolutely, Yosh. We can be as structured as you want."

"Great. I've never had much structure, so I'd like to be as structured as possible. Let me rephrase that," I said. "I'd like to be as structured as you think would be useful for me."

"Well, I might have to think about that for a bit," he said with a smirk. "I wasn't thinking you would want such regimentation."

I smiled back at him. "Thanks a lot. Go ahead and rub it in."

"Fine," Mideol said with a smile. "Let's begin then. What we discussed earlier this month regarding the dilemma, the self, and The

Spirit, is a description of the predicament that you've created for yourself."

"Don't you mean the predicament in which I find myself?" I asked.

"No—I mean the predicament you have *created* for yourself. What you have earned for yourself so far is a blueprint detailing the structure of your dilemma. You can think of it as a roster of the players involved in the creation, maintenance, or dismantling of the dilemma. You still have little idea about the journey of the *self* before, within, and after the dilemma.

"Beyond that, you have no knowledge of how to proceed at different points within the journey. These details can be worked out by trial and error, as you mentioned, but that may take a very long time. It's commendable that you have already made enough progress in addressing your pride that asking for help took only two weeks this time."

"Thanks," I said. And I meant it. I knew it was real progress.

He nodded. "Over the next week we'll look at the journey and then more deeply at the mind. In the new year we'll begin the process of aligning the mind more closely to The Spirit. If the mind can be brought to a closer alignment with Source, then the frame becomes less dense. Once this happens, the canvas of the Changeless Self becomes the object of focus for the 'I.' The object of focus is no longer the frame of the changing self—I hope that's clear. Since you already know that the mind consists of both cognitive and emotional elements, you can expect that our work on the mind will consist of cognitive and physical/emotional aspects. But as I said, that will have to wait. Today, we'll begin with an exploration of the journey itself."

"That sounds wonderful," I said, looking at him in astonishment for taking my concerns and turning them into anticipation. "How do you *do* that?"

"Do what?" Mideol asked.

"How do you manage to replace my fear of being bored for the next five months with anxiety over not having enough time to finish everything you've laid out for me?"

He smiled in acknowledgment. "This journey does not end until you want it to end, Yosh. There is even more to be done than you imagine, but fortunately the journey is the reward itself—because every step is a step further into clarity and joy. This journey is unique among journeys because the rewards are not intermittent. The goal of this journey is built into every step, and every step creates the ability to proceed to the next step.

"Each next step may look impossible at first. Fortunately, a different 'I' arrives to meet that step than the 'I' that thought I was impossible. The questions are *whether you wish* to see beyond these limited senses of 'I,' and *how much desire you carry* with you into the journey."

"I do want to see beyond my assumptions of my self—beyond the constraints of my mind. I want to see myself clearly. I guess I'm not afraid. I'll do what it takes."

"Very well, then. Let me tell you about your predicament. It is not a dilemma that you fell into. This life of conflicted interests is a dilemma that you have *chosen*. This dilemma cannot be separated from 'you' because the dilemma *is* 'you.'"

Mideol paused to let his words sink in before he started speaking again.

"The reason you have not been able to see your dilemma clearly is that you've always seen it as existing *outside* of yourself. In reality, your dilemma has two causes—two roots. First, it exists because you do not clearly understand *who you are*. Secondly, it exists because you do not understand who you are *in relation to your world*. We have to examine both of these causes if you want to proceed on the journey."

"Proceed on *which* journey?" I asked, confused about whether this was the same journey as the path to the solution or something entirely different.

"To proceed on the journey toward the awakened life, of course," Mideol replied.

"Is that the journey that I'm on?"

"It is the journey that Abe felt you were on. It is the 'other way of thinking' that you recognized earlier. In reality, there are only two ways of being—asleep and awake. You have been asleep for most of your life, and you are not alone in this. Most of the world mostly sleeps throughout the course of its existence."

"How can you say that? I know a lot of people who are very much alive. They have exciting jobs, they travel, they move in influential circles. Some excel at sports, music, or art. I may not know them personally, but I know they exist."

"An excellent observation, Yosh. It's the reason I say 'most.' It's quite common to have lucid moments. For some people those moments of lucidity are more frequent than for others. Still, they are *moments* in which they awaken. These moments are not *being awake* in any stable way. They rarely last very long.

"As you'll see, it is also possible to be awake in *certain aspects* of one's life without being awake in a *global sense*. The image of accomplished athletes or artists who are asleep to many other parts of their life is so common it has become a cliché. This does not diminish their accomplishments in any way, but it would be wrong to assume they experience similar lucidity in other aspects of their lives."

"I see what you mean. It does seem that some people can 'connect' pretty well in one part of their lives and still be 'unconnected' in many others. I'm sorry to say I haven't experienced that level of connection in any particular area myself. I have had the other experience that you mentioned, though. I mean, I've had moments of *lucidity*, as you call them. There are times when I've felt totally alive in a certain moment. Those moments have never lasted long, but I remember them vividly."

"Exactly. These moments of awakening are experiential—like the intense activity of sports or the deep resonance of making music. Some can be moments of profound insight, like literally waking from a dream. They are the experience of an awareness that extends beyond the intellect but that is not separate from thought or cognition. In the Zen experience, such profoundly 'awake' moments have a name—*Kensho*."

"It actually has a name?"

"Several names, but Zen is very precise in this distinction, so let's use Kensho."

"So is that what you teach? Are you a Zen teacher?"

"No, Yosh. I find value in Zen, but I find value in a great number of traditions, as you've seen. What I have to teach you is not the path of any one tradition, but the habit of seeking that which is of value across traditions—and at the heart of our great traditions. Anyway, we should return to our discussion."

"You already told me about Kensho—that momentary awakening," I said.

"Yes, Kensho is a transient experience, but there is a *deeper* experience, too. Because it is not transient, it cannot rightly be called an experience. It is more like a state of being. This state of being is called *Satori* in the Zen tradition. It is the state of being awake. It differs from Kensho in that it is stable."

"So you mean that Satori is a stage in which you stay once you get there?"

"Not necessarily, Yosh. Some have sought to define degrees of Satori that vary by their length or stability, but that isn't relevant to you at this time. It's enough to understand that this stability may range from tenuous to absolute, and that your goal at this time cannot be defined more clearly than even the most tenuous aspect of Satori.

"The journey I speak of is the journey from sleep to a Satori that *approaches* its greatest stability. It's a journey of six steps and six stages. The threshold of that sixth step marks the limit of a perception that the rational mind can contain. This is the Satori of which I speak. Beyond the approach to that step there is little to discuss. But there is considerable territory to cover through this sixth step.

"Your birth was the First Step—that step brought you into *being*. It was the step that made the journey possible. When you take Step Two as a child, you separate yourself from *being* and become conscious of your role as an active participant in your world. You enter into the realm of the little-e-ego. This is stage two, and it is marked by contentment in limitation. Here you accept your condition because you have no knowledge of any other state of being. Therefore, the dilemma does not yet exist because you cannot recognize it. You could call this 'ignorant bliss' if you'd like.

"Eventually, though, you become aware that you are asleep. That moment marks the onset of the dilemma because in that moment you understand you have some ability to affect the very way your world is shaped. You become both empowered and aware of your powerlessness.

"This recognition marks Step Three. Before taking this third step, you are asleep but do not even know that you are sleeping. The desire to take this step and the knowledge that it exists come from the same source. This is the beginning of your *conscious* participation in the world as a creator of that world. It is at once a liberation and an imprisonment—as you've seen. The stage which you enter after taking the third step is marked by both an ability to see your potential and a sense that this potential exceeds your grasp.

"It is the desire to possess these visions of potential, while retaining your identity as little-ego, that marks stage three as the birthplace of the Big-Ego. In this stage, you are firmly enmeshed in a mistaken sense of self. The frame of your 'I' is dense. It may be marked by an ornate structure that reveals the degree to which you revere your mind or your changing self. You arrive at this third stage because you experience a *dilemma of mistaken identity*.

"As this stage progresses, though, you may catch glimpses behind the curtain of illusion that holds you within your mistaken identity. These are those fleeting *Kensho* moments—those first, momentary flashes of recognition into your true nature. No wonder you feel such a deep affinity for it. But this sense of a *divided identity* is often mistaken for a dream and is not validated by most communities. While movement from stage one to stage three is common and necessary to operate effectively in any society, stage four comes only to those who know that reality lies beyond society's mutual agreements. Stage four comes only to those who reconcile that *divided identity* into acceptance of a *loss of identity* that questions the Ego itself."

"So, let me back up a second," I said. "Are you saying that my dilemma started when I took this fourth step?"

"That's right, Yosh. This fourth stage, entered by taking the fourth step, is a product of the *dilemma of divided identity*."

"Okay, I think I understand. Then how about the fifth step?"

"Step Five is marked by both an intellectual and emotional *understanding* of the dilemma of divided identity. Taking this step means confronting the inconsistencies of our former attachments *and* maintaining the desire to do so, regardless of the consequences. The stage that may follow is marked by wisdom. The wisdom that defines stage five is only arrived at by wrestling with a certain paradox within Step Five. Do you remember the paradox of inaccessibility and approachability that we spoke of earlier this month?"

"Yes, I remember that," I said.

"Good, Yosh. What you need to understand, then, is that this fifth step is characterized by uncertainty that is marked by this paradox. You feel that you've lost your identity as the changing self but have not yet assumed the identity of the Changeless Self. You feel unable to commit to either identity because the first one is a lie, and the second one is just speculation.

"This inability to define yourself has been called a *void* or an *abyss*. You feel untethered, as if confronted by a great emptiness or nothingness. It is also known as the *dark night of the soul* or *existential angst,* and it is in Step Five that you first encounter it. It can be hard to think of such angst as marking progress beyond the *dilemma of divided identity*. It *is* progress, though—but subtle progress.

"You yourself experienced this, Yosh, when you looked out and saw the void."

"That makes sense to me now," I said. "That *is* what I was feeling."

"Yosh, progress within the fifth stage is marked by a growing frustration with this paradox. You ask yourself, 'How is it possible to have an inherent inconsistency in my identity and at the same time utterly lack any identity?' The resolution of this paradox is the goal of the fifth stage."

"You mean the paradox of the split personality or divided identity?"

"No," Mideol replied. "I mean the paradox of being stuck *between* the two dilemmas—the dilemma of divided identity and the dilemma of a lack of identity."

I looked at Mideol in confusion. After starting to feel like I was getting somewhere, I was now feeling even more in a fog with all of these steps and stages.

"I never realized that the dilemma had all these stages," I said. "It just seemed like one big problem."

"The main purpose of my explanation is to help you see these stages and the progression between them, Yosh. Only then can you see the journey more clearly. Maybe I should draw this out for you. It's too early to look at this progression in all of its detail, but an outline might be helpful."

"That would be wonderful," I said. "But why not the details?"

"As complicated as this sounds, the progression I'm sharing with you is only a linear outline of a non-linear process. What we're discussing here is your *internal* journey, but I think I should incorporate elements of your wider social journey into this model. You haven't encountered these elements yet, so discussing them at length would only complicate matters. Limited as an outline might be, it may still be of assistance."

With that, Mideol pulled out a fresh sheet of paper and began to write:

Steps in the Journey: Transition of Perspectives

Stage 6—Awareness = Being
    Step Six—Awake – confronting the void
Stage 5—Wisdom – emotional & rational integration – The Diamond Rule
    Step Five—confronting inconsistencies – encountering the void
Stage 4—Loss of Identity
    Step Four—Fullness of Ego - dilemma of divided identity
Stage 3—Ego
    Step Three—Development of Ego - dilemma of mistaken identity
Stage 2—little-ego – no dilemma – blissful ignorance
    Step Two—separation
Stage 1—being
    Step One—birth

"That helps," I said. "I'm just not sure I'll remember them."

Mideol thought for a moment, put his hand on the paper with his fingers spread apart, and began to draw. "Does this help?"

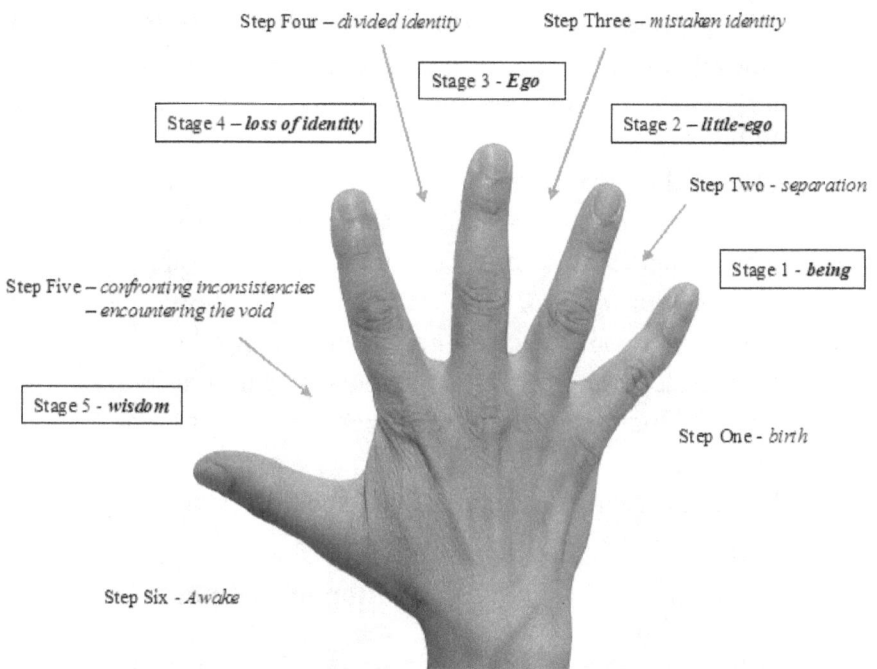

"Yes, that helps a lot," I said.

"Good. Now that you have an outline of the steps and stages, can you tell me where it is that you feel you might be?"

"I guess I've had a bunch of divided identities, and now I'm feeling like I don't even have an identity."

"Very good, then let's go back and look a little deeper at the dilemma of a lack of identity. A feeling of a lack of identity is the height of this entire set of dilemmas. A lack of identity seems more unstable than a divided identity, but that instability is its greatest value. The intense discomfort of lacking identity implores you to seek a resolution.

"You see, Yosh, any action—even walking—requires you to become unstable before you can move forward. It is a question of what you value more—either stability or movement in your desired direction. One takes you where you want to go. The other leaves you standing still. In this case, the direction you wish to travel leads to the fifth step because you have decided that you will not move backward."

"Okay, that makes sense."

Mideol gestured to the list of steps and stages. "Just as Step Four marks entry into *understanding* the dilemma, Step Five marks entry into *wisdom* and the *resolution* of the dilemma. The dilemma must resolve itself here because unlike the two previous stages of the dilemma, stage four is too unstable to persist. There is no place else to go. For this reason, stage four is a terrifyingly uncomfortable place to be."

Mideol leveled his gaze on me, and I could tell that Step Five and the approach to it were particularly relevant. He took a deep breath and began again.

"You have to understand, Yosh, that this is not an esoteric discussion. Sooner or later, everyone who becomes sufficiently aware of the journey takes Step Five. Residing in stage four that precedes it is marked by a sense of being tired of sleeping but unable to awaken.

"In other words, they are stuck," Mideol said with a tone of inevitability.

Yes, that's what I felt like—stuck. He was describing me.

"So what happens to them when they're stuck?" I asked.

"Well, there are four possibilities. Having progressed within the fourth stage to the point where they can perceive the void and not look away, they are faced with a decision. It is then that four options present themselves. Option One is chosen when such a person, tired of remaining in the dilemma, sees no way out. They may choose to return to sleep, resuming life with a divided identity. Returning to Stage Three is often characterized by quiet resignation. Or they may return to Stage Three with cynicism and hatred for a world that they now see as enslaving them. In either case, the pain of being awake in a world that sleeps is too great, and the hope of awakening is too remote.

"In the case of quiet resignation, it is possible to adjust well in a world that also exists at stage three. The cynical ones, however, feeling their own sincere efforts thwarted, often come to embody hatred—deep hate for themselves because they fell short of a goal they could once see, and hate for everyone around them who they feel is complicit in their downfall.

"Feeling themselves cast back into a world of enslavement, these individuals fight to enslave others rather than be enslaved themselves. In so doing, they justify as *fate* the conditions they've willingly chosen."

"What a terrible place to be."

"It's the darkest existence, Yosh—and such a shame because these people had been capable of reaching the fourth stage of the journey. Yet, the deepest hell is created by those who have seen heaven and then rejected it."

"What do heaven and hell have to do with it?" I asked, surprised.

"Heaven and hell have a lot to do with it. You may think of heaven and hell as physical places, but such concepts have nothing to do with it. The heaven and hell I speak of exist eternally as frames of mind."

"They exist in my mind?"

"No, they exist as *frames* of mind. We'll discuss it later," said Mideol. "For now, let's return to our four options and explore the remaining three.

"Option Two is not the way of quiet resignation, nor of cynicism or anger. But this second way out is also a product of progressive fatigue, like the first option. It differs in one way, though. The second option is to end the journey by ending your life. It is a choice to move neither forward nor back. A person who chooses this way out may mistakenly feel that he possesses a greater commitment to honesty than the person who chose Option One. That thinking is flawed, however, because he or she has not yet become aware of the largely emotional nature of the mind."

"So the second option is worse... because it's less honest?"

"No, Yosh, the second way out is worse because it fails to see that there is a value greater than honesty. That value is *life itself*, because life offers the possibility of the journey, and on that journey honesty is a choice. Without life, honesty cannot serve you.

"Yosh, you've already seen how your emotions have driven your behavior in the guise of *partial* honesty. If you elevate honesty above life, you forsake the opportunity to realize this because life itself has been lost."

He said it with such finality, all I could say was, "I see."

"Option Two, the second way out, is neither more honest nor better. After all, you can return from resignation, or even from the hell of your own making, to continue the journey. That is the meaning of redemption. You cannot return to continue the journey if there is no 'you' to make the journey. Killing yourself is not an option if your purpose is the journey."

"I understand that now," I said with equal finality.

"I know you do, Yosh, but you need to recognize that this is the second option. The next way out of the dilemma is Option Three. It is a sort of paralysis. It is the path of the *perpetual seeker*—a type of *limbo*. Choosing this way out leaves you unable to act but unwilling to fall back into illusion. Choose this option, and you may remain stuck for so long that you assume 'being stuck' as your identity. Then the dilemma of a lack of identity *becomes* your identity."

"That sounds sad."

"It can be unfortunate, but it is not a lie and not disingenuous. It is simply a combination of fear and fatigue. Both must be addressed if the *fourth* option is to be chosen by such an individual. Unfortunately, the other two options still remain open to this individual as well."

"Back to being stuck," I said with a sign of resignation.

"Yes, I believe it's a feeling you know well, Yosh. This means the fourth path remains available to you. Option Four is the path of the solution to the dilemma. It marks the resolution of the dilemma and movement beyond the fourth stage of the journey.

"When you choose Option Four, you are taking Step Five to its conclusion. They overlap—they are one and the same thing. This step is the way out of both the anguish of hell and the oblivion of the dilemma of a lack of identity. Choosing Option Four is choosing to follow the insights of *Kensho*. It's the choice you make to continue the journey to *Satori*, the fully awakened state. It is this fourth option that I offer you, Yosh. You have prepared yourself to make this choice."

"What do you mean, 'I've prepared myself.' Prepared myself for what?"

"Your honesty has brought you to the fifth step of the journey, Yosh. You have moved in and out of the first option and grown tired of it. You have contemplated the second option, suicide, and rejected it. You've remained mired in the third option. All that remains now is to accept the dilemma and true self-respect.

"In fact, you've chopped your way to the gate of acceptance over the past month. You now know that no magic formula or pat answer will serve your need. If you wish to proceed out of the dilemma, you will need the self-respect that allows you to take yourself very literally. Anything short of that will obscure your path."

"I think I understand."

"But simply because you have moved from knowledge to understanding does not mean that you are free of the dilemma. You may now understand its construction, but that doesn't mean you have moved beyond it."

"But I thought that's why you explained it to me."

"All that I have given you is a blueprint detailing how your dilemma is structured. That does not mean you possess the wisdom to escape it. Escape requires more than a fundamental understanding of the dilemma. It requires *action*.

"Escape from the dilemma of a lack of identity is not possible without action because it is our actions that define us unequivocally. By action I mean closing certain doors of possibility and walking through others. Only through action can you truly make a transformative choice."

"But you haven't outlined any action for me," I objected.

"You're right, I haven't. Right now I'm simply giving you a map of the journey. This map describes the route but does not adequately assist you in navigating the terrain. You can either navigate by trial and error… or you will need a guide. Either way, you will need to navigate it, and that's the action I'm talking about. Our discussion today occurred because you had requested a guide. That is why I've given you this map."

"So is that what you are—a guide, a teacher, or some kind of guru?"

"I'm many things to many different people. I've been known as a friend, a peacemaker, a student, a teacher… and yes, a guru. I know that in your popular culture that word is often used dismissively, but it's actually a very useful word. It could be used to define my role with you. So could other words.

"A guru is a teacher but a teacher of a specific type of under-standing. The word 'guru' is composed of two roots—'gu,' meaning darkness, and 'ru' meaning light. So a guru is actually an individual who helps you become aware of how to move from the darkness into the light, from error into alignment with Source, or from the kingdom of man toward the kingdom of God.

"We might say that a guru can assist you in moving from sleep to *Satori*. A guru is a guide to an *understanding* of your divided nature who enables you to grow, through *wisdom*, into an *awareness* of your true nature. Do you understand these distinctions?"

"I think I understand," I said. "Your blueprint of the dilemma defined the relationship between my mind and my changeless self in the different steps of the journey. The distinctions between under-standing, wisdom, and awareness are what Jim spoke about with me in the progression from data to awareness."

"Good, then you understand the full value of such a guide. Let me ask you, Yosh—why is it that you asked me to provide you with such guidance?"

I thought to myself. I *had* asked him, hadn't I? I mean, not in so many words. But I'd sought his help in getting over these areas that kept tripping me up.

I said, "Well, at first I guess I didn't ask you. I mean, it's been a couple of weeks since we had our discussion about the dilemma. Then the more I read and the more we spoke, I realized that my understand-ing really hadn't taken me that far. It felt like I was heading back to being stuck. The difference was that now I knew *why* I was stuck. I've gotten through so much by trial and error on my own that, at first… I guess I just fell back into that habit. I thought I'd work my way out of the dead end by myself."

Mideol nodded as I continued.

"Then I thought about it like this—I'm trying to build a ladder out of this pit of the dilemma I've fallen into. All the pieces for a ladder are there, and I probably *could* build it. The main thing is that I know I need a *ladder* because now I know that I'm in a *pit*. Before our conversation about the dilemma, I didn't even know this was what the dilemma looked like. So in my mind, over the last couple of weeks, I'd already started to build that ladder… but it was slow going.

"Then, one day earlier this month, I turned around and I saw that right behind me was a fully made ladder. I just hadn't seen it because I was so focused on doing it myself. I thought about our talk and about how the 'I' can see itself in all of these dimensions that you've described. I saw that trying to do it myself was a way of ignoring larger definitions of 'I.' Like you said about action—*seeing myself take this action* was what clued me in to how I really defined myself.

"It struck me that I was just going back to an old habit of my mind because what I wanted was to 'do it myself.' When I *looked at myself*, I saw that what I was doing was acting more on 'doing it myself' than acting on 'trying to find a way out.'

"Once I saw it that way, it became easy to say to myself that I want to put 'try to find a way out' above 'do it myself.' That's when I asked you if you could show me how to use the ladder."

"That's fantastic, Yosh! You really have learned the lesson well."

It was strange to see him so elated. I thought a *guru* would be all reserved and stoic. But he loved to see me make progress. He loved to laugh and paint and make music. He loved being outside and he loved ingenuity. He simply loved to be alive.

"So, Yosh," he said, "can you give me a name for the sentiment you confronted in yourself while searching for that ladder in the pit of your dilemma?"

"I guess it was my stubbornness."

"No, Yosh. It was something greater than stubbornness. It was one of the greatest obstacles that prevents escape from the dilemma—your *pride*."

"My pride? Again? It feels like I'm back at the ranch talking to Jim."

Mideol grinned. "Yes, your pride. There was a time, not long ago, when you would have preferred to remain in the dilemma rather than seek help. Do you recall that time?"

"Yeah," I said in soft voice, a little embarrassed.

"Well, one of those sentiments will always be ascendant over the other. This is your choice. It's either pride or the desire to pursue the journey. The fact that you recognized this choice implies you've developed an ability to step outside of yourself—to see your 'I' from a position *outside* of the dilemma. There is a point of paradox here that is subtle but essential. 'You' cannot take the sixth step on the journey if you're the same 'you' who arrived at stage five."

"I don't think I really understand what you mean by a different 'you.' I know what you're saying, but I can't picture what that would look like."

"Yosh, moving through this stage of the journey requires a metamorphosis of sorts. That is a gradual process. It's necessary because you cannot crawl into Stage Six as a caterpillar. You must fly into it as a butterfly. Yet without crawling through Step Five, you can never acquire the perspective needed to transform yourself into something capable of flying beyond the wisdom of stage five. The transformation required is no less dramatic than that of a caterpillar rearranging its molecules to become a butterfly."

"I'm sure you're not talking about rearranging my physical structure, are you?"

"No, but there will be *physical* changes that accompany the *internal* change. Still, physical change is not the goal. It's only one of the hallmarks of moving to stage five and beyond. But even those physical changes are hard to see. As a people, we have a long habit of seeing the goal and the journey as physical in nature when the most important journey is internal. As such, the change that's demanded is internal as well.

"Jesus of Nazareth spoke of this very situation about two thousand years ago when asked about the physical arrival of the kingdom of God. He answered in response to others who conceived of it as a physical location requiring a physical entry. The New Testament says that when asked by the Pharisees when the kingdom of God would come, Jesus replied, 'The kingdom of God does not come with your careful observation, nor will people say, *Here it is*, or *There it is*, because the kingdom of God is within you.' That's from Luke, chapter seventeen."

It seemed odd, Mideol quoting the Bible. Or maybe not so odd, since he knew so much about so many different religions. "So, Jesus is saying that the kingdom of God is internal?" I asked.

"That's what I believe he's saying… that it will not come visibly. Also that the kingdom *already* exists within you. I believe he's saying that it is arrived at by making a change in yourself that puts you in consonance with Him, just as He expresses consonance with The Father. Once that change is made, it allows you to see the kingdom of God which is within yourself."

"So does he talk about the nature of this change or metamorphosis?"

"He talks about it many times and in many ways, just as many of our other great teachers have taught in their own ways. His parables regarding the kingdom of heaven, or the kingdom of God, speak about the 'fruits' by which such a transformation can be realized and demonstrated. His explanations regarding eternal life seem to point to the same state of Being—the same process of the internal journey manifesting external fruit."

"Are those all the same thing?"

"I believe they are. Other traditions have their own names for this unique state of identification with The Spirit. Of course, Jesus would not use the term *Satori*. It would have had no meaning to his listeners. He does, however, use the term 'the kingdom of heaven' interchangeably with 'kingdom of God.' By doing this, he reminds us that this state of *Being* can be contained by no single name, even within his own tradition.

"At the same time, Jesus demonstrates that it is the *concept* he refers to that is important, not the name for it. I follow his lead and equate 'the kingdom of God' with concepts such as Satori, Nirvana, Joy, Heaven, Samsara, or Nibbana."

"How did *Joy* get in there?"

"Yosh, we're talking about the goal of the journey. You may recognize parts of our discussion in the discussions that you had with Jim or Shuren. The discussion of joy as distinct from happiness was such a discussion. Siddhartha Gautama—The Buddha—describes Nirvana as the 'highest happiness,' a happiness that is not derived from temporal or impermanent things."

"That does sound like the same thing as joy, as I discussed it with Jim."

"It is. The practice of seeing things for what they are, rather than as they happen to be labeled, is a practice that is intrinsic to the journey. This is a demonstration of that. In fact, most Zen Koans, Sufi stories, Sikh paradoxes, or parables of Jesus are aimed at creating within us a realization of the impediments we create that prevent us from taking Step Six."

"I'm not sure I understand what those impediments might be."

"Yosh, Step Six has little to do with *understanding,* and this is why the mind has trouble grasping it until it has arrived at stage five that precedes it. For now, it will be enough for you to focus on the needs of Step Five."

"Then why are you describing anything beyond it, if I won't be able to understand it?"

"It may be valuable for you to know of it so that you recognize it."

"Recognize it without understanding it—I'm not sure I follow you."

"Unless the desire to focus and see things clearly is your motivating principle, you will not be able to escape the dilemma. Once it *is* your highest principle—above all others—then moving through Step Five of the journey becomes inevitable. Entering stage five brings new questions that test the limits of *understanding.* W*isdom* is born out of this struggle, and the final level of the dilemma is created."

"So stage five is where this transformation occurs?"

"No. Stage five—the stage of wisdom—is where you stop wanting to hide behind lesser definitions of yourself. Here you come to see yourself as more than your past. The act of moving beyond this stage to Step Six requires you to have addressed this movement across many aspects of yourself. It is the cumulative caterpillar movement through Step Five that makes Step Six possible.

"Flying across Step Six to the sixth stage is like throwing a lifeline to the remainder of yourself. You feel some degree of arriving but recognize you still have to drag those other parts of yourself across. I know that you'll have questions about this, but let's wait until it becomes relevant to you."

"All right," I said. "I've got enough to handle just taking all of this in."

Mideol smiled again and continued. "Now, taking Step Five is the pivotal action. Once that critical action is taken, you will not turn back. Step Five marks entry into a stage of stability within the journey, but don't confuse it with arriving at the goal. Though you will have moved past all three definable levels of the dilemma, you are still not free from it. This is because habits of mind from your previous identifications persist. They need to be addressed in order for you to proceed.

"Step Five—your current focus—ushers in a period of study, contemplation, and application with the goal of living more fully in *Kensho* moments and growing into ever more stable periods of Satori. Progress within Step Five involves forays back into your third stage *and* the third stage of others to align the various aspects of your being to your new identity. This takes time and effort, but the accumulated wisdom of these efforts may create the building blocks for your progression to awareness."

"How long does that stage of the journey take?"

"There's no set time. The stage ushered in by taking Step Five can last an entire lifetime. For Buddha, Jesus, Lao Tzu, and Guru Nanak Dev of Sikhism, it ended—and they took the sixth step while they were still young men. For other men and women that stage of the journey has taken much longer or has started much later in life.

"Once the fifth step is taken, though, the sixth step comes more clearly into view. But again, paradoxically, it is the *effort* devoted to trying to see Step Six with increasing clarity that allows Step Five to be taken. Interestingly, once the fifth step is taken, time becomes irrelevant to the seeker of Step Six."

"I don't understand," I confessed. "So you get through Step Five by trying to reach Step Six, and then you forget about Step Six altogether? That makes no sense."

"Yosh, Step Six marks entry into the process of moving ever deeper into the kingdom of God. But the distinction between *moving deeper* and *arriving at fullness* is not one that we can adequately discuss at this time. It's enough for you to know the map of the journey."

"Thanks," I replied. "I'll have to take your word for that last part. I'm not sure I get all of this, but the beginning and middle parts of the explanation help."

"You are welcome. The understanding is difficult because it exists in two dimensions of activity. This means that the journey is both *linear* and *non-linear*, but I'm afraid that will also mean nothing to you right now.

"For now, remember that this is *only a map*. So now you know where you are on that journey. If you wish to proceed beyond the dilemma, it will mean committing yourself to earning clarity of vision. Only with clarity of vision can you proceed past the fourth stage and take Step Five of the journey. That requires further inquiry into both the dilemma and the 'I' that wishes to make the journey.

"Yosh, this is the journey that is open to you. How far you wish to travel is a choice you *will* make. The ease or difficulty of the journey depends upon the choices you have already made and the choices made by those around you. In turn, the choices you make will impact the ease or difficulty that others will encounter in making the journey themselves.

"The journey can be as difficult or as uncomplicated as you allow, but it can only proceed if the 'you' that arrives at any particular step has grown able to recognize the 'you' that is capable of taking that step. Allowing yourself to *be* that higher self you have newly recognized *is the act* of taking that step. You will know this when you encounter it."

THE MIND THAT JOURNEYS

The next few days passed quite uneventfully. It was almost the end of December. The winter solstice had come and gone about a week before, and I wondered at how the bulk of the winter lay ahead of us even as the days were already growing longer. I mentioned my thoughts to Mideol and he chuckled, just shaking his head. I didn't find any humor in it, but apparently he did.

"So why is *that* so funny?" I asked.

"It's not funny. It's just such an apt metaphor."

"Do you just go around looking for metaphors?"

"Well, I have to entertain myself somehow, don't I?"

"So, are you going to share it with me, or do I have to guess this one, too?"

Smiling back at me, he said, "It reminds me that someone may have been given a blueprint, provided with a map, and have a willing guide—yet it still may be just the beginning of a long winter before any of those benefits become apparent."

"Well, there's not much I can do about that, is there?" I said, smiling back.

"Actually, the most important decision lies ahead of you," he said. "Your recognition of your intrinsic consonance with The Spirit—the recognition that your changeless self is at once part of, *and* the whole of, the Changeless Self—has the *potential* to transform you. To realize that potential, however, requires *action*, and the first step of that action is a *decision*."

"But I told you that I'd already made that decision. Haven't we already discussed this... or did I miss something?"

"You've made the decision to accept a ladder as a way out of the pit of your dilemma rather than constructing one yourself. That is a significant decision. But there is another decision that remains."

"Well, will you share that with me?"

"Of course not. It is not my role to tell you what questions to ask. If you cannot ask a question, then you have not earned the right to assistance with the solution. It is enough that I've informed you that such a decision remains to be made. That itself may be too much to offer. Consider it a gift that honors the sincerity of your inquiry, which has brought you so far in the span of two short months."

"I appreciate that. I'll give it some thought."

"You're welcome. Now, why don't we take a walk?"

We spent most of the next several days outside. The snow had come down heavily, and Mideol enjoyed walking the hills and the forest. There were several snowshoes in the west storage area, and they made for much easier travel. I put them on over my boots and swung the door open. The cold hit me immediately. At first it was a shock. Then I welcomed it. This first step out of the cave each day was like waking from a dream.

Every morning I cherished that first breath outside. I always breathed it in through my nose so that I could take in the smell. I'd never smelled snow, and if I'd been told that snow had a smell I wouldn't have believed it—but it does. I came to love that smell of snow in the mountains, which was never as sharp as the first breath of the day.

Each day Mideol would join me on the ledge, and we'd walk up the path with Keeley leading the way. Even though we were together, I felt such solitude walking in the forest during the winter. The snow fell straight down in a fine white haze of single flakes before tapering to utter stillness. Then it would return as a dense curtain of clumps that parted before us, only to close back as we walked through it. The snow seemed to breathe in a pattern of starts and stops. At times I would try to match my breath to the stirring of the snow.

Maybe I only thought of the snow as breathing because that's what Mideol had been teaching me at the time. Those last few days in December, he seemed to have lost all interest in talking about anything other than breathing. We hadn't even spoken about *the journey* since the day he'd described it in such detail.

He *had* referred to some kind of formal teaching, but for whatever reason he seemed to have no interest in discussing that or anything else. He just wanted to work with me on breathing. Mideol said that everything else could wait, but breathing could not.

When we weren't outside on those days, we sat at the table or on the carpet and he would have me breathe. That sounds strange because I thought breathing was something I'd done since I was born. I quickly found out how wrong I was.

As Mideol explained, "There is taking a breath… and then there's breathing. We will start with breathing, Yosh. That is the basis of the activity of the body and the most frequent and constant physical interaction you have with your world. It is also largely separate from your conscious processes.

"Your breathing communicates with and reflects that aspect of your mind that is distinct from cognition. At the same time, breathing is a function that allows for conscious control. Because breathing possesses these twin qualities, it can serve as a gateway to integrating the conscious and unconscious aspects of your being.

"By becoming aware of your breath, you become more aware of your connection with your world. As this awareness grows, your breath can start to act as a bridge between your thinking and your emotions and between the mind and the biological processes that support the mind."

He stopped for a moment, and I asked, "Do you mean that by controlling my breathing I can control my mind?"

His brow furrowed as he thought about my question. "A bridge allows traffic to move in both directions, Yosh. But before it can be of use, you must become familiar with its construction and the flow of traffic across it. Only then can we discuss utility. Let's begin at the beginning, shall we?"

With that, he began to demonstrate the *observation* of breathing and the observation of thought along with breathing. Over the next several weeks and months, he would go on to show me how to use my breathing to interrupt my incessant thoughts and how to use it to help focus my thinking. He showed me how to use breathing to calm my disruptive emotions and how it could enhance my flagging emotions. I never knew there was so much to learn about an act that I'd always taken for granted.

In the beginning, when I objected that I knew how to breathe, he told me frankly that I did not. He then showed me how to breathe intentionally, first breathing in with my lower abdomen, then with my lower ribs and mid-abdomen, and finally with my upper chest. I never considered holding my breath to be part of breathing, but I learned to be as conscious of the spaces *between* my in-breath and my out-breath as I was of the breath itself. Exhaling, I learned, is just the opposite. It starts with the upper chest, then the lower chest and mid-abdomen, and finally the lower abdomen until the last of the breath is squeezed out.

He was right, of course. I had never taken such deep breaths. And I had never truly exhaled either. It was incredibly calming. Our work on breathing began during those last few days of December and continued each morning and evening the whole time I was with him.

Between our time outdoors and the breathing exercises, we spent little time in discussion. But Mideol's comment about a *decision* played through my mind over and over during those days. I still had no idea what he was talking about, so I thought I would at least ask about the concepts he had already shared with me.

It seemed that the key lay in the *dilemma of a lack of identity*. Even though I understood the relationship between the changeless self and The Spirit, something was missing. Part of that was all the discussion we'd had about the Ego and how the Ego fit into the steps and stages that Mideol had outlined.

We were sitting together after dinner, two days before the end of the month, when I looked across the table at him, past the dirty dishes, and felt I had to get an answer. "Do you mind if I ask you a question about what we were discussing earlier?"

"Not at all. Please ask."

"I understand the steps and stages you told me about, but I can't seem to bring that together with the discussions I've had with you and the Cramfords about the Ego. When I think about all of this together, it starts to feel like a jumble again."

Mideol listened and then took several slow, deep breaths, just like he had demonstrated to me. We sat together for a couple minutes before he responded.

"Yosh, the map of the journey I shared with you is complete in all six steps and the stages those steps define. A more detailed map will *not* help you. I believe what you may need is a clearer picture of the *traveler* within that journey. That traveler is the 'I,' but from Step Three to Step Five the Ego is an intrinsic part of you as that traveler."

"Right," I said. "I can see the journey pretty well now, thanks to your description, but I can't see how the Ego fits in. If I could see how the Ego got there, then I might see a way to get rid of it."

"Yosh, I believe you are requesting insight into the structure of the human mind as it relates to the origins of the Ego. I think you want to understand how the Ego insinuates itself into human nature."

"That's it!" I said. "That's exactly what I think I'm missing. If I can find out how the Ego got there, then maybe I can start to see what part of *me*, or 'I,' is *not* the Ego. If I saw that, then I might see how I fit into these steps and stages."

"That is an admirable request," said Mideol, already drifting off into thought.

I got up to clear the dishes while he sat there thinking. After wiping the last plate dry and putting it away, I came and sat back down. No sooner was I sitting than Mideol got up without saying a word. He walked over to the shelf in the west room and picked something up. Then he went to the eastern stairwell and walked downstairs, returning empty-handed. Finally, he sat back down at the table saying nothing about his actions. He simply began where he had left off.

"Yosh, I know that we've spoken only briefly about the mind. In our model of the 'I,' we equated the changing self with the mind but didn't discuss the mind in detail. We simply saw how mind is composed of both rational and emotional parts. We saw how mind, together with the changeless self, forms your concept of 'I.'

"It seems now you want to look deeper into the concept of mind so that you can understand how it creates an Ego. Why? Because it's that Ego that stands apart from the changeless self in the dilemma of divided identity. The process that you're asking about is *the creation of habits of thought* within the mind. In other words—why is it that you begin by seeing yourself as the mind?"

"Wow!" I said. "That is what I'm trying to get at. I just couldn't find the words to say it."

"You were almost there, Yosh. At least you were reaching for it. When you think about it, the mind is actually a very difficult concept to grasp. It's not as if the mind is sitting there waiting for you to look at it under a microscope. The mind itself is a concept."

"How can the mind be a concept? I *know* I have a mind."

"The mind is like the *lap*," said Mideol. "We know that it exists by virtue of its functioning and its usefulness. But it is difficult to say that the mind resides in any particular location. In the same way that your lap only exists because you are sitting in a particular way, your mind exists because you process information in a particular way. Even the concept of mind *beyond* your own mind is an extension of your internal experience. Projecting that experience onto your fellow human beings is an *assumption*. The only thing that you can know for sure is that *you have a mind*.

"You cannot really know that others have a mind or know if their mind is similar to yours. You assume that they are having a similar experience, and so long as your assumptions explain their actions in a way that is predictable or acceptable to you, you continue to maintain your assumption."

I felt sick. As soon as I thought I had things nailed down, he mixed them all up again. He'd been talking about the mind—the changing self or Ego—in such detail, with all the steps, and now he tells me that we can't even be sure that other people have minds!

"I'm confused. It seems like what you're saying is right, but I thought we had just talked through the self—and the mind, which is part of self. Now you're telling me that the mind might not even exist. Well, which is it?"

"I'm happy that you can sit with this apparent contradiction, disturbing as it may be, Yosh. Your confusion is understandable. Let me see if I can help. One of the problems with this question is that inquiry into the nature of the mind and the construction of the Ego is not restricted to one field.

"Historically, this inquiry has been made within religion or philosophy. Then it fell within the purview of psychology and psychiatry. Recently, the mind has become the subject of biology, neuroscience, endocrinology, and radiology, as well as other disciplines. So the question becomes *where to begin.*

"I prefer to begin with science… not because it is superior to the other schools of inquiry, but because it provides common ground not generally contested on the basis of familiarity. Remember, this is only an overview. We will look at what our traditions have to say about the mind and the Ego later."

"I didn't realize I was asking something so complicated."

"Let's simplify it then. Think of religion and philosophy as our traditions. Now think of the inquiry of our traditions as the *experiential aspect of inquiry into the mind.* To spend time in the company of those who have sought to understand their traditions from the perspective of Source is invaluable to validating your personal experience within the journey.

"Learning how to identify common denominators within our collective journey away from them can be rewarding. That is what inquiry into *our* traditions, religions, beliefs, cultures, and civilizations has to offer. That sentiment stands in opposition to the habit of inquiring with the intent of justifying *your* tradition as superior to others. You can learn as much by avoiding the latter sentiment as you can by emulating the former."

"I'm not sure I understand how you would go about identifying these common denominators," I replied.

"We'll discuss that later too, Yosh. For now, you can take the map of the steps and stages of the journey as an example of this process. That map has been constructed by reviewing the similarities in the human experience across many traditions. Earlier I focused on that similarity to identify the *changeless*. Now I will focus upon that which is subject to change—the Ego. If we let science take the lead, perhaps it will allow us to begin on common ground."

I was happy with that. I didn't know how all of these traditions could possibly come together in one map.

Mideol got a glass of water then sat back down. "Now, think about science as the *experimental aspect of inquiry* into the mind, since science is pursued through verifiable experimentation. This aspect of inquiry represents the desire to build from the ground up, rather than boiling things down to a common denominator. Science accepts nothing until it is proven—that's the hallmark of scientific or experimental inquiry.

"Most people think of 'experiential' inquiry and 'experimental' inquiry as separate things, but I think they each address part of the puzzle. To me, each has the capacity to answer questions that the other may not see or may be unable to address. The habit of identifying ourselves with like-minded individuals as a 'science tribe' or a 'religion tribe' speaks more to our primate desire to be included in a group than it does to a desire for earnest inquiry."

"That makes sense," I said.

"Good, then let's look at what *the scientific aspect of inquiry* has to say about mind and see if it can't help us understand the journey more fully. Since science builds up from the bottom, let's look at the beginning of the individual mind. This is an aspect of inquiry that science handles well—the construction and evaluation of theories. Your first question might be, 'Have I always had this belief in the existence of the mind?'"

"Sounds like a good place to start."

"Good. Much of this line of inquiry began in the late 1970s, though it continues to this day. Many studies have looked at the development of certain abilities of children at different ages. These studies revealed that abilities of the mind *develop in stages*. This means that the question 'Have I always had this belief in the existence of the mind?' might need to be preceded by the question 'Have I always had a mind?'

"Now, first it was determined that the mind is actually composed of many pieces, and that these pieces develop in stages. So that question might better be rephrased as, 'When do I develop pieces of my mind?' This is a question that science can address, so science did just that.

"Early on, studies conducted by Premack, Woodruff, Baron-Cohen, and others on children showed that precursors of the concept of mind present themselves at different ages in our development as children.

"Let's look at just one of these pieces. The capacity for *directed attention* was typically found to develop between the ages of seven to nine months. This means that a child of this age is able to perceive an object as being *of interest* to another person and is capable of having their attention directed by a person pointing to an object."

"You mean that before seven months of age we can't do that?"

"Yosh, the fact that we can't do it for the first half year of life is *interesting*. The fact that we can do it as early as seven months is *amazing*. The capacity to perceive and respond to directed attention by members of your own species normally *develops within us* but is not present from the beginning."

Mideol paused, then continued. "The capacity for directed attention is not unique to us, but it is deeper than in other species."

He called Keeley, who had been sleeping in the corner. She came and sat down in front of him. He told her to stay and she remained where she sat. Mideol got up, went to the shelf he had gone to before, and found a small piece of bread. Then he walked over to the western stairwell, bent down, and pretended to place the bread where neither Keeley nor I could see it.

Keeley watched him intently.

Mideol came and sat back down. She looked at him.

He pointed to the eastern stairwell *opposite* of where he had just gone and then told Keeley to "take it."

Keeley looked at him confused but then went straight to the area where he had directed her attention. She retrieved the bread, which he had earlier placed in the eastern stairwell, and ate it right away.

We watched her enjoy it.

She returned, begging to go to the other stairwell as well. Mideol gave her permission and off she went.

Mideol turned back to me. "You see, Yosh, Keeley and other dogs have the capacity to have their attention directed by humans. But this capacity has been shown to be absent in wolves—even if they are raised by humans. Wolves may be able to have their attention directed by *other wolves*, but can't generalize directed attention *beyond their species* regardless of their upbringing. *You*, however, at seven to nine months of age possessed the ability to have your attention directed."

I sat there thinking about this. I had never given it much thought before.

Mideol continued. "You see how Keeley moved quickly from having her attention directed *by* me to expressing her intention *to* me? So let's follow her lead from *attention* to *intention* as an example of a *piece* of mind that develops later but which incorporates the previous piece of mind. With these examples, you may begin to see how the mind develops its early pieces instinctively but quickly moves to *conscious involvement* in its own development.

"Of course, an understanding of *intention* is much deeper in humans than in dogs. In humans, it typically begins to develop around the age of four. At this age, children are able to perceive that another person must have a mental representation of a situation, just like they have such a representation. In other words, they are capable of *projecting the concept of mind*. Even more interesting, a child at this age is able to understand that their mental representation can differ from that of another person. Such a child can appreciate the value of possessing information that another person lacks. At the age of four, a child is already aware of the *framing of Reality into separate personal realities*. And they are aware of the power that goes along with this framing."

"How does science know all this?" I asked.

"Well, much of this knowledge comes from experiments using something called a false-belief task. The best known of these tasks is called the Sally-Anne task because it involves two dolls named Sally and Anne. Sally has a basket and Anne has a box. Sally also has a marble that she keeps in her basket. The child being tested is shown a scene in which Sally leaves the room, leaving Anne alone with the basket, the box, and the marble.

"While Sally is gone, Anne takes the marble out of Sally's basket and puts it into her box. Sally then returns to the room. The examiners ask the child, 'Where will Sally look for her marble?' If a child says that Sally will look for it in her basket, then the child *passes* the test, meaning this child understands that Sally and Anne have a separate reality that is influenced by each doll's own assumptions."

"That sounds like when we were talking about personal reality and Reality. Did you say that kids normally can do this when they are four years old?"

"That's right. By the age of four or five a child *innately* knows what we've been discussing. At that age, *you* knew that your personal reality was not Reality... just a *representation* of Reality—a *model* of Reality."

"So if I knew this when I was four or five, how come it came as a revelation so recently?"

"Ah, that's a very good question! Simply because you *now* know that the mind works this way does not mean that you were aware of it before when you were constructing your habits of thought. Until science demonstrated it, we had no idea that this capacity of mind developed at this point in our childhood. Think about it. How far back do your memories go?"

"I guess the first things I remember are around the age of four or five."

"Exactly. For most of us, our memories begin around this age. They may be *vague* memories, but they are memories nonetheless. When you say that your memories begin around this age, what you're saying is that your *construction of a personal view* of Reality, or a personal reality, began around this age. In other words, you were beginning to construct your picture frame around this age. You were beginning to slice off a part of Reality to call your own.

"That, Yosh, is the origin of *your* mind and *your* reality. What we are discussing is the timing of this process of moving from ego to Ego, which we talked about earlier. Around this age, that process begins within us as individuals."

That made a lot of sense, and I could see how science added to my understanding of the mind. I thought it would jumble things up, but it did clarify things in a way I hadn't imagined it would.

Mideol continued. "To the extent that you were rewarded for having your personal reality, it became firmer—the frame grew denser. Gradually, you became convinced that your model of reality was Reality itself. You thought, 'If it works for me, it should work for everyone else.' It became easy to justify your position.

"If you found yourself in a situation where you were surrounded by people who had a similar reality and whose frames largely overlapped your own, it became easier to reinforce the belief that your personal reality was indeed Reality. Later, if you sought to remain in such a community, your belief in that personal reality as Reality Itself would become even more concrete. There's just one problem, though… it's a lie."

"Well that's pretty blunt," I said.

"It is as it is. You have already seen for yourself how this lie plays out."

"Yes, I have, and your explanation makes perfect sense."

"There's more. Can you see the other implication of the Sally-Anne task?"

"Not really."

"There is another implication. We've seen how the mind has learned to distinguish personal realities from Reality. We've also seen what the mind does with its own mistaken identity. But now the mind has created *another* mistaken identity, hasn't it?"

I thought for a minute and said, "I see what you're getting at. The mind has also created a mistaken identity *in the other person*!"

"Exactly, Yosh. The mind has not just separated itself from Reality. It has also separated itself from the other person. Three-year-olds may be thought of as participating in the same Reality. This Reality can be thought of as 'no-mind' because the construct of mind has not yet been formed.

"Five-year-olds have their own personal realities. And as we grow older, we gradually lose our ability to participate in Reality. When we look *internally*, our attachment to our own framed reality leads us to believe that it serves us. But what do we see when we look *externally* at other minds, or other framed realities?"

"I guess we see them as *separate*, like you said."

"Yes, that's correct, but think about it a little deeper, Yosh. What else were the four-year-old children seeing in the interaction between Sally and Anne?"

I had no idea what he could be talking about. It sounded pretty straightforward to me. He could see that he'd lost me again, so he asked it a different way.

"What if you add the children to the scene? Look at *them* as well as the dolls. What do they see as witnesses to the drama of Sally and Anne?"

I started to see what he was talking about. I had been looking at the scene from the perspective of the *children in relation to the dolls*. If I looked at the scene from the perspective of the *examiners*, then the children were part of the scene as well. I tried to figure out what this change in perspective revealed. Then it hit me.

"The kids can see that *Anne is fooling Sally*. They recognize what she's doing."

"Excellent, Yosh. That's exactly right. Children at this age are beginning to recognize the utility of owning and controlling information. Other studies have confirmed that by the age of four or five, humans are capable of understanding the implications of *misperception* and the value of *manipulating information* for their own benefit. That is an incredible realization.

"We've already looked at the internal implications of this information. Now let's look at the *external* implications. When we look out at the world from a perspective of our framed reality, we see a world populated by framed realities that often do not agree with our own reality. We look down and see that we have, in our hands, a tool that possesses great power. It is the power to manipulate and control information. With information we can manipulate and control the framed realities of others."

"It sounds kind of scary."

"It is as frightening as you imagine, Yosh, because the next question is, 'What do we do with that power?' Seeing ourselves as separate from the world, we seek any advantage to fulfill our needs and advance our perceived interests over the interests of others.

"Those others may be other *human minds*, or they may be other *living beings* that we are convinced do not possess minds. But we are especially interested in establishing our advantage over the other members of our own species, those we frequently compete with for the same resources."

"But how could it be otherwise?" I asked. "We can't contain all of Reality within our thoughts. Didn't you say that we can be aware of 'It' but we can't contain 'It'? We have to act in the world. How would we do that without framing Reality?"

"Yosh, this is our dilemma. No sooner do we learn about the power of information than we are forced to use that power or be faced with the knowledge of its use against us. We quickly learn that the conscious use of knowledge is ponderous because so much of it comes at us so fast. If we are capable of pushing the bulk of that information into our unconscious, then we can process more information at a faster pace. To do this, we create mental models of reality and continuously test them for their utility within our world.

"As we get rewarded or praised for the outcomes of these models, we start to identify ourselves with those models—the ones we have created and refined. Without intending to, we forget our original state, the state of no-mind within Reality, and come to believe that we *are* our models of Reality.

"This is the point at which we move from little-ego to Ego. We then become so invested in our models of reality that we forget about the very existence of Reality. We come to reside in the dilemma of a mistaken self. This is our general condition. And even this assumes a relatively healthy childhood and a relatively consistent environment that is amenable to modeling."

"No wonder we're so messed up," I replied. "Do any of these models actually serve us?"

"Forming models is not the problem, Yosh. We have evolved, as all animals have, to form models of our world. The problem lies in our gift of being able to consciously create our models and the curse of our tendency to unconsciously identify with those models. Stuck in this cycle, we seek to defend our *self* by withholding and manipulating information, otherwise known as *deception*. It is a slippery slope that leads from deception of others to self-deception.

"History, with all of its contending waves of defense and attack, counterattack, preemptive attack, and defense, is born out of this predicament. It becomes the story of this never-ending cycle."

"That all sounds so depressing," I responded.

"It isn't depressing when the Ego feels it has obtained an advantage through its manipulation of information. The Ego actually feels pretty good about that. In fact, it feels *proud* of itself because it has proven that it is better than the other Egos.

"What the Ego doesn't see is that the other Egos are just biding their time. No advantage lasts forever. Eventually, one of them is able to use the manipulation of information to *its* advantage. Then, the first Ego doesn't feel so good.

"In reality, it never truly felt 'happy' for long, because as soon as it was done gloating over its victory, it began to fear losing the advantage and had to start preparing its defenses. This is history, summarized."

"It sounds exhausting."

"It has become exhausting for you, Yosh. You have become tired of this game. That is why you are here. Eventually, all Egos that allow themselves to be confronted with the truth become tired of the game. It is a question of honesty. Once you see how you have framed your personal reality out of Reality, and you see the consonance of your 'changeless self' with The Spirit, you can see what you have been doing for what it really is. This is the point of realization that you have already experienced. It is for this reason that it appears exhausting to you. To many others, it remains quite interesting."

"I'm glad that I'm free of it."

"I never said you were free of your dilemma, Yosh. I said that you could *see* it."

"I thought that those were the same thing—that seeing it *was* being free of it."

"Then you were mistaken. Realization is conceptual—and it is important—but change does not occur without action, and thought is not action."

"I don't understand. What action do I need to take?"

"You have all the pieces, Yosh. You simply need to integrate your realization of the blueprint of the dilemma with your understanding of the map of the journey. You need to see these together through the eyes of both the Ego and The Self."

"I don't think I can even repeat that back to you, let alone try to do it."

"You are not far from it, Yosh. All of the pieces are there. You need only to put them together. If you can formulate the *question*, then the answer is not far off. Why don't you sleep on it? Tomorrow we can look at it again."

He got up to finish his evening routine.

I just sat there looking at the fire in the stove. I was still staring at it long after he'd gone to sleep. Mideol's words kept coming back to me, but no question came to mind. As I watched the flame flicker, turning to embers of gold, my mind wandered over the past few months.

I added a couple of logs to the fire and went to bed.

ACCEPTANCE

It was the last day of the year, and we had been outside all morning. All our discussions had really gotten to me. I just wanted to be outside not thinking about any of it. Mideol had thrown so many concepts and so many new ways of thinking at me. It was as if I'd seen the emptiness, and he'd thrown me into it. At first, his concept of losing identity had only been a concept to me. Lately, though, I'd come to feel that I actually had *moved into* this *dilemma of a lack of identity*. It was not a comfortable place to be, and I couldn't find any escape.

As much as I tried to get rid of all these thoughts, they seemed to keep coming back. I was really getting tired of all this thinking. Even being outdoors didn't help. It had taken an hour for us to get down to the valley after spending the first three hours on the forest trail. We walked through a world blanketed in white, following the river as it wound down into the valley.

The river was beautiful in the winter. It flowed between the banks like a small canyon cutting through the snow. The boulders were covered in thick snowcaps and looked like so many cupcakes frosted in white. The thin covering of ice was broken in a few places by the constant flow of the now-small stream.

Except for the occasional bird and the sound of the river, there was silence. It was a silence that must have played itself out for as long as these mountains had been here. It was a silence that would be here long after I was gone. Strangely, I found comfort in being around something so permanent... and the emptiness of it no longer scared me.

I had come to feel much better *being* in the changeless than I did talking about it. It felt like home to me now, and I realized what I had missed earlier in my life. Before I knew it, all of our discussions had fallen into place.

I felt the answer before I even formulated the question. I should have been excited. This was the answer that I had been searching for—for so long. But I just wanted to be here. Everything else could wait. The question and the answer were like the shadows of the trees in bright sunlight… sharp and clean against the perfectly white snow.

I sat there all morning admiring the play of light and dark in this magical black and white world. I was so lost in thought that I didn't notice the clouds move in. The shadows faded and the outlines blurred, but that was okay. The simplicity of the answer was still perfectly clear to me. It hadn't faded a bit.

It started to snow quite heavily, and we began our climb back up through the curtain of white that embraced us toward the path that led home to the cave. The falling snow contracted my world to the few feet around me. But in my mind I could see the valley and no amount of snow could shrink it. I walked on, comforted by the immediacy of the snow and the vastness of reality—Reality.

At last we entered the cave. I was as grateful for the warmth as I had been earlier for the chill of the fresh morning air. Mideol cooked lunch while I put away the snow gear. We ate together, watching the snow come down. I was still lost in my experience of that morning. Mideol must have sensed it because we barely spoke after lunch. It kept snowing till late in the afternoon, and I sat on the armchair just staring off into the storm.

I remember focusing on the snowflakes falling nearby and losing focus on those farther away. Then I would focus on those far away and lose the focus I'd had before. After an hour of this, I thought how that shifting external focus contrasted with the steady focus I now felt inside. Finally, I felt the need to tell Mideol what I'd experienced.

"I have the answer," I said as we sat at the table.

"You do?"

"Yes. It came to me by the river this morning."

"Well, I guess it's my turn to ask if you would like to share it," Mideol said.

I started to explain. "When I looked at what you said, it was really pretty simple. First, I looked at the map of the journey and remembered what you'd said about Stage Six being a growth in wisdom. I believe you said that this stage was marked by my recognition of my changeless self as part of The Spirit, and at the same time as the whole of The Spirit, like Kabir mentioned.

"I didn't realize it at the time, but the understanding that led to that wisdom was a mixed blessing. Sure, I felt like I was out of the dilemma of a *lack of identity*, but now I was stuck in a new place. Now I was stuck in a dilemma of *being beyond identities*. Then, all our bouncing around in different traditions just seemed to make that worse, not better. It seemed like any reality was just an illusion, so why choose any of them?

"At some point, though, I remembered you saying that the next step was an *action*, not just some understanding. That meant it had to be an action *based* on that understanding. That was the next piece of the puzzle."

"That's pretty good, Yosh. Go on."

"The final piece of the puzzle was the part you told me about yesterday—the part about the original identity in Reality before the framing of Reality starts at four years old. I think you called it 'no-mind.'

"So then I thought about what you'd said earlier about seeing things through the eyes of the Ego and through the eyes of The Self. That's when I realized I had been looking at the whole thing through the eyes of the Ego. I'd been looking at it all through *my* eyes, but those eyes were still my *same old eyes*! I had gone through all of our discussions and had just been *thinking* about them. I never actually thought *to do* anything about them!

"That thought hit me when I was down at the river today. There was a feeling of actually *being* timeless. All of a sudden I was looking at everything from that perspective, and it became clear. It was only by *being* timeless that I could see through the *eyes* of The Timeless—The Spirit!"

Mideol started to laugh. I thought he might have lost it. Then I started to laugh with him. It was an infectious kind of laughter, and I couldn't stop. Before I realized it, I was laughing at how utterly simple and how utterly impossible the whole thing was at the same time.

We laughed ourselves to the point of tears. Those tears captured the senselessness of the whole thing, but after the tears were gone I felt clean. There's no way to describe it. I felt totally clean—like I had just now been born into this world, and like I was seeing it for the first time.

Mideol finally said, "Congratulations, Yosh. You have become aware of the *sixth step* on the journey. I do not say you've come to understand it, because understanding falls short. That is why I said you were *not far from the answer*—and why I could not give it to you. I also know that you do not wish to discuss it because even talking about it detracts from being in the stage that the sixth step opens to you.

"Tomorrow will be the first day of the New Year. We will discuss *nothing* of the journey for the next month. Arriving at Step Six requires some time to settle. Taking that step is a monumental achievement, but becoming *established* in the fifth stage is not easy. Still, that's necessary if you wish to return to lower stages to assist the other aspects of yourself to join you on your journey. Without a critical mass of those aspects of yourself, you will only be stuck at the entry point of this new level.

"Now we will begin to lay the groundwork for advancing into the space opened up by taking Step Six. Tomorrow you'll begin training within this new state of being. Today, though, we must finish the work that you began two months ago.

"You've traveled a great distance, Yosh. I congratulate you. The reward for your effort is the *experience* of union in The Spirit. Guru Nanak called this way of being *Gurmukh*. In Buddhism, it is 'encountering your Buddha nature.' It is what Jesus called 'entering the Kingdom of Heaven' and what Abraham experienced as the 'presence of God.'

"You now know that The Spirit has no name. You will learn why the Upanishads of Hinduism refer to it simply as 'Tat' or 'That' and

231

will recognize this relationship between the changeless self and 'Tat' as *Tat-tvam-asi* or, in English, *That art thou*. There is still much for you to learn, but little to know. You must give this new experience your clearest expression so that it becomes fixed in your intellect."

He was right. I really didn't want to leave the space of being in that presence. It was new to me, and part of me was afraid that if I left I'd never find my way back. I just wanted to *be* there. But I didn't want to leave the job unfinished, either.

"Well, I guess it would help me to state it as clearly as possible, so I'll give it a shot," I said, floundering for where to begin. I shuffled through my thoughts for what seemed an eternity. Finally, I tried to put them into words.

"I suppose that 'I' cannot ultimately have a divided identity. If 'I' do, then I'm still stuck in the dilemma. To understand that my change-less self is consonant with The Spirit is to fully embrace the 'dilemma of a divided identity.' I now see that all of my steps in the journey have been necessary to bring me to this realization. None of them could have been avoided. I was looking for something that I couldn't put my finger on but felt it was there—that it had to be there. But it was this process of seeking, and the habit of sustained inquiry that you and the Cramfords helped me with over these past few months, that led me to it.

"Ultimately, though, to make use of that space—to move on— requires recognition and action. The recognition I needed was seeing that my dilemma had not really resolved itself. It had simply taken on a new shape. It had become a 'dilemma of a lack of identity.' The action I needed to take was a choice. If 'I' was going to escape the dilemma of a lack of identity, 'I' had to choose between one of the two identities."

I felt like I was on a roll.

Mideol just nodded silently, waiting for me to go on.

I continued. "Looking back, I realize that several times I chose my temporal identity, my changing self, by default. I intellectualized my eternal identity or changeless self. This was my default decision because I had been conditioned to make that choice since I was four or five years old. That is the habit of a separated and framed self, or *personal reality*.

"My decision to choose that identity was reinforced by my fear of having information used against me and by my desire to use information against others. This alternating fear and desire resulted in the creation of mental models that I came to see as myself. Those insights into the development of the mind, which you shared with me yesterday, helped me to see my actions for what they've been."

I paused to collect my thoughts, took a deep breath, and continued. "Now, finally, the needed action was to actively *choose the opposite* and *actively deny my default desire*. I had been unaware of one part of this—that the simple act of choosing the other relationship as my identity and actually acting upon it, *changes everything*. When I made that choice, all the *changing self* and *mind* pieces of myself no longer felt like they were welded onto me. They felt like they were just taped on and could fall away at any moment. And that's what they did. They just fell away.

"I can't explain it. It felt like they were just these shoddy additions I had built onto my house. They'd looked great when I'd built them, and they'd been comfortable at first, but they just didn't fit together when I stepped back and looked at the whole thing. Today, for the first time, I was able to put enough distance between me and my old way of putting things together. I was able to look around— to look away from what I'd built. And now I saw this magnificent home that I'd never seen before. For the first time, I realized I'd wasted my time building all of these useless additions when I could have been living in this *awesome* house instead. I guess that's the way I would sum it up."

"What an excellent summary, Yosh. I wouldn't change a thing. I like your house analogy—it's quite fitting. This habit of summarizing your internal achievements can be quite a useful tool. I think that your summary will serve you later when the activities of the past three months are not so fresh in your memory.

"Now, before we celebrate the New Year and your achievement, I have two final observations I'd like to share with you. Neither of these could have been made understandable for you previously, and both will serve you well as you proceed in the months and years to come.

"The first of these is a summary of the animating principles of the two extremes of identity. The second is a formula to reverse the habit of the 'decision by default' that you identified. That habit will diminish, but it will not stop seeking to re-establish your identity with a changing self and a once-familiar framed reality."

"But it feels like I'm beyond them already."

"Yosh, you must guard yourself against that sentiment. The state with which you have become familiar today is not yet a stable state. Until your dedication to this identity extends to enough aspects of your self, this state will remain unstable. And without stability, significant progress will be difficult. The experience you've had today is more than Kensho, yet less than stability in Satori. There is no need to discuss this now, but the articulation and the formula will assist you when the need arises."

"I'll try to remember that."

"Very well, let's start with the animating principle of the Ego as the perspective of the most densely framed reality that defines itself in separation from The Spirit. The animating principle of the Ego within you and your society would read:

> I will seek relative advantage for myself over the
> other members of my own species."

"That sounds pretty straightforward," I said.

"It needs to be straightforward to capture the essence of the thing, Yosh. We've already seen how this perspective of the Ego extends beyond the members of your own species. But seeking advantage over other human beings goes to the heart of the sentiment. As far as 'relative' goes, you don't need to look far to see how we can fight over scraps while ignoring that we've chosen to live on a scrap heap.

"Now, Yosh, what about the animating principle of The Spirit? What do you think that would look like?"

I thought about it for a while but was relieved when I heard him begin to answer his own question. To be honest, I wasn't feeling like thinking very much. Still, I understood how important it was to not drop the ball at the last minute.

Mideol stated, almost solemnly:

> "The Spirit is my highest nature,
> as it is for my brothers and sisters.
> To be Whole while being a part, is for me to Be."

"How wonderful," I said, "You've actually captured what I feel. I could never have expressed it that way."

"You will find your voice in time, Yosh. As you pointed out, however, the perspective of The Spirit has nothing to do with striving or seeking. It is about *Being*. This is why the Ego cannot see it. The Ego is looking for something like itself. The Ego looks at The Spirit and wants to know what *It* wants. 'Does the Spirit want offerings? Do the spirits want us to stay off their sacred land? Do the gods want a sacrifice? Does this god prefer a sacrifice of our crops, our animals, or one of us? Does God want my chastity? Does He want my obedience? What does he want?' These are questions asked by the Ego.

"But The Spirit does not want. It *is*. It simply *is*. In that simple statement, joy, peace, and love converge and the distinction between the three becomes irrelevant, as do many other distinctions. The aversion to thinking—which I suspect you currently feel—reflects a recognition of this irrelevance. But this is not the end of inquiry, Yosh. Your desire to simply *be* in this space of awareness *without the intrusion of thought* is quite natural. This space of alignment with The Spirit is your true home. But you can only act from there through an awareness that informs your thought.

"You are threatened by the realization that thinking will draw you out of this space. But in time you will learn how to move in and out of this space in which you have come to have an awareness of Source. Then you will learn that thought and inquiry can actually *deepen* the 'you' that returns to this space. That is why you must actually *increase your inquiry*—not end it.

"Going forward, that inquiry will need to be both broader and deeper. But that is not a discussion for today. We'll begin that inquiry tomorrow, but it will not begin with discussion. It will begin with *breadth* before we dig deeper. Before that, though, there is one last thing I want to share with you."

"You've already shared so much," I said. "Just hearing the animating principles of the Ego and The Spirit is helpful. I see what you meant by the value in seeing them plainly."

"Yes, there is value in that, but now we come to the issue of sustainability—of being in the perspective of The Spirit. You have had your first intimation that such a state may be sustainable. But there are three challenges to this stability.

"First, you must deal with habits of the mind that persist from your previous personal realities. Most of the next five months will be devoted to addressing misperceptions of reality that underlie those habits.

"Second, you must challenge the efforts of the Ego to reassert itself by self-deception or distraction. Though it has lost this battle on the center stage of conscious identity, it will continue to challenge you in the many other aspects of your being.

"Finally, if the Ego fails in these efforts, it will attempt to exploit the gap between your intentions and your actions. If it is able to thwart your efforts by rewarding you for your intentions, it may yet succeed. To address this, you will need a tool that you can rely upon, and which is readily available to you."

"A tool?"

"Yes, a tool. But not a physical tool. Since the challenge of the Ego is both a mental and a spiritual challenge, this tool must possess both cognitive and spiritual capabilities. And it must apply to action as well as thought."

"Sounds like a lot to ask for."

"It *is* a lot to ask for, but the best tools perform the most important functions. This tool performs such an important function that I call it the *Diamond Rule*. It has the capacity to confront the animating principle of the Ego and remind you of your highest nature."

Mideol took out another sheet of paper and then wrote at the bottom of the page:

Accept no benefit from another that is not freely offered to you.

"That's it? That's the Diamond Rule?"

"Do not let its brevity fool you, Yosh. The *application* of this rule will assist you in addressing the challenges of the Ego. *Thinking about* the rule does not offer the same power. This tool can be of great use even if you don't fully understand it. In fact, using it before we discuss it will make the discussion even more productive."

I accepted what he said. It was more than I knew what to do with, but he had an uncanny way of giving me pieces of the puzzle before I needed them. Mideol handed me the paper and asked me to write the animating principles of the Ego and The Spirit above the Diamond Rule. I did and then decided to call it my 'perspective page.' Afterward, I didn't want to think about anything. As the sky grew darker outside, my brain might have been full, but my stomach was again feeling empty.

Mideol and I wrapped up the day with a meal. He said it was as much in celebration of my progress in the journey as it was about ringing in the New Year. Our meals had always been small but flavorful. This one was different. It was huge.

There was fresh cornbread sweetened with honey and rich with ground flax seed. There was tofu, which Mideol showed me how to make from the soybeans that he farmed during the summer. We had beans and carrots that Fitra had canned for us, all spiced with herbs that Mideol had collected earlier in the year.

It was also one of the rare times that we had meat that Keely had discovered—venison from a mule deer that had recently died after breaking its leg and getting stuck in the snow. It was all delicious. We ended the meal with cake and the only sugar frosting I would see during my whole stay with him.

I was content and feeling finally at peace. In that moment, there was nothing else that I wanted.

We finished the day with music. Mideol played while I joined him singing some of the lyrics he had taught me. I had never really played music before. I'd tried my hand at piano when I was a kid, but I'd never stayed with it.

Mideol was pretty talented. He had two instruments he played most often. The first was an acoustic guitar with rich tones and plenty of spare strings. The second was called a harmonium, a wonderful little instrument that looked like a wooden box with piano keys on top. It worked like an accordion that sat on the ground. He sat behind it and pumped the bellows at the back with his left hand, using his right hand to play the keys. It sounded like an organ and filled the whole room with sound.

With a beautiful voice, Mideol sang in several different languages. I understood the English and he'd translate the others for me. He explained how playing music and familiarity with several languages helps to keep the brain healthy because both activities force the brain to think in different ways.

He valued the music more than the words, but when they came together it was wonderful. After he played, we did our breathing exercises. Then Mideol did his evening routine while I sat next to the fire.

When he was finished, he sat next to me. "Yosh, tomorrow you will begin the practice."

"What is the practice?" I asked.

"The practice is the beginning of the next step on the journey. Until today, you have been moving back and forth between the fourth and fifth steps of your journey. That area of the journey has its own practice and has appeared to involve thought and rational consideration. This has been the reason for our lengthy discussions. Today, you have taken the sixth step and have come to realize that emotional movement is central to this journey. That sixth step was hidden from you because you were looking for a cognitive or intellectual step. Integration of reason and emotion in a structured way is a faculty and a habit that you do not yet possess.

"When you encountered Step Six today, you recognized it with the deeper faculties of your mind. Those faculties exceed your cognitive capacity. It was the act of allowing yourself to be greater than your cognition that revealed this step to you. In *choosing* to act upon that recognition, you've encountered a definition of self that is aligned with your changeless self.

"The sixth step has brought you into a stage that is a further expression of that alignment—the realm of the 'awakened state,' and it is marked by both the *act* of awakening and then the *process* of awakening. Step Six is the *act* of awakening. Recruiting the other aspects of your being into this same alignment with Source is the *process* of awakening. Creating the conditions for this alignment to proceed more fully is the purpose of the practice.

"This practice is aimed at increasing your alignment with The Spirit. It will occupy you for the rest of your life, Yosh. But you must understand that the practice is only partly intellectual. It is also emotional, physical, and spiritual. In each of these other areas, the practice is mostly experiential.

"Ultimately, the fullness of the awakened state will only be available to you if you succeed in actualizing the wisdom you gain in stage five. This often means returning to stages four and five *in particular areas* to actualize the understanding and wisdom associated with those areas of activity."

"What do mean by all that?" I asked, again feeling overwhelmed by the complexity.

"I mean that just as your entry into this stage was experiential, so your growth within this stage will be experiential. It will require you to integrate your awareness with the actions of your life. As you grow toward awareness, the potential conflicts and complexity of application will also grow.

"If you fail to actualize your knowledge, understanding, and wisdom across many aspects of your being—well, then the journey devolves into a simply intellectual exercise. When that happens, the power it has to transform you becomes lost. You can become stuck all over again. But this time, you get stuck in an even more intractable position."

"So how would I avoid that? I mean, how would I avoid getting stuck there?"

"By engaging with your world—but in a particular way. First, you avoid getting stuck by being *deeply honest* with yourself in a way that *aligns your interests with the interest of all other honest seekers.* Aligning yourself with their honest aspirations is a guide to aligning yourself with Source.

"Second, you avoid getting stuck there by becoming familiar with all aspects of mind, even those aspects that you have not previously considered. That process of familiarization will feel quite different. It will begin tomorrow morning."

"*Tomorrow* morning?"

"Yes, Yosh. There's a great deal to cover and only five months to establish a base for your practice. Tomorrow morning we'll start with the *daily practice.* This is a daily anchor to your overall practice. We'll begin early morning because early morning is a time when certain possibilities of being are available to you, possibilities that are not always available during other times of the day."

"That makes no sense to me."

"A great deal will not make sense to you at first, and that's another aspect of the experience which will change. Do you recall our discussion regarding the Self and the twin aspects of the relationship between the 'I' and The Spirit?"

"I do," I said, quickly finding that piece of paper in the drawer.

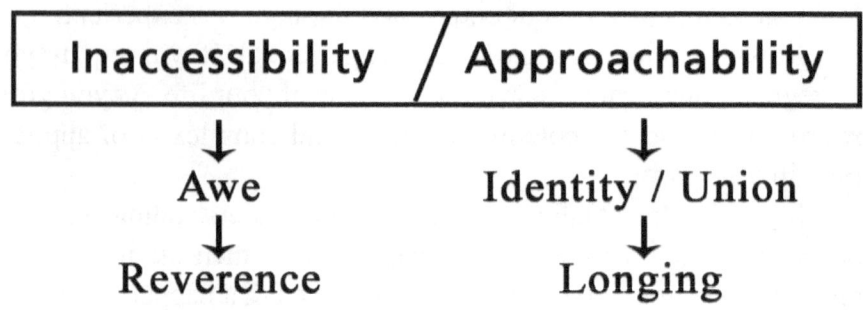

"Good, then as you move into this new stage, you will understand that a new relationship exists now between these two aspects of *inaccessibility* and *approachability*. In this stage, you will see that inaccessibility is greatly *reduced*, and approachability has greatly *expanded*."

"You're right," I said. "In fact, it feels like The Spirit is totally accessible."

"It may feel like that right now, but that's because you are in unfamiliar territory. In reality, there is still much that remains inaccessible—but you cannot see it. This means that you cannot adequately question it, either. There are two ways to deal with this.

"You can spend your life independently acquiring familiarity with this stage. But then you will not be able to act upon that familiarity because your life will have run its course. Alternatively, you can accept guidance and reserve questions for that time when your familiarity with the terrain is adequate.

"The choice is yours, Yosh, but you must understand that questioning without familiarity and failing to act as instructed both constitute the *first choice*. The *second* choice is a matter of transmuting the reverence for honesty demanded of yourself previously to the reverence for instruction provided to you now. If you can manage this transition, then you will have made the second choice. Once again, it is your action and *not your thought* that will mark your decision."

I thought about what he was saying, and I trusted him. I knew there was only one choice that I could possibly make.

I stood up, pushed my chair in, and turned toward him.

"What time do I get up?" I asked.

Mideol smiled, walked over to me, and put an acknowledging hand on my shoulder. Then he led me to the west rear storage area and handed me a large bucket, similar to the one he was now carrying. He filled his bucket with water from the basin and set it next to the storage room door. I had seen him do this each night, and now I did the same thing, setting my bucket of water outside the east rear storage area door by my bed.

Though there were quite a few questions going through my mind, I didn't ask any of them. It was my first step into a new way of learning. I could still hear Jim's last words of advice at the H.R.C. about the need for respect. I finally understood what he meant. Ah, I thought to myself, this is yet another piece of information that has arrived before I needed it.

We said good night, and Mideol gave me a hug that welcomed my decision more than any words could have. Almost without knowing it, I bowed slightly and thanked him, then returned to my room.

That night I lay in bed staring at the ceiling, filled with awe at the thought of all that had happened to me that day. Had it all just happened in one single day? This day felt like it had been years in the making, but it had really been just one day.

My thoughts couldn't contain the wonder that I felt, but they no longer needed to contain it. I was fast asleep well before any imaginary stroke of midnight ushered in the New Year.

ABOUT THE AUTHOR

Bikram Dhillon, MD has been a life-long student of the interplay between our internal and external realities. The founder of Physicians Total Wellness in Chicago, Illinois, he works with patients nationally and internationally to help them establish the foundations of well-being, deep preventive care and optimal functioning in their personal and professional lives. His experience of the personal journey has led to the thoughts expressed in this book. Other books to follow will attempt to further his far-reaching ambition, as both writer and doctor, to help motivated individuals heal themselves as the path to healing our world.

www.ingramcontent.com/pod-product-compliance
Lightning Source LLC
Chambersburg PA
CBHW020830260626
47169CB00003B/922